WE ARE READY

READY

AND OTHER SHORT STORIES

BY MASTER STORYTELLER

WALTER G. ANDERSON

MILTON & HUGO L.L.C.
4407 Park Ave., Suite 5
Union City, NJ 07087, USA

Website: *www. miltonandhugo.com*
Hotline: *1- 888-778-0033*
Email: *info@miltonandhugo.com*

Ordering Information:
Quantity sales. Special discounts are granted to corporations, associations, and other organizations. For more information on these discounts, please reach out to the publisher using the contact information provided above.

Library of Congress Control Number:		2025913227	
ISBN-13:	979-8-89285-551-8	[Paperback Edition]
	979-8-89285-550-1	[Digital Edition]

Rev. date: 06/18/2025

We Are Ready

(Walter G. Anderson)

We left Earth. The ones we left behind called it the Rapture. We call it Evolving. We are many. We are waiting. We are ready.

It is as if a dark stage awaits you while you wait in the wings. Cutting through the darkness center stage, one lone spotlight beckons from directly overhead. On your left is a vastness filled with a murmuring audience that cannot be seen through the dark. Though apprehensive, you will yourself to move across the dark stage and step into the light.

The noise dies down to a silence so complete you can hear your own heartbeat. The light is warm and comforting. Looking down at yourself, you raise your arms out at your side, basking in the peaceful bliss of the light.

Then, like magic, the things that were a part of you come streaming out like the radiant beams of a star going nova. Experiences that shaped who you are push back against the darkness as the spotlight dims. There is a collective gasp from the audience; and the music begins, soft at first, barely discernable, raising in volume. From nothing *to a force* all around you, and you realize the music has always been there. You just couldn't, wouldn't, hear it. It is beauty incarnate. It is you. It is life.

Welcome home. We are ready.

Departure 153

(Walter Anderson and Liz McGuire)

A young man sits on a long wooden bench and watches from a distance as an old woman enters the train station. The old woman shuffles forward, stooped from a lifetime lessons in living. She is carrying a simple paper shopping bag with string handles.

"It doesn't hurt anymore…"

She stops and wonders where *that* came from. Five years earlier, those were the last words her husband of sixty years had said to her as he lay in their bed dying of cancer the doctors could not cure.

"Excuse me, can I help you?"

She looks up from her reverie. A man in a conductor's uniform stands before her, smiling.

"I was…," she starts to say.

"Come over here and rest for a while, Mrs. Peterson. I'll check you in and bring you your boarding pass."

She moves to hand him the paper bag.

"Oh no, ma'am, you must carry that," he says with the same kind smile.

She follows him to a bench and sits by herself. She sits the bag between her feet and gives a heavy sigh as she sits back. A scarf covers her white hair. She is dressed in a housecoat that covers a faded print dress. She looks around the train station: A vast cavern contained the train station with a seemingly endless row of long wooden benches, most of which are empty. She doesn't remember it being this big. The benches separate the desks where people line up to get their tickets and the trains that comes and goes.

The old woman looks down into the bag and notices a picture frame. She leans over and reaches for the object as her old body protests. She sees her old boney hand, the sagging skin covered with age spots. She

3

notices her hand is steady today, no shakes as was before. Harry loved her hands. So graceful and beautiful, he'd say. She pulls the picture frame from the bag and sits it on her lap. She remembers the picture. It is from her and Harry's wedding. How young they were. She marvels at how clear the picture is. She is standing there beside her new husband in her beautiful wedding dress, oblivious to the joys and hardships that awaited them in their lifetime adventure together.

Would you do it again knowing? she wonders. "Yes," she says as her fingers stroke the glass over the picture. "Yes, I'd do it again," she whispers to no one.

Right after that picture was taken, she tossed her bouquet; and Ralph, the dog, caught it. The women chased that dog everywhere, and oh, what a mess they made, tripping over tables and falling in the dirt.

She laughs out loud, wiping a tear from her weathered cheek. She sets the picture frame aside and looks into the dark maw of the bag. Leaning forward, she reaches into the bag, pulling out an item of cloth. No, it's knitted. A knitted orange-colored doll. She gasps. This doll was knitted over forty years ago. She and Harry had tried to have children but never could. They gave up trying, and low and behold, Kassie came into their lives. Harry's sister had a baby girl she didn't want. The old woman remembers giving this doll to Kassie when she was only three. That child was so happy to get it she shook with pent-up feelings she didn't know how to express. Just then a small hand reaches in and snatches the doll from the woman's lap.

"Hey!" the woman starts to protest; but standing before her, gripping the doll, is Kassie. She has the most excited smile and is shaking with pent-up delight.

"But you're…," says the woman in confusion.

You see, Kassie had been taken from her and Harry tragically in some cruel joke God sometimes plays on his children without no rhyme or reason. The little girl bounds forward and leaps onto the woman's lap, hugging her fiercely, and departs with the doll just as quick. The woman reaches for the departing child.

"Wait!" she says, and then she notices her hand again. Only this time it's full, not sagging. It is clear of age spots. She sits back, holding both hand out, looking at them in wonder. These are young beautiful hands. The nails are perfect.

"Oh," she says, and her eye is pulled away by something shiny in the bag. She reaches in, pulling out another picture, no, it's a mirror. She remembers this mirror. It was an old mirror her mother had, but that mirror was broken. She remembers packing it away in the attic. This mirror wasn't broken. She looks into it and gasps. The young woman looking back at her is her sixty years ago. She reaches up and pulls the scarf away, to reveal a lustrous head of brown hair with not a trace of gray. She also notices she is wearing a pink dress with red trim that Harry loved to see her in. She stands up, setting the mirror aside. While holding her arms out, she twirls around, billowing the skirt out. She laughs and stops, seeing the shoes of someone standing before her. She looks up, and there's Harry.

"Hello, Kathryn."

She covers her mouth, astonished. It's Harry all right. He is young and dressed in a suit, smiling at her, with his arms out reaching for her. She is in his arms in an instant. As they embrace, a huge train rumbles into the station. She is sobbing into his neck as he holds her.

"It doesn't hurt anymore, Kat," he whispers as she pulls back and looks into his eyes.

"All aboard!" the conductor shouts.

Kathryn looks behind her to see the conductor standing there holding her boarding pass.

"*Now* will you get on the train, Mr. Peterson?"

Kathryn turns back and looks at Harry. He is smiling at her.

"I waited," he says.

"He waited, I waited, we *all* waited," the conductor says, shooing the couple toward the waiting train.

Kathryn stops and looks back at the bench. It is bare. Nothing remains.

The End

Note: I personally love this story because it could happen without anyone knowing. God does move in wonderful ways.

Giraffalo

Nobody knows how the baby giraffe came to be alone on the prairie of the African savannah. He was curled up in the grass when Hazel, the momma water buffalo, approached him. They touched noses. It was a bonding that would last the two lifetimes.

He was as different as buffalos and giraffes could be. He had long skinny legs, a long neck, and big eyes, whereas a water buffalo was all brown or black. He had spots in unusual patterns all over his body. Even though he was very young, he was taller than most full-grown water buffalos.

The other young water buffalos teased him by calling him names because he was different.

His adopted momma told him, "Of course, you're different. We are *all* different."

"Am I a water buffalo too, Momma?" he asked her.

"You, my son," she said, smiling at him, "are Giraffalo."

And that's what they called him—Giraffalo.

The older water buffalo accepted him as one of the herd, and though he was teased, he made friends among the herd.

Bruno, the lead bull of the herd, taught Giraffalo that the herd was the most important thing.

"Why?" asked Giraffalo, who by now was much taller than even the biggest water buffalo in the herd. "Because, alone, most of these couldn't survive on their own."

Bruno told him as they walked that there are lions that would eat them or they would not be able to find water when they're thirsty, and sometimes someone in the herd might know something that will help the entire herd.

Giraffalo thought about that. "So together we are stronger?" he asked.

Bruno looked up at the young Giraffalo. "Yes, together we are stronger, as long as we *trust* each other."

Over time Giraffalo grew, and the water buffalo who teased him came to accept him. They knew he was different, but now he was part of the herd. When one of his friends wanted to know where the greenest grass was, they would ask Giraffalo because he could see over the backs of the herd. He could see danger before anyone and spot the watering holes and let the herd know in what direction to go.

One day, smoke filled the valley where the herd was feeding. A prairie fire had started, and was burning toward the herd. Bruno bellowed the alarm, and the herd started moving away from the smoke. At first, the herd moved slowly as they continued to feed, but the wind was blowing the fire toward them, and the smoke was getting thicker. The herd started trotting.

"Can you see the fire, Giraffalo?" asked Hazel, his momma.

"No," he said, looking back. "The smoke is too thick."

By now they could hear the grass burning. Bruno lead the herd at a fast pace away from the fire, but it seemed there was no way around the flames.

After a while, some of the buffalo were too tired to keep going. Bruno was a good leader and was always there to urge them on. He kept Giraffalo with him to spot those buffalos.

"I can see the fire," Giraffalo yelled over the roar of the flames.

"Can you see a break in the flames that we can run through?"

Bruno asked as he pushed an older cow to get her moving away from the oncoming fire.

Giraffalo could not. The fire seemed to stretch from one end of the valley to the next, getting closer.

As Bruno and Giraffalo caught up to the herd, they noticed that it had stopped moving.

Bruno pushed through and asked, "What's wrong?"

Another bull answered, "There's a cliff, and we can go no further."

Buffalos could be heard bellowing out their distress. The smoke grew thicker, and the noise from the approaching flames grew louder.

As the fire grew nearer, Giraffalo, because he was so tall, noticed that the smoke was not so thick up there, and he could actually see the fire closing in on the herd. He called for Bruno, who was trying to figure a way out of the situation. The herd packed up against the edge of the cliff.

Bruno pushed his way toward Giraffalo and nudged him. "Is there any break Giraffalo? We need a way out, now!"

Giraffalo bent his neck and told Bruno what the bull had feared. "There is no break that I can see, but I think we can run through it where the fire is thinnest."

Bruno looked around at the herd almost totally lost to panic.

"I can see over the smoke now," Giraffalo said, "and the smoke is thinnest over there." He indicated with his head.

It went against the buffalos' nature to run into the fire.

"Remember when you said we have to trust each other?" Giraffalo yelled.

Bruno looked at the herd milling around him and knew something had to be done.

"They will follow you, Bruno. Will you follow me?" asked Giraffalo.

The lead bull studied the situation and looked at Giraffalo. He knew this was the herd's only chance. Bruno bellowed that there was a path out of the fire and started the herd moving.

"*Go!*" was all he said to Giraffalo, who started moving toward the spot where the flames were thinnest.

The herd was completely engulfed in smoke and could only see the buffalo in front of them, but they could hear Bruno, and they trusted him to lead them to safety.

Giraffalo ran at the fire and could only hope the herd followed. He passed through the flames that were barely a foot deep, and just as soon as he passed into the area already burned, the danger was passed. For just a moment, Giraffalo couldn't see the herd. Then through the smoke came Bruno with two big bulls on either side running with a thousand water buffalo right behind him.

Oh, they still tease Giraffalo, calling him Stretch and Beanpole, but everyone remembers how one of the herd saved the rest because he was different.

Everyone remembers Giraffalo.

SECOND CHANCES

He was a data entry clerk for an accounting firm. He was one of twenty that made up the pool of office cubicles. The accountants themselves had offices on the next floor and were promoted from his office pool. He was the next clerk in line to be promoted, and everyone knew it. For five years, Jimmy Daniels had paid his dues, and today a spot upstairs was ready to be filled.

Jimmy had a wife and daughter whom he adored, and was adored in return. They lived on the second story of a fourplex apartment building. Jimmy's sister, Janice, and her son, Carson, lived in the apartment next door. Janice was a single mother bringing up seven-year-old Carson, who was a good playmate for little Katy, Jimmy's daughter. Katy was five, and she thought the world of her cousin, while Carson tolerated Katy because—well, she was a girl.

It was Friday, and Jimmy, who had been counting on this promotion, sat in his cubicle, half-heartedly listening to the radio, waiting on the call from his supervisor. He ate his lunch and listened as the local radio station told of a millionaire who had lost a wedding ring that was precious to him, and was offering a $15,000 reward to anyone who found it. None of that could fully penetrate Jimmy's preoccupied mind and the financial freedom the promotion held for him and his family.

"Hey, Jimmy Dan!" Sal, the guy in the next cubicle, said, poking his head around the corner of his workstation. "The big guy wants to see you in his office. I think it's about your new job, pal."

"Man, I hope so." Jimmy got up and followed Sal down the aisle between the cubicles.

"I hear they pass out box seat tickets to the game now and then," Sal said.

"That's what I hear," Jimmy replied, wiping his sweaty palms on his suit pants and straightening his tie.

"You won't forget about your old pal, Sal, when they pass them out to you, will ya?"

Jimmy winked at him and, smiling, pulled open the boss's door and left Sal outside.

J.J. Boyle was a good supervisor. Never demanding of his people, he was fair and went out of his way to make them feel like they were all in it together. He was built like a bulldog, with jowls to match.

J.J. was behind his desk, talking into the phone and waving Jimmy in as he spoke. Jimmy came into the room, trying not to appear as though he were eavesdropping on the boss's conversation.

"No, no, he's right here… yes, I'll be sure to mention it," J.J. said to whoever was on the other end. "…Yes, sir, I will." He waved Jimmy into a seat. "I'm sure it won't be a problem… okay, sir, goodbye." He hung up the phone.

Jimmy's heart beat fast. J.J. looked at him across the desk.

"Jimmy, I've got some bad news for you, son."

Jimmy's stomach lurched.

"I know you've been counting on this promotion and…"

He sat, watching his boss's lips move, feeling his body go numb as he took in what J.J. was telling him.

"…So next time, Jimmy, I guarantee it. Don't let this set you back, Jim—these things happen, and it has nothing to do with you personally."

Dejected, Jimmy left the office and shuffled back to his cubicle.

"Well?" Sal had been posted up, waiting for the good news. "How'd it go?"

Jimmy looked at his friend.

"The owner's sister's kid, Winston, got the job, Sal. I guess I'll get the next one," he said, falling into his chair.

"Winston? The playboy from the mailroom?" Sal asked.

Jimmy nodded.

"Say, man that stinks." Sal felt awkward standing there. "I'm sorry to hear that, Jimmy."

Sal left to spread the word. Nobody bothered Jimmy the rest of the day. He was well liked among his coworkers, and no one wanted to partake in his misery.

Five o'clock rolled around, and Jimmy called his wife, Sarah, with the bad news. He delayed his trek to the parking garage with the phone call and listened as she told him it was okay, that she and little Katy would hold dinner for him till he got home.

"Don't worry, honey, you'll get it next time."

As she spoke this familiar line, he found himself gripping the phone tighter, willing himself not to be short with her. Sarah only wanted to make it better. Calmly, he agreed and signed off, telling her he'd be home soon.

With a heavy sigh, he sat back and listened as the radio was the only other noise left in the office pool.

"...And finally, this..."

The radio droned on.

"The millionaire who lost his precious ring has upped the reward to twenty thousand dollars. When asked why so much, he replied that his late wife had given it to him to commemorate a special day in their lives together. He claims there is a special inscription on the inside of the ring, and he would know the ring from this. When asked what it was, he wouldn't say. Be sure to stay tuned, as a man and a goat—"

Jimmy turned the radio off and stood to shut down the office. It was no accident that he was the last one out on a Friday night. He wasn't in the mood to face a bunch of rowdy weekenders in the parking garage.

He walked across the deserted structure and unlocked his seven-year-old Chevy. Sliding into the seat, he pulled the door closed and stared at the concrete wall in front of the car, thinking about the day's events. He reached to start the engine.

Nothing.

Jimmy sat still, then turned the key again. The starter rrrrr'd but didn't catch.

"Damn!" He hit the steering wheel.

Once more he tried the key, this time until the engine wore the battery down to a click, click, click.

"Damn, damn, damn!" he yelled, pounding his fists against the steering wheel and kicking the floorboard. "What do I gotta do to get a break around here?!"

He shouted the words to the concrete wall as if it had the answers.

For a minute, he just sat there, collecting himself. Then, with a heavy sigh, he opened the door, climbed out, and slammed it shut behind him. Running his hands through his hair, he glanced around the empty garage.

Just then, a Lincoln Town Car came down the ramp from the upper floors, radio thumping. The car pulled up beside him. Its tinted window slid down, and the volume of the music lowered.

Jimmy stepped forward and leaned in to see who it was.

In the passenger seat sat a buxom blonde, cleavage front and center. Behind the wheel—of course—was Winston.

Perfect, Jimmy thought.

"Jimmy!"

He straightened up and looked around the otherwise empty garage.

"Hey, Jim, we're all going over to Tillie's to celebrate. Come with us!"

Jimmy wondered if Winston even knew whose promotion he'd just stolen.

"Can't, Winston. My car won't start, and I've gotta call someone," he said, leaning back down to speak into the open window.

Just then, Helen from the mailroom leaned over the front seat.

"Hi, Jimmy. Come with us—you can be my date tonight," she said, all provocatively sweet.

"I'm sorry about the promotion thing, old boy," Winston added. "Let me buy you a drink, and then I'll take you home. You don't have to call anyone."

"No thanks. You three go on—have a good time. I'm not really in the mood to party tonight," Jimmy replied.

"Nonsense, Jimmy Dan," Winston said, motioning for Helen to open the back door. "I insist. I feel like such a heel and want to make it up to you. It wasn't my idea to get bumped up ahead of you. At least let me give you a ride home."

He straightened up and checked his watch.

"Come on, Jimmy, I won't bite… hard," Helen said, and she and the blonde in the front seat shared a giggle.

Jimmy sighed, walked back to his car to make sure it was locked, then climbed into the back of the Town Car. Helen scooted closer, purring, "Hi, Jimmy."

"Look, I just need a ride home," he said as he shut the door.

"We'll get you home, Jim," Winston assured him, guiding the car down the garage ramp and out into the street. "Come have a drink with us, buddy. It's Friday night, and the night is young."

Winston glanced back at Jimmy through the rearview mirror.

"No, Winston, I really gotta—" Jimmy started, but Helen slid over and pressed herself against him. Her perfume was intoxicating, her body a deliberate distraction.

"Oh, Jimmy, come on, honey. I know you like me," she whispered into his ear, sultry and teasing. "Because I sure like you, Jimmy."

He tried to pull away, wedged between her and the door with nowhere to go.

"Helen, I'm married."

"I won't tell," she said with a sly grin.

Winston smiled in the rearview mirror, clearly enjoying the scene unfolding in his back seat.

Helen opened her hand, revealing two small pills. "Look what I got," she said quietly.

"What's that?" Jimmy asked, a little too sharply.

Helen leaned back, feigning surprise at his tone. "It's X, silly. You know—ecstasy."

"Drugs?"

"Don't be like that, Jimmy," she said, drawing back slightly, her playful tone cooling as if he'd ruined the vibe.

"Pull the car over, Winston," Jimmy said, leaning over the front seat.

"Aw, come on, pal, lighten up a little," Winston replied, steering the car around a corner.

"I said stop the damn car!" Jimmy yelled, his voice sharp against Winston's head.

Winston pulled the car to the curb barely three blocks from the garage. Jimmy opened the door and got out.

"Say, Jim, no hard feelings, right? We were just trying to be friendly," Winston said through the open door. "I mean, this doesn't have to be an issue at work, right?"

Jimmy could tell Winston was worried he might say something about the drugs at the office. Three pairs of eyes watched him closely as he formed his reply.

"I'm not going to say anything," Jimmy said, knowing it was true. "What you do on your own time is your own business. I just need to get home." He closed the car door and backed away as they drove off, leaving him alone beside a vacant lot.

He looked around, checked his watch, and with a random kick at a rock in the road, started walking back the way they had come. He stepped onto a cracked sidewalk beside the empty lot. Across the street was another empty field, with a freeway pillar holding up the highway above.

Fifty feet up the walk stood a dilapidated phone booth—a standing relic of the past.

"Hey, you!" someone yelled from behind him, across the street.

Jimmy turned to see two thugs hurrying to cross and jogging toward him.

"Hey, can you spare some change, man?" said one of them.

Both looked to be in their early twenties, with the menacing air of street life hardened into their features. Jimmy quickly glanced around, his instincts screaming trouble.

"Yeah, I'm talking to you," said the taller one.

"What do you want?" Jimmy asked, suddenly feeling conspicuous in his suit coat and tie.

"What do you think we want, punk?" said the shorter thug, pushing Jimmy roughly.

Jimmy turned to face the one talking to him when the taller thug punched him square in the mouth, splitting his lip. Before Jimmy's head could recover from the blow, the shorter thug drove a fist into his stomach, doubling him over.

This was a dance the two thugs had practiced to perfection. Jimmy never stood a chance.

After the first two blows, all he could do was curl up on the sidewalk and take the kicks raining down.

"Get his wallet!" one of them barked.

Jimmy's wallet was ripped from his pocket.

"Eighteen dollars!" said the mugger in disgust. "You're going to have to do better than that, asshole."

"What about credit cards?" said the guy trying to roll Jimmy over to get to the pockets underneath him.

"Cops!" And Jimmy's dismantled wallet bounced off his head as the two thugs raced back the way they had come.

Jimmy slowly sat up. He checked his lip with the tips of his fingers as he watched the cop car slowly roll up and stop at the curb where he sat. The flashing lights came on. There were two officers in the car. Nobody got out.

The officer in the passenger seat rolled down the window and asked Jimmy if he was alright.

"Yeah, I'm just peachy," Jimmy said, sitting on the sidewalk and nursing his broken lip.

"You want to file a complaint?" asked the cop. "We can run you down to the station, and you can look at the mug books, maybe I.D. your muggers."

Jimmy shook his head as he got to his feet. "Yeah, I'd like to, officer, but see, I got this other thing to go to." He paused to spit blood out of his mouth. "And other people are expecting to kick the crap out of me too. Wouldn't want to disappoint them, now would I?" He said sarcastically as he took off his scuffed-up coat and loosened his tie.

"Look, mister, this isn't the best neighborhood to be roaming around on a Friday night dressed in a suit and tie. Now, I know you're mad, and if you lost anything like jewelry, maybe we can get it back for you," the officer told him. "But you must file a complaint and identify your attackers. Otherwise, can we contact someone for you, or take you somewhere?"

Jimmy dusted off his pants and, after a deep calming breath, said, "No, officer, I'll just walk back to the garage and call someone from there. It's only a few blocks from here."

"Are you sure? Because it's no problem."

"Naw, it's been a long day," Jimmy said, looking up and down the street. "Those guys are long gone and probably still running. Besides, the walk will do me good."

He stretched, pretending to be better than he felt.

"Alright, sir, we'll be in the area if you need us," the cop told him.

Jimmy watched as the car pulled away from the curb and drifted down the street. The strobing lights went out. He started walking in the opposite direction, toward the broken-down phone booth.

"We'll be in the area, he says," Jimmy muttered under his breath. "Couldn't be in the area when Pete and Repeat started their little kicking contest."

He punctuated this by kicking a rock across the street. The rock shot off with a sharp pain in his leg causing him to wince and look down to see the tear in his pant leg and a bloody knee poking through.

"Great," he said and limped up to the phone booth, barely noticing that most of the glass had been broken out and that it looked like it was about to fall over.

Oddly, the overhead light was on.

Jimmy was preoccupied with his misery and paid it little mind. As he passed, the phone started ringing. It startled him for a moment but only earned a quick glance over his shoulder as he limped past.

The phone kept ringing. When he did stop and look back, he knew if he went back and answered it, it would probably stop before he could pick it up.

It continued to ring with the persistence of a dreaded midnight call.

He limped back to the phone and stepped in under the neon light. As he reached for and picked up the handset, he noticed a bunch of frayed wires sticking out of the back of the phone.

He felt his whole arm start to tingle as he brought the handset up to his ear. Light-headed, he had to reach out to brace himself as the tingling seemed to reach his head.

"Jimmy!" said a voice over the phone.

"...walking for a minute," said the voice.

"Boy, I thought you were going to keep—"

"Who... who is this?" Jimmy asked in a slight daze.

"Well," said the voice, "I guess you could say I'm your guardian angel, but after the day you're having, I wouldn't be a very good one, would I?" The voice laughed out loud.

Jimmy didn't think that was very funny.

"What do you want?" he asked, looking around outside the booth for some clue as to who this was on the phone and how they were seeing him.

"Jimmy, I'll be straight with you, son. You asked for a break, and I've been authorized to give you one. But—and this is important, Jim—one is all you get, so don't waste it. You picking up what I'm laying down, son?" said the voice.

"Who is this?" Jimmy asked again, looking behind him. "Where are you? And how'd you know my name?" He turned back and noticed his reflection in the polished metal surface of the phone.

"None of that matters, Jim. You remember what I said—don't waste it."

Looking at his swelling eye and bloodied lip in the metal face of the phone, he heard the connection break—no dial tone, just dead silence.

Jimmy pulled the phone away from his ear and looked at the handset as if it might provide some clue to the caller's identity. Instead, he noticed someone had pressed a wad of chewing gum—already chewed—into the listening cup of the phone, and one side of the mess was still stuck to his ear.

He pushed the handset away, reaching for his ear to feel the gum attached.

"What the..." This seemed to be Jimmy's breaking point.

"Gum?" he said, looking at the sticky mess on his fingers still trailing from the side of his head.

He let go of the phone and backed out of the booth, wiping his hand on his pants and angrily scrubbing the side of his head.

"Good one, God!" he yelled to an empty sky. "That's exactly what I needed! Somebody's nasty-ass gum in my ear! You call that a break?"

He kicked the phone booth, causing the light to flicker and then go out.

Jimmy turned and marched down the street toward the parking garage, oblivious to the pain in his knee.

Jimmy was mad.

He had a cell phone in his glovebox for emergencies, and he planned to call someone to come get him.

When he got to his car and dropped into the seat, on impulse he put the key in the ignition and turned it—starting it right up.

For a moment, he sat there stunned.

He expected the car not to start. He knew the car wouldn't start. Yet it did.

Jimmy wasted no time putting the car in gear and started to leave the garage for home.

That's when the front tire blew.

A twenty-minute drive from work took him an hour and a half.

When Jimmy pulled into his parking area, he did so on a temporary tire that he'd had to change before finally leaving the garage.

Jimmy walked with a slight limp up to the fourplex apartment building and climbed the stairs.

His sister, Janice, was coming from his apartment with a bucket of steaming water headed to her own across the porch.

"Your hot water broke again?" he asked her.

"Oh my God, Jimmy, what happened to you?" she said, stepping back to let him pass.

"I got a flat," he told her as he went into his apartment.

She followed him in and heard the same question from her sister-in-law.

"It looks like you had more than a flat, honey. What happened to your lip?"

Sarah assessed the damage done to her husband. His shirt sleeves were rolled up, and his hands were blackened from changing the tire. His lip was split and swollen, with a smudge on his forehead.

"And what's that on the side of your head?" she asked.

Janice stood back and watched her brother and his wife sort out this day.

"Look, honey," Jimmy said as he disengaged himself from her, "I really need a shower. You wouldn't believe the kind of day I've had." He left the two women and started down the hallway to the bathroom.

"Jimmy, honey, are you okay?" Sarah asked, still concerned.

He waved as he disappeared into the bathroom down the hall.

Janice ducked out to empty the bucket and got back just in time to hear her brother yelling from the bathroom, "Son of a bitch! Can't I even get a hot shower in my own bathroom!?"

The bathroom door opened, and he came out wrapped in a towel, disappearing through the door across the hall.

"If it isn't one thing, it's another!" the two women heard from the closed bedroom door.

Sarah turned to Janice in time to see tears spill from her eyes.

"He knows the pilot light won't stay lit on our water heater," Janice said through her sobs. "He's the one who told us to get the water from over here and not use the water heater."   She cried.

"I know, honey," Sarah soothed. "He doesn't mean it. It's been a bad day for him. He'll feel better in the morning."

"I waited till after nine to take my bath," Janice said, wiping her eyes.

"It's not your fault, honey," Sarah told her sister-in-law as she walked her back to her apartment door across the porch. "You know Jimmy — he'll be over first thing in the morning to apologize. Don't let it bother you."

She left Janice and, after locking up, went to take care of her husband.

Meanwhile, the radio droned on unattended. "...next up, the reward for the missing ring hits twenty-five thousand..."

The next morning, Jimmy was up early. After a hot shower, he came down the hall to the sound of Saturday morning cartoons.

"Hi, Daddy," little Katy said, perched in front of the TV. Her hair was disheveled; she was still in her nightgown and clutched her favorite pink bunny.

Jimmy went over to her in his robe, picked her up, kissed her cheek, and carried her into the kitchen to start the morning coffee.

"Daddy, what happened to your mouth?" Katy asked, poking her little finger into the wound.

"Ow!" he said, pulling back. "Be careful, sweetpea. Daddy got in a fight with ten lumberjacks last night, and it wasn't pretty." He gave her a raspberry on the side of her neck, causing a fit of giggles.

"Really, Daddy?" she asked.

He told her it was true. Her eyes wide with little girl wonder, she asked, "Did you beat them up?"

"Of course I did," he said, getting her cereal bowl and pouring her favorite cereal. "Where's Carson?" he asked, sitting her back in front of the TV.

Through her first bite of cereal, she told him, "He didn't come over yet. We're gonna watch G.I. Joe." Then, as an afterthought, "Daddy, can you beat G.I. Joe up?"

"If he gets out of line, I can," Jimmy said.

He heard the morning paper hit the porch and left her to go get it. With a cup of coffee and the paper, he sat down in the adjoining dining area, turned on the radio, and opened the paper. Carefully sipping his coffee, he almost burned his mouth when he read page two.

"I don't believe it!" he said as Sarah walked into the dining area on her way to the kitchen.

"What?" she asked, pouring her first cup and coming over to sit with him.

He showed her the paper, pointing to a picture of two smiling idiots holding up a check for the missing ring.

"Huh," she said, reading aloud. "They found that millionaire's ring."

"Those are the two assholes that attacked me last night!" Jimmy said, exasperated.

She shushed him and told him to keep his voice down, pointing toward the living room where their daughter sat.

"That's incredible," he said. "So much for karma, huh? Where did they find it?" she asked, sipping her coffee.

He read for a moment. "It says here they found it in the coin return of an old, broken-down phone booth." He sat back, staring off at nothing. "You don't suppose it was the same—"

He was cut off by an explosion that blasted through the dining area window. Jimmy instinctively ducked and covered his head. The noise left his head ringing.

Rising up to take stock, he saw Sarah was okay.

"Katy!" Both parents bolted for the living room. Katy was crying, but Jimmy picked her up. She didn't appear to be harmed. He handed her off to Sarah and ran to the front door, flinging it wide to look across the porch, where he saw his sister's apartment on fire.

The damn water heater, he thought.

"Janice!" he yelled, starting across the porch with Sarah, carrying Katy, one step behind him.

He stopped and turned to his wife, shielding her from what he'd just seen.

"The stairs, Sarah," he said.

The door on his sister's apartment had been blown completely off its hinges and lay across the porch. The dining area windows of both apartments faced out and sat side by side.

Jimmy's window had been blown inward, while the explosion from Janice's apartment blew out her window.

It was this window where Janice's body hung out, burnt and bloodied, her eyes fixed and open but seeing nothing. Smoke billowed out, and fire flickered inside.

"Go!" he yelled as tears from the smoke and the enormity of the situation spilled from his eyes.

"Get her down!"

"What about Carson?" Sarah yelled over the roar of the fire, pressing her daughter's head into her chest to keep her from seeing the flames.

"Carson!" Just then, Carson's screams came from inside the apartment.

"Go, Sarah," Jimmy urged again. As she took Katy down the stairs, he started to enter the apartment—but had to stop. The heat was unbearable.

His nephew called for help again.

Jimmy ran back across the porch to the kitchen, stripping off his robe as he went. Reaching the sink, he threw the robe into it and turned on both taps. The water couldn't come out fast enough.

Spinning around, he yanked open the refrigerator, grabbed the water jug, and emptied it onto the robe. Kool-Aid, orange juice—anything he could find—soaking the robe completely. He snatched it out of the sink, struggling to put it on as he ran back next door.

Smoke billowed out, flames licking down the path he had to take.

Crouched low, he started into the burning apartment, figuring Carson would be trapped in his room.

As he moved down the hallway, he pulled the wet robe over his head and heard Carson cry for help again—this time giving him a bearing.

Jimmy burst into the bathroom and slammed the door behind him.

"Uncle Jimmy!" came the boy's voice from the bathtub.

Jimmy rushed over, scooped him into his arms, and climbed into the tub with him. He turned on the water and activated the shower. Steam still rose off his wet robe from his trek down the hall.

Quickly, Jimmy glanced at the only window in the bathroom and sighed in despair—it was too small for Carson to fit through.

"Come on, buddy, we've got to get real wet to get out of here," he told the boy, soaking them both.

Carson clung tightly to his uncle's neck.

"Are we going to get burned up, Uncle Jimmy?"

"Of course not, Carson. But we have to be fast," Jimmy said, trying to smile reassuringly.

He clutched Carson tightly, climbed out of the tub, and headed for the door.

Jimmy pulled the dripping robe over himself and Carson, wrapping his nephew up and holding him close.

"Hang on, Carson. Uncle Jimmy's going to get us out of here."

He opened the bathroom door and took an involuntary step back from the heat.

Crouching as low as he could, he ran into the burning hallway. He felt the skin blistering on his back as he passed beneath the flames. The noise was deafening.

At the end of the hall, the apartment opened up. To the left was the kitchen and dining area, to the right the living room, with the front door between them at the farthest point.

Jimmy was running all out. As he reached the end of the hallway, the gas main in the kitchen exploded, filling the entire left side of his path with intense blue fire.

Jimmy never slowed. He kept running, right through what was left of the front window in the living room.

One story below the burning apartment, a crowd had gathered, watching as a smoking ball of Jimmy launched himself from the upstairs window and fell onto the grass below.

Time seemed to slow for Jimmy then. He was aware that Carson was curled up in his arms and that the air suddenly felt cooler. He caught glimpses of the people below as he and Carson made their descent. He could see the plush green grass scattered with pieces of glass and debris from the blast.

Then, everything sped back up as he hit the ground. Jolted by the impact, he gasped for breath. Carson was coughing but still clinging tightly to him.

Someone lifted Carson from his arms. Jimmy noticed his nephew was covered in blood. This confused him.

"Jimmy?" he heard through the crowd. Was that Sarah?

"Jimmy?" Sarah called again, and then she was there beside him.

He reached for her, trying to say something, but all that came out was a gurgling sound.

"Oh my God! Somebody do something!" she cried, pressing her hand to the side of his neck. She was sobbing, trying to speak through her tears.

"It's okay, baby. Oh Jimmy, honey, say something!" She clutched him tightly, and he tried to respond.

She was a silhouette against the morning sky. He saw the blood covering them both and wondered where it was coming from.

The pulse from the wound in his neck started to slow, and his sight began to fade.

"Jimmy!" Sarah called from far away, and he stared into the sky, watching smoke drift upward.

Then the light faded too much.

"Jimmy! Jimmy, honey, please…" Sarah sobbed, rocking her dying husband.

He wanted to tell her something to stop her tears, but he didn't know what.

He was fading, confused, unable to grasp it all.

The blackness took him.

For a moment, there was silence—peace, even—until the blackness began to fade.

He started to regain vision; things began to lighten.

There was an image before him.

Was it a face?

"Jimmy?" he heard, trying to make out a metallic reflection of his own face.

His whole body tingled.

"What the..." he thought.

"Jimmy, honey, is that you?" Sarah's voice.

Sarah? He thought.

Then he said it.

"Sarah?"

His daze cleared as he realized the reflection he was seeing was the metal face of that dilapidated phone booth.

"Jimmy, where are you?" Sarah's voice came over the phone pressed to his ear.

He pulled the handset away and glanced at it. The wad of gum was still clinging to his ear. Involuntarily, he chuckled and scooped it off with his fingers, suddenly aware of his freshly split lip.

"Jimmy, honey, you're scaring me. Are you alright?" she asked, worry threading her words.

He put the phone back to his ear. "Sarah, is that you, baby?" he asked, nearly giddy with joy.

"Jimmy, are you drunk, honey? Do you want Janice to come get you?" she pressed, concern rising.

He laughed into the phone, then whoo-hooed. "Am I drunk? No, baby, I'm fine. I'll be home just as soon as I can. Tell Janice not to use the water heater—she can get all the water she needs from us tonight."

"Okay, are you sure you're okay?" she wasn't convinced.

"I'm fine, really. I'll be home soon... I gotta fix a flat... or maybe I'm getting one. Honey, I gotta go. I love you."

"Okay," she said softly, and he hung up.

Jimmy danced out of the booth on a sore leg and a light heart, whoo-hooing again as he wiped the gum from his ear.

Suddenly, he stopped.

Slowly, he turned and looked back at the little phone booth. The neon light flickered—almost as if it were winking at him.

He went back and stepped inside.

Tentatively, he reached up, pulled down the coin return cup, and stuck his finger inside. His fingers closed around something round.

He pulled out a shiny gold ring. Just a simple gold band.

His heart hammered as he held it up to read the inscription inside: *To second chances, love Phoebe.*

"Well, I'll be," he muttered to himself.

He tucked the ring into his pocket and left the phone booth, smiling.

As he rounded the corner and disappeared from sight, the light in the booth flickered one last time—and went out.

THE END

Billy Schultz and the
Fantastic Time Machine

It was obvious Billy Schultz was special when he was barely walking. At age four, he shaved the family cat, claiming that now she, being in heat, wouldn't be so hot and always crying to go outside. Unfortunately, Dad's electric beard trimmer was never the same, neither was the cat. The cat's new name became Baldilocks. When Billy was six years old, a small dog followed him home and took up residence in Billy's bedroom. The dog's name became Spike. Spike seemed to treat everybody, but Billy, as a suspect in the ongoing criminal investigation that was Spike's life. In short, Spike was a grump and would nip at you if you got too close to the crime scene. Billy's mom was an exception, for she fed him, and he even allowed her to pet and stroke him and sometimes bathe him when he developed his "dog odor" that only Billy's mom could smell, according to Billy and Spike anyway.

Billy was as busy as a boy could be. Billy's best friend, outside of Spike, was Allen Tasker. Bart had Millhouse, Ren had Stimpy, Batman had Robin, Sherlock Holmes had Dr. Watson, and Billy Schultz had Allen Tasker. Allen was almost frail looking and always one step behind Billy with Spike bringing up the rear, well out of reach of the fast-moving feet of the two little boys. Allen trusted Billy explicitly. He was the perfect assistant. Spike trusted no one and always let the boys know when anyone, except Billy's mom, approached.

One day, while the trio played outside, a thought came to Billy that he could transport living matter through time by the use of high intense light. Billy and Allen were kneeling down in the backyard in a two-boy huddle with Spike keeping watch. They were looking at ants and or other insects crawling in the grass through a magnifying glass.

"And see how when the light from the glass hits them, how fast they age?" Billy was telling Allen as he unintentionally burned the unsuspecting insects.

"Why do they smoke and squirm like that?" Allen asked, which was a valid question.

"Time friction," said Billy. "They are aging so fast that the friction from their time travel makes it seem like they are burning under the light." Billy was seven years old.

As the boys further explored their discovery, Billy's dad walked into the backyard. Spike gave a warning growl as he approached.

"Hey, you two, what's up?" Dad asked, looking over the two boys, while blocking the sunlight.

The two boys looked at each other and answered that nothing was up.

"Have you two seen Baldilocks? Those darn squirrels have got to go!" Dad said, indicating the large tree beside the house.

The two boys looked at the tree.

Dad continued, "They're tearing up the wires in the attic, and that cat does nothing about it. Why do we have a cat if..." He wandered off toward the tree.

The boys followed.

"Billy?" Billy's mom called from the back porch. Spotting her son, she called across the yard, "Now you boys help Billy's father." She was shaking out a towel, and the cat Dad was looking for was rubbing against her legs. The boys reacted. Billy, shoving his magnifying Time Machine glass into his back pocket, ran over and grabbed the cat that noticed the approaching boys too late and was captured.

Just then Dad came around the corner.

"There you are!" he said, taking Baldilocks from Billy. Mr. Schultz carried the cat over to the tree, Billy and Allen in tow. "It's time you earned your keep," he said, while stroking Baldilocks. He squatted down, putting the cat between his feet while looking up at two squirrels chattering on the upper branches.

"See those nasty little pests up there?" Dad said to the cat. "They're laughing at you. They're not afraid of *you*." He pointed the cat's face toward the squirrels watching from above.

Baldilocks, enjoying the attention, started to purr.

"Maybe put her in the tree, Dad," Billy said, trying to be helpful.

Dad picked up Baldilocks and reached up to put her on the lower branches just above his head. Baldilocks, ignoring the chattering squirrels above, looked at the trio below. A nut from above banked off her head.

"Did you see that?" Allen said.

Billy laughed, and Dad looked up at the squirrels, while shaking his head. Baldilocks made a break for it down the tree, past the boys, and dashed under the porch. The squirrels seemed to chatter louder as if they were laughing.

"Yeah, laugh all you want," Dad said. "I'll get you, you little bushy-tailed rats!"

The two boys laughed behind their hands.

Dad looked down and gave a heavy sigh. All of a sudden, he looked up. "Hey, there's a new state lottery," he said, changing subjects. "I'm gonna give it a try. Wanna help me pick the numbers?"

"Sure, Dad," Billy said.

The trio, Spike in tow, walked back into the house.

As it turned out, that lottery ticket hit four out of six numbers and was the closest he had come to hitting the jackpot. Mr. Schultz always included Billy in the picking of the numbers. As for squirrels, it was another year before Billy figured out how to get Baldilocks to chase them off the property.

Billy was a boy who did not believe in quitting. Okay, the time machine wasn't exactly right, but he was convinced that the magnifying glass played a part in time travel. Like all good inventers and scientists, his mind was always striving for the answers that hindered his projects.

It was a normal day, and Billy and Allen were in his bedroom discussing the elements that make up a young boy's life.

"My dad says that when he wins the lottery, we're getting a great big swimming pool."

Allen grunts as he is using a laser pointer to tease the cat. Spike watched from a corner. Baldilocks chased the point of light around the room with the intention of killing it. The closer she gets to Spike, the higher his lip rose, exposing his teeth in warning. Allen raced the light across the floor and up the wall, losing it in the curtains. The cat ran straight up the curtains, causing the curtain rod to give out. This caused Baldilocks, the curtains, and the curtain rod to come crashing down.

The door suddenly opened, and Billy's mom stood there with her hands on her hips.

"What are you two doing that you have to destroy this bedroom?" she said in a stern manner.

Baldilocks untangled herself and ran into the open closet. Spike quietly slinked under the bed.

"It was the cat, Mom," Billy said.

Mrs. Schultz came in, picking up the pile of curtains.

Billy jumped to his feet. "That's it!" he said, looking at Allen.

Mom looked at Billy, and Billy dashed forward and disappeared in the closet, coming out a moment later carrying Baldilocks.

"Come on, Allen," he said while running out of the bedroom.

"Don't run in the house, Billy," Mom said as the boys left the bedroom.

Allen caught up with Billy as he was going out the back door.

"Close the door so she doesn't run back in," Billy said.

"What are you gonna do?" Allen asked as he followed Billy off the porch into the yard and around the corner to the tree, where Billy placed Baldilocks on the ground.

"Where's the pointer?" he said, taking the laser pointer from Allen. "Watch." Billy placed the point of light in front of the cat.

Baldlilocks saw it and tries to put her paw on it, only to have it move. The squirrels were chattering up in the tree, positioning themselves to watch the cat. Billy moved the light around, and the cat chased it. Billy raced the light up the side of the tree, with the cat chasing it right behind. Two squirrels appeared to brace themselves as the cat bolted up the tree. Billy traced the light right up to the squirrels with the cat in hot pursuit, bounding down the branch. The squirrels panicked and took off in the opposite direction. All of the instincts in the cat took over, and Baldilock's attention was distracted from the uncatchable point of light to the catchable squirrels running away from her. The chase continued across the house roof as the nimble little squirrels made their escape across the power lines to the telephone pole. The cat does not follow.

"Well, will you look at that!" Dad had walked up as the chase unfolded.

They all watched as the cat walked across the roof, swaggering like a gunslinger. She hopped back into the tree and down the side into a hero's welcome.

—◊◊◊—

Billy always thought time travel was possible. His mind would not release how magnification through glass made things appear larger or smaller depending on how you turned it. Many times he would pull out his magnifying glass, studying it, trying to unravel the mystery of the device. At age twelve, he and Allen conducted numerous experiments altering magnetic fields and trying to magnify these fields using various magnifying devices. They reasoned that the magnetic field from a strong magnet may assist matter transformation when its image was projected through a magnifying device.

"I bet when one is set in a magnetic field that is sped up and harmonized through magnification, they're pushed through a rift in time," Billy said to Allen, who by now was taking notes.

Spike watched from his corner. Older and more tolerant of intrusion to his space, he rarely left the room except to do his business and eat.

Without warning, the door burst open.

"Mom wants you to mow the lawn." Kathy, Billy's older sister, stuck her head in.

"How many times do I have to tell you to knock?" Billy said in frustration.

Kathy ignored him, looking around at the mess that was Billy's laboratory. "What are you two geniuses doing now?" she said, taking a step into the room.

"Get out, now!" Billy told her.

"I came in to see Spike," she said as she moved over to Spike's corner bed and started scratching his happy spots.

Allen, having a crush on Kathy, tried to explain, "We're in the process of trying to fluctuate magnetic fields to create a portal in time and project through."

Kathy looked at Allen, then back to Billy, then at the array of things lying around the room. "Yeah," she said, standing back up. "Well, Billy better project himself out to that lawn mower, or Mom's going to create a portal for his allowance to fluctuate." At that said, she left, leaving the door open and Allen staring after her.

Billy gave a heavy sigh and said, "Come on, Allen," as he went out after her.

—◊◊◊—

"Do you think the Earth's rotation is maintained by the magnetic field?" Billy asked Allen as they rolled out the lawn mower from the garage.

Billy's dad came from around the corner, pen and paper in hand. "Quick, I need six numbers."

The boys were used to this by now. They rattled off the numbers.

"Thanks, wish me luck," Dad said and was gone.

The boys mowed and raked the yard like they did every Saturday. Finishing up Billy's yard, they headed over to do Allen's.

"We need gas," said Billy, going in to get money from Dad.

"I need you to get a lottery result ticket from Mr. Gentry while you're there," he said, handing Billy the money.

Gas can in hand, the two boys head out on their bikes to the local convenience store.

"What if...," said Allen as they peddled, "the magnetic field around the Earth is maintained by the Earth's rotation."

They both rode in silence for a moment. Billy was musing over what Allen had said. They arrived at the store and went in to pay for gas.

"So," said Billy as he paid, "instead of the Earth's rotation being maintained by the magnetic field, the magnetic field is created by the Earth's rotation?"

The store clerk looked at the boys. Billy asked for a lottery result ticket. This ticket gives the winning numbers to the last drawing and the number of winning tickets sold, if any, for the previous drawing.

"Pump six," said the clerk, handing the ticket to Billy. "Tell your Dad better luck next time."

Billy looked down and saw that the number of winning tickets was zero.

"Okay. Thanks, Mr. Gentry."

The boys went outside to fill their gas can.

"If that's true," said Allen, "we should be able to create our own magnetic field."

On the way back, Billy thought about this. "Just having a magnetic field isn't enough. There are magnetic fields all around us. We need to create several fields that we can control."

They filled the mower and pulled the rip cord to start it. The mower coughed but did not start. They pulled again, and after sputtering, it climbed to a steady spin.

"That's it!" cried Billy.

Allen, now familiar with these revelations, waits.

"All we have to do," Billy yelled over the mower, "is make a rotating magnetic field and overlap it with another, magnifying it in the overlapping....come on!" Billy shut off the mower and ran toward the house.

The rest of the day was spent with various spinning objects finding their way to Billy's bedroom. Every speaker Billy owned sacrificed its magnet to Billy's and Allen's project.

"Oh well, holy moley, Mr. Man. Look at this mess!" Mom said, coming in to see if Allen was staying for dinner. "Does your father know you've dismantled his truck in here? For the love of Pete, where's Spike?"

Spike, hearing the word *dinner* spoken by Mom, came through bicycle tires on Dowling rods, roulette wheels, pie pans, fan blades, and various other circular objects while making his way out of the door.

Mom shook her head and pulled the door closed as she left.

Later, while counting piggy-bank change for new magnets, Kathy pushed the door open, poking her head in. She sees the mess.

"What in the world are you up to now?" she said.

"What do you want?" Billy said, dumping change back into the piggy bank.

Still looking around, she said, "Mom wants you to wash your hands for dinner." She stepped in and spun a bicycle tire with magnets attached. "What's this for?" she asked.

"You wouldn't understand," Billy said, stopping the tire.

"It's to create a stable rotating magnetic field," said Allen, hoping to impress his crush.

"It isn't very stable if you have to keep spinning it by hand," she said, looking at her brother. "How are you gonna keep your speed constant?"

Billy just stared back as Kathy spun another wheel.

"Mom!" Billy yelled.

Kathy moved toward the door. "Dweeb," she says while she looks at Allen and winks.

Allen's face turned red.

"Fans, Einstein. Electric fans. You can attach your magnets to the blades and splice into the power source with a voltage regulator in order to control the speed." And with that, Kathy ducked out the door.

Billy and Allen looked at the open door, each thinking different things. Billy's mind was absorbing this new idea. The little brother in him rebelling against anything *she* could say, but the scientist in him could find no flaw in this new information. In fact, it was the very solution to several problems that had plagued this project. Billy bolts from the room, throwing a "Come on," to Allen over his shoulder.

They run through the living room into the dining area.

"Don't run in the house, dear," Billy's mom said. And to Allen, she said, "I spoke with your mom, dear, and she knows you're staying over."

"Thank you, Mrs. Schultz," Allen said, taking a seat at the table.

Billy's dad was already sitting at the table, as was Kathy. She was seated across the table from the boys.

"Dad, I need some stuff from the store to do my project. I gotta have an advance on my allowance. Please," Billy said as he reached for the potatoes.

"How much?" Dad asked.

Billy started thinking.

WE ARE READY | 37

Kathy watched. "He needs a fan and a voltage regulator and magnets and epoxy, don't cha', Billy?" she said, teasing him.

Billy looked at her, torn between saying something mean or admitting she was right.

"I know my truck needs washing and the rain gutters need cleaning," Dad said, seizing the opportunity to get some stuff done.

Mom, imagining her boy perched at the top of a ladder scooping crud out of the rain gutters, falling and breaking his neck, said, "Oh, now, I don't know about that, Ted. It sounds too dangerous."

Billy, quick to see an opportunity to make a buck, said, "Allen can help, and we can wash your car too, Mom."

"How much money are we talking about, Billy?" Dad said, spooning meatloaf onto his plate.

"Einstein gonna invent time travel with a magnetic fan and a nuclear yo-yo," Kathy said, teasing Billy.

Billy looked at his sister from across the table, not wanting to upset his parents while fighting with her at the dinner table, so he said, "That's right, and the first person I'm gonna thank is my genius sister who told me about the fan."

This comment was so unexpected that for a whole minute no one said anything.

"Well now, that was a nice thing to say," Mom said, smiling at Billy.

Allen, feeling the moment, couldn't control himself. "And beautiful too." Every eye turned to Allen, who promptly turned purple. "I mean… it…was beautiful…how…"

Everyone laughed openly, adding to Allen's misery.

For years, Allen had been as much a part of this family as Billy was at Allen's house. Allen's crush on Kathy was not a secret, but until now…

The boys discovered they needed well over $200.00 to fund their project. They set about mowing lawns; cleaning gutters, yards, and garages; washing cars; collecting aluminum cans; even walking Mrs. Hanson's barking, furry land shark of a dog.

They did anything and everything to earn money.

—m—

"Boy, when I win that lottery and we get our swimming pool, I'll be able to pay you boys to clean it," Dad said as he collected a drawing results ticket from Billy. "Only two numbers! That ain't worth squat," he said, crumpling up the lottery ticket. "What is all this stuff, Billy?" Dad asked as he looked at the array of equipment all over Billy's bedroom.

Billy, who was adjusting the position of fan no. 3, said, "It's going to be my time machine, Dad."

Dad, noticing his feet getting tangled in one of the many electric cords all over the room, asked, "Where's Allen?"

And as Dad backed out of the room, Allen answered, "Here, Mr. Schultz," from the closet where he was coiling more electric cords.

"You boys be careful you don't start a fire with all these electrical cords." After once more surveying the room, he asked, "Is Spike in here?"

"Mom and Kathy are giving him a bath," Billy replied.

Dad slowly pulled the door closed, only to have it pushed open again by Billy's mom. A fluffy Spike smelling like flowers came in and made his way through the obstacle course that is Billy's room, to his corner, where he started licking himself, trying to get the smell off.

"Oh now, honestly, Billy, whose car is all this?" Mom said, stepping into the room. "Allen, are you under there somewhere? I swear you need to clean all this up. It's so...a person can't even walk in here."

Allen stepped out halfway from the closet and waved at her.

"Oh, there you are, Allen. Billy, a package came for you from the university. It's in the den, hon."

Hearing this, Billy and Allen raced by her.

"Don't run in the house..."

The rest was lost as they ran to the den. This hadn't been the first time Billy had written to the Science Department at the State University, asking if there was any way to see a magnetic field.

By now the school was supportive of a young scientist's inquiries.

"It's here!" Billy exclaimed, grabbing the small package off the table. He ripped it open to reveal what appeared to be a pair of orange sunglasses. Billy held them up as Allen gathered the papers that had fallen to the floor.

Back in the room with the door closed, Billy put on the glasses.

"Turn the fan on," he said, while looking through the glasses.

Allen flipped on the fan as he read the paper.

"It's not working," Billy said.

"It says here that we need an ultraviolet light," Allen said.

Billy removed the glasses and bolted from the room. He came back in minutes holding a black florescent light with peace signs and flowers painted on it.

"My dad's hippy light," he said, plugging it in. "Black out the window." He put the light near the fans and picked up the glasses, putting them on. "Wow," Billy said, looking at the spinning fan. "Turn on the other two," he said, stepping back.

Allen does this and again.

"Wow."

"Let me see," Allen said.

Billy handed him the glasses. Allen put the glasses on and saw what appear to be fine lines of a magnetic field emanating from the spinning magnets. He looked around and saw the same lines coming from almost every electrical device in the room.

—◊◊◊—

After three days of experimenting with different configurations involving the fans and coiled electric cords and using Dad's timing light to coordinate the spinning fans and the voltage regulator to adjust them just right, Billy said, handing the glasses to Allen, "See how the lines disappear in the center?"

By now the bedroom floor was bare, except for three fans and three electric extension cords. The three coiled cords on the floor created three fields that overlapped in the center. Above and also part of this configuration, the three fields from the three fans above the coils overlapped each other as well as the lower ones, indeed creating a central area where there appeared to be no lines.

As Billy watched, Allen walked over to the fan array and slowly stuck his hand into the center of the field. Billy gasped as Allen's hand disappeared. Billy ran over and turned the overhead light on.

"Do it again," he said.

And Allen did.

Billy came over and asked as he looked at Allen's hand, "Did it hurt?"

"No," said Allen, "it didn't hurt."

So Billy put his hand in and watched as it disappeared. He pulled it back and looked at it. Everything seemed to be fine. Billy looked at Allen, removing the glasses. "We did it!"

They both gripped each other by the upper arms and hopped up and down, laughing. It seemed that they had the same idea at the same time. They both stopped. Both boys turned to look at Spike. Spike, observing from the corner, lifted his head. They picked him up.

"Don't worry, Spike, this won't hurt a bit," Billy said while patting Spike as he carried him to the fans.

Spike started to squirm. Billy needed Allen to help feed the dog into the center of the spinning fans.

"Be careful," Billy said.

"I am," said his assistant as Spike disappeared into thin air.

The boys stepped back. Spike was gone. The two boys stared at the fans, too stunned to say anything. All of a sudden the bedroom door opened, startling them visibly.

"Mom said…" Kathy poked her head in and noticed the two boys looking guilty. Something was up. "What are you two doing?" she said, stepping into the room.

Billy recovered first. "Nothing," he said, reaching over to turn off the fans. "What do you want, Kathy?" he said, throwing an elbow into Allen.

Slower, still convinced she's caught her little brother in an act of something she could later hold over his head, she said, "Mom wants you two to come and eat lunch."

Nothing appeared to be out of place, and then her eyes fell on Spike's empty bed. She looked at Billy and then back to Spike's corner.

"Where's Spike?" she asked.

Allen said, "What?" with guilt written all over his face.

"Get out, Kathy!" Billy said, pushing her back out the door.

"What are you two up to…?" she said as Billy succeeded pushing her into the hallway, closing the door.

With his back pressed up against the closed door, he asked Allen, "Where *is* Spike?"

Allen, still stunned, shrugged his shoulders.

Billy almost jumped out of his skin as a knock sounds on the door. "You boys come and eat, now!" Mom said in passing.

—◊◊◊—

The day passed with the two boys cleaning Billy's bedroom as if it was a crime scene. Allen went home early, leaving Billy in his room trying to figure out what happened. Dad came by seeking lottery numbers.

"Wow, what happened in here?" he said, indicating the spotless room. "Where's Allen?"

"He went home early," said Billy and then rattled off six numbers.

Dad wrote them down, thanked his son, and, already preoccupied, left the room.

—◊◊◊—

The next day Allen came over, and they both hung around the backyard. Billy's mom came out on the porch carrying Spike's bowl.

"Here now you two go and get Spike so he can eat. This isn't like him to miss his dinner. Where is he anyway? Spike, here Spike," she called.

Billy volunteered to take the bowl to him. "He's around the house, Mom, I'll feed him." Billy stood there, holding the dish after she left.

"What are we gonna do?" Allen asked.

Billy didn't have an answer.

—◊◊◊—

Billy went to bed that night thinking about his time machine and Spike. He just couldn't believe Spike was gone.

What were you thinking, and where is he? Those were the last thoughts he had before sleep took him.

It was late at night or early in the morning when Billy is awakened with some smelly thing rubbing against his face. Still half asleep, he pushed it away.

"Go away, Spike," he said, only to have Spike come back to lick his face again. "Stop it, Spike!" Billy said, and then it hit him. He sat bolt upright in bed. "Spike!" he said, taking the dog by the side of his head and looking into his face. "Holy moly!" Billy said, checking Spike out to see if he was okay. He then wrapped his dog up in a hug of pure relief. Billy let Spike go and checked the clock. It's nearly 3:00 a.m. He jumped out of bed, hopping across the room as he puts his tennis shoes on. He dashed out the front door and ran all the way to Allen's house.

Billy knocked on Allen's window until he opened it, rubbing his eyes. "Spike's back! He's in my room, and he's okay."

Allen was instantly awake.

The two boys spent the day setting up the time machine and discussing what to do next.

Billy's mom came into the room.

"Billy, I'd like you to go to the store and get some milk. Here's the money and please don't take all day. And your father wants a lottery ticket result thingy. I swear that man needs another hobby…," she said, walking away.

Convinced they had sent Spike into the future, they discussed how to go into the past as they ride their bikes to the store.

Mr. Gentry, the store clerk, listened as the two boys discuss possibilities as they walk in.

"Because if we sent Spike into the future at 750 revolutions per minute clockwise, all we have to do is reverse polarity and…oh, hi, Mr. Gentry, can I have a lottery result ticket, please," said Billy, placing the milk and money for it on the counter. Billy looked at the ticket and noticed no one had won the jackpot.

"Tell your dad better luck next time," said Mr. Gentry as the boys left.

"I will. Thank you."

All the way home the boys discussed the possibilities of slower or faster spinning magnets. Coming up to the porch, Billy saw his old magnifying glass and picked it up, stuffing it into his back pocket. They went into the house and gave Mom the milk, but they noticed the lottery result ticket had got wet and was stuck on the side of the milk jug. Billy peeled it off.

"Thank you, boys," Mom said, taking the milk.

Billy and Allen walked into the living room. Billy stopped, still holding the wet ticket by the corners. He turned to Allen. "What if we send this ticket back through time, and Dad plays *these* numbers?" Billy looked down at the wet ticket. The ink had faded from the wet milk jug.

Allen said, thinking out loud, "If we do that, then we'd have already got the ticket two days ago."

Billy looked at his friend, realizing he was right. If they send the ticket through today, then they had already got the ticket two days ago, and Dad had already played… Billy looked closer at the ticket but could not make out the part that said how many winners hit the jackpot. He pulled his old magnifying glass from his back pocket, and as his heart seemed to beat faster and Allen crowded in to also look, the ticket came into clear focus. Through the lens, they both watch as the number of winners turn from zero to one.

Just then they heard tires screeching out front and a crash as someone ran over the mailbox at the curb. The boys ran to the living-room window in time to see Dad jump out of his truck that was parked on top of the mailbox.

He was yelling and waving something as he dashed up the path and through the front door.

"I did it!" he yelled as Mom came into the room.

"Here now, what's…," she started to say before Dad cut her off by placing a big kiss on her mouth. He pulled back and told her, "I did it, honey. I hit the lottery!" He turned and saw the boys. "We did it, boys. We're rich!" he said, dancing around with Mom, still waving the winning ticket around. "Twenty million dollars!" he said, showing the boys the winning ticket.

They looked at the ticket and the results ticket, and then they looked at each other and began to dance around like idiots too.

Unobserved, the world's first time traveler had come out to see what all the fuss was about, and after seeing the humans jumping around like maniacs, Spike turned and walked back into Billy's bedroom, where he turned to circle his bed three times before lying down and, with a heavy sigh, took a nap.

Megan's Story

Our light of observation shines first on a woman in despair. She is alone in a child's room, crying over the absence of its occupant, yet she clings to the last item left in Pandora's Box—hope, the purest form of faith in things not often reasonable and not always seen. A total disregard for the reality that her child, a five-year-old boy is, in fact, gone and might not return. Yet still she clings to hope as a drowning victim clings to a life ring from the very boat that tossed him in the sea. A little girl of six watches from the doorway as her mother clutches her brother's favorite toy.

"Don't cry, Mommy. Timmy will come home," she says.

The woman looks up at her daughter and tries to smile through tears of grief. Words escape the woman, and the girl can only watch her mother as both of them struggle to understand.

"Megan, honey, come away from there," her father's voice draws her attention from down the hallway. The man gently pulls the little girl away from the doorway into the darkened hallway and squats before her, taking her shoulders in his hands and looks into her face as he explains, "Mommy needs to have some space right now. She misses Timmy and is sad." He sees the little girl for the first time in days since his son has gone missing. He realizes that in their grief in missing their son and the drama of the search has caused them to neglect their other child. The tracks her tears had made attested to her grief as well. Megan's unwashed hair, naturally curly and a luscious brown just like her mother's, lay stringy on her shoulders. Her clothes are dirty, and her eyes are sad. A father's heart aches anew. He pulls her to him and hugs her, feeling her trembling six-year-old body soaking up his love.

"I miss him too, Daddy," she tells him, hugging his neck.

"I know, honey, I know," he whispers. He holds her away from him and tells her, "I gotta take care of Mommy now. Take Rufus into your room for now, and I'll come to tuck you in, in a little while." Rufus, being the standard-size Chihuahua watching from the end of the hall.

"Okay, Daddy. Come on, Rufus," she says, sniffing and pulling away from him as she enters a door off the hallway and turns on the light. The dog follows.

There is a princess clock on the dresser that shows 9:00 p.m. The room is painted pink and white. The only contrast being the dark window framed by gossamer curtains and a vintage ventriloquist's doll that sits in a small wooden chair in the corner of the room. The doll is dressed in a black tuxedo with its inanimate face facing forward and oversized eyes looking away from the bed where Meagan and Rufus sit. Stuffed animals are scattered around the child's room. It is quiet in the house. The door to the room is open but, unnoticed by Megan as she clings to the dog, starts to close on its own. Slowly, it shuts out the hallway, where her parents might appear, until it fits into the doorframe with a sounding snap as its mechanism shoots home. Rufus's head comes up, and he issues a little growl-whine. Megan pulls him to her as her attention is also drawn to the door, and all is quiet again.

"Don't worry, Rufus, they'll find Timmy. And then Mommy and Daddy won't be sad," she says almost in a whisper.

The dog shivers next to the child and whines his reply.

Megan's attention shifts to the dark window and then to the ventriloquist doll. She gasps as its eyes slowly move by themselves from the opposite wall to settle on her sitting on her bed with the dog.

"They won't find Timmy."

She can hear the dolls ceramic mouth click and clack as it speaks.

"You were supposed to watch him, weren't you?"

Rufus yips and tries to pull away from Megan to get to the doll, but Megan holds him fast to her side. Eyes wide, mouth forming a silent *O*, she stares at the doll, afraid to move.

"You know where he is," the doll teases.

Slowly, she indicates, no, with her head.

"Yes, you do," the doll insists.

Rufus cannot be restrained any longer as he bounds to the edge of the bed and barks furiously at the doll.

The doll's eyes move to the dog, and it hisses, "Shed-up ya lap rat, or I'll sic the cat on you!"

Rufus attempts to jump off the bed to get to the doll.

Megan scampers across the bed and grabs him.

"No!" she says to the doll.

"Yes!" Its eyes move back to Megan as it insists.

Megan, almost trancelike, whispers, "He's in the house on the hill."

"Bingo!" says the doll and then laughs.

"But the police say there's no one up there," she reasons. She watches as the doll's eyes roll up into its head and then find her again.

"*She* is up there…"

Rufus struggles to get free.

"And," adds the doll, "*she* has children—*all* the children." Again, the doll laughs, and as Rufus finally gets free and bounds down off the bed, the doll's eyes return to the wall and again becomes lifeless. Rufus reaches the doll and, with an angry growl, grabs its lifeless leg, pulling it off the chair, angrily shaking it side to side. Suddenly, the door to the hallway opens and Megan's father comes in.

"Rufus!" he says as he sees the dog attacking the antique doll. He stepped over and separates the two, sitting the doll back on the chair and trying to hand Rufus to Megan. "I think he wants to go outside, honey. Take him out and then it's your bedtime."

Megan's eyes are riveted to the doll.

"Megan!" her dad says as she absently takes Rufus, then slowly looks up to her daddy. "Megan, are you all right?" he asks, feeling her forehead. "You feel all right. Listen, make sure you stay in the front yard and put a jacket on. It's cold out there," he says as he leaves the room.

The doll comes back to life as Dad disappears into the dark of the hallway. Its eyes roll slowly back toward Megan.

"*You* have to go and get him, Megan," the doll teases the girl.

"But I'm only little," she says under her breath while clutching her dog.

Rufus looks up at her and licks the side of her neck. Tears pool in her eyes. Rufus whines.

The doll chuckles. "If you don't..." He lets the rest of the sentence hang. Then its eyes return to the far wall, and all is silent again.

Where Megan and her family live is a typical tract home neighborhood of the middle class Main Street, USA, where all the neighbors know each other. As Megan descends the four steps from her porch to the front yard, she is dwarfed by the night. The front yards in her neighborhood are empty of life. Cars line both sides of the street, but there is no movement except for one page of a local newspaper being pushed by the wind down the middle of the quiet street. On Megan's left as she faces the street, she sees the cross street and can just make out the stop sign. To her right, where the paper continues its windy path, her street, Maple Street, continues into a cul-de-sac. There are three street lights on Maple Street that hold off the dark of the night, the furthest being at the end of the cul-de-sac. Beyond that there is only darkness, but Megan knows what's beyond the light. The sky is dark, and the moon is hidden behind clouds that are only visible when they thin before the moon as they pass. A dog barks in the distance. Otherwise, all is still and ominously quiet. Rufus returns from doing his business and dutifully stands next to Megan looking up at her expectantly. Megan looks down at him and makes a decision.

"Come on, Rufus, we have to go get Timmy," she says with a heavy sigh. Then she walks across her yard, past the cars parked at the curb, and starts to walk down the middle of the street. Rufus whines his little dog whine but follows nonetheless.

As she walks down the middle of Maple Street, between the parked cars, passing unnoticed by the windows of the houses that line her path, a gentle breeze presses her back as she and Rufus close in upon the darkness at the end of the street. As she gets closer, she can see the two stone pillars that support two sides of a huge wrought iron gate that have stood there for at least one hundred years. The two-piece gate is chained together, but the left side is separated from the upper hinge and sags into the right, creating a triangle of space at the bottom where curious children can dare each other to pass. The newspaper page that blew past Megan moments before is spread out across the bars of the gate, caught in the wind. It is the front page of a local newspaper with headlines that read, "MISSING CHILDREN PLAGUE COMMUNITY,

LOCAL PRIEST CLEARED OF WRONGDOING." Below this headline is the picture of a priest in his Catholic vestments. Megan has eyes only for the darkness beyond the gate. She stands before the gate, gathering her courage, and watches as the clouds part from in front of the moon, revealing the house on the hill. A dark Victorian silhouette stands out of place in these modern times. Abandoned to decay and neglect, this house, surrounded by trees stripped of their leaves by the season, stands as the urban legend of the neighborhood. A constant challenge for schoolchildren to test their courage and dare their friends. Megan stands transfixed as Rufus shivers beside her ankle.

"Hey!" a man says as he steps from the darkness beside the left-hand pillar.

Megan jumps, startled by his sudden appearance.

Rufus yips and presses into her leg.

"What are you doing here, little girl?"

She recognizes him and breathes a sigh of relief. "Oh, hi, Father Spivey," Megan says with a smile.

Father Spivey is unshaved, wearing a tattered dirty black frock coat covering a black shirt, also dirty, with a white square beneath his chin, marking him as a priest of the Catholic order. The very man whose picture is pressed into the iron gate beside the opening that Megan must go through. He is clutching a simple wooden cross with a silver icon nailed to it. His eyes are wild, his hair unkempt, while his demeanor is that of desperation.

"I gotta go get Timmy," Megan tells him matter of fact.

"Oh, Christ, child!" Father Spivey says, stepping away from his place beside the pillar. "You *can't* go up *there!*" His eyes dart around looking for what he *knows* lurks in the dark beyond his vision.

"I have to!" Megan says and starts for the opening in the gate.

"No!" he hisses and steps in front of her.

She plants her foot in frustration, placing her fists on her hips and cocking her head at an angle and says, "Mommy and Daddy are sad, and Timmy has to come home, *now!*" She tries to step around him, but he is reluctant to let her pass. "I'll scream," she threatens.

He steps back, looking horrified. Larry Spivey cannot be seen pestering a screaming child in the middle of the night, not in the wake of his woes with the community.

"I *have* to!" Megan insists, passing him and ducking under the opening in the gate.

Larry is forced to finally approach the evil he knows is in this place.

"Wait!" he whispers as loud as he can, afraid the surrounding houses might hear him.

Megan stops and looks back at him.

"I…I…"

The scene hangs for a moment as he stands up straighter and resolves his fear. He crosses himself and kisses the wooden crucifix clutched in his hand as he too passes below the gate opening, and together, the three move into the darkness beyond the streetlight.

"You're Megan Carpenter, Tim Carpenter's sister, right?" Larry asks as they start walking up the driveway between gnarled oak trees and the reaching branches of the maple trees that give the street its name.

"Umm, hmm," Megan says as they walk.

It is quiet but for the leaves blowing across the driveway and through the branches overhead. Rufus is practically riding on Emily's foot as they walk. The moon is still partially visible and illuminates their path. Megan reaches up and takes the priest's hand, and he is grateful. They round the last curve of the driveway that goes passed the front of the house. Suddenly, the moon hides, putting the place in almost pitch black. As they come near the house, they can make out a soft glow behind several downstairs windows. The front yard is in pitch darkness, but they find their way to the bottom step of the porch. As they ascend the wooden steps, the boards create a melody of squeaks and creaks that fray the last nerve of Father Larry Spivey. The oversized front door is flanked by windows with some sort of covering obscuring most of the light on the other side. The priest quickly steps beside the door and presses his back into the wall beside it, facing Megan. He flattens himself there so as not to be seen when it opens. Megan can just make out the shape of his face and the little white square of his priest collar in the dark. The door opens without them knocking, spilling a soft light out. Rufus growls and whines, uncertain whether to charge or retreat.

Megan squints and raises her hand to the light. A women's silhouette is standing before her with one hand on the door. Megan looks once more at Larry beside the open door. He is vigorously shaking his head "No," with a finger pressed to his lips in a "Quiet" gesture.

"Well, look who came to visit!" the women says. "Shelly, right?" the women asks, pushing the door all the way open and stepping back to allow Megan to enter.

"I'm Megan," she says.

The woman looks past the girl standing on the porch as if she was expecting someone else. The women notices Megan's brown stringy hair framing an almost round face, dressed in a light jacket and dark pants. Rufus lets out a string of barks, which draws the women's attention. She is in a print housedress with an apron that wraps around a pudgy frame and reaches over both shoulders covering an ample chest and reaches to the hem of her shin-length dress. Her hair is pinned back but half has escaped the pins and, with the light behind her, forms a halo-like appearance. She is young by no means but is not an old hag either.

"What the hell is that!?" she says while eying Rufus.

Defiantly, Megan tells her, "That's my dog, Rufus. We came to get Timmy, my brother."

The women's attention returns to the girl as Rufus gives a trembling whine.

"Your brother, Timmy, huh." She pauses to look one more time past Megan into the darkness behind the girl. "Well, why didn't you say so," she says, becoming the hostess. "Come in, sweetie, come in."

Meanwhile, Larry is on his tiptoes pressed so hard against the wall next to the door he is in danger of going through it.

Megan enters the house with Rufus pressed against her ankle. Both watch as the woman steps back up to the doorway and looks out one more time as she slowly pushes the door almost closed.

"Step over here, dearie," she says, directing Megan to move into what looks like a dining area behind the front door.

Larry breathes a sigh of relief as the light from the doorway diminishes. Megan steps over to an antique table that is shoulder high to a little girl. The table is cluttered with various old stained papers, vintage kitchen items, and a candelabrum with half the candles burning.

Suddenly, the women flings the front door open and reaches out and around the door jamb to grab the cowering priest one handed by his coat in the middle of his chest, dragging him into the room as if he weighed no more than a rag doll. She pulls him to her and, with her face two inches from his face, says, "Hello, Larry." And with superhuman strength, she throws him across the room by the dining area, to crash into the far wall, where he falls to the floor below the back- sized crater he leaves from the impact. Rufus barks furiously at the woman as she slams the front door. Dust, cobwebs, and pieces of plaster from the ceiling rain down as the house is rocked from both jarring impacts. The woman, although pudgy, is quick in a lunge for the barking Chihuahua. Rufus yips as her fingers brush against his flank.

"Run, Rufus!" Megan shouts.

The women is motivated by her near miss and is bent over, zigging and zagging with the dog as he scampers to stay just out of reach. She chases him past a gasping Larry who is on his hands and knees recovering from the impact with the wall.

"Run, Rufus!" Megan yells again.

Woman and dog disappear into a dark hallway where Rufus is forced to choose between a flight of stairs to the right or the uncertain dark hallway to the left. He darts up the first few steps, and the woman launches herself in a desperate grab, which lands her full out on the stairs with the dog's back paw in her grasp. Quick as any survival instinct, Rufus whips around and bites her hand. The woman lets him go with a grunt and gathers her legs under her again to continue up the stairs.

"Come here, you little son of a *bitch*!" She emphasizes "bitch" as she is sprawled out across the top of the steps, reaching for the departing dog.

Rufus follows the only light at the top of the stairs and runs to the left, disappearing from her view as he scampers into a vacant room. Gasping for breath, the women laughs and balls up a psychotic fist and pulls it to her breasts as she lay across the top of the stairs.

The door to the room Rufus entered swings shut and slams closed. Inside the room, Rufus sees that other than the window letting in the moonlight, there is nothing else. He looks back to the closed door and whines. He turns back to the room. The plaster on the walls is fractured with age and gone in some areas. One such place, low on the wall, is almost big enough for him to crawl through. He walks over and sniffs, smelling the scent of rats. It's dark between the walls, but he starts to dig at the hole. His paws moving as fast as they can, making a "chick-a, chick-a, chick-a," sound in the room.

Meanwhile, the woman comes back down and goes into the room to find Megan trying to open the big front door. Both of her hands on the knob frantically trying to turn it, but the door won't budge.

"Looks like we'll be having *dog* for supper."

Megan spins around to face the women. Wide eyed, she looks for Rufus.

"Oh, he's alive...for now." She tilts her head and looks up to the ceiling above. The "chick-a, chick-a, chick-a" can be faintly heard.

"Rufus!" Megan says in a whisper.

"You know? By George, I think you're right," says the woman in a jovial manner.

Larry moans. The woman looks over her shoulder to where Larry is trying to get to his feet. She sees the wooden crucifix on the floor in front of him. She looks back at Megan. "Have a seat, dear, I'll just be a minute." The woman waves her hand at Megan, who launches backward toward the antique table. A ladder-back chair rights itself and catches the girl like a catcher's mitt and a cord falls from the window behind her, wrapping her into the chair with her arms trapped to her sides.

"There. Now, that should hold you." She turns back to Larry, grabbing him by the hair on his head and pulls his head back to spit in his face. "Father Larry Spivey, remember me? Nice of you to join us." She pulls him to his feet and pushes him into the wall.

Larry grabs the wrist of her hand that holds his hair, and with his other hand, he takes a swing at her.

She catches his attempt with her free hand. "Oh, you wanna fight, huh?" She shoves his head into the wall several times, dislodging several items from the wall and a fireplace mantel beside him. An ornamental dagger that had been hanging on the wall, crossed with its mate, falls to the floor. She reaches over and plucks the mate off the wall, and bracing her elbow across his throat, she holds his hand to the wall and drives the dagger through his wrist. Larry screams and thrashes around. Megan screams while the woman laughs.

"Oh, that didn't hurt, ya big baby."

Larry is thrashing against her as she reaches over and picks up a heavy block that sits on the mantel as a bookend. Larry is pounding on her back as she presses her shoulder into his body, holding him against the wall. She hammers the end of the dagger in his wrist, driving it deeper into the wall. Three good whacks and she steps back and bashes Larry in the forehead once with the heavy block.

"Shut the fuck up, asshole, you're scaring our guest." Her free hand supports him from slumping too much as she tucks the block up under her arm and "wills" the other fallen dagger into her hand, driving it into Larry's other wrist as she holds his arm out from his shoulder.

"Jesus!" Larry's dazed head whips around to watch as the woman hammers it home.

"Not quite, but it'll do," she says, stepping back. She turns her back on the priest, facing Megan across the room. She smooths down the front of her apron with both hands, leaving twin bloody smears down an already stained and dirty-white piece of material.

"There now," she says while tucking her hair back up on both sides, "where were we?"

Megan watches in horror as the woman starts toward her.

"You're a bad, bad lady," Megan says as she struggles against her bonds and starts to cry.

Still breathing hard from her tumultuous greeting of her guests, the woman approaches and stops a step from Megan. She leans in and examines Megan's face intently.

"Oh my," she says and moves into what looks like the kitchen part of the house.

Megan is bound to a high ladder chair between the table and a wall. The table comes to her chest. Her point of view shows the parlor to her right that looks to have been the house's primary living room, complete with dark rotting furniture placed haphazardly throughout the room. Father Spivey hangs from the wall to the left of a large dormant fireplace. Above the fireplace mantle is a broken mirror with two lit candles burning in front of it. Various items sit or lay across the mantle.

To Larry's right was the hallway where the women chased Rufus. A wall separates this dark hallway from the parlor and the kitchen space, where the woman is searching for something in various cabinets that hang above the counters. She pulls a cut crystal perfume bottle with an eyedropper stopper in it and rushes back to Megan's side.

"Oh, I *need* these!" she says, removing the stopper and sitting the bottle on the table in front of the girl. The woman takes Megan's hair in her hand and yanks her head back until the girl's face is pointed to the ceiling.

"Owe!" Megan cries.

"Hold still!" the woman orders, placing her knee in Megan's lap and leaning in to work. "Oh," breathes the woman, "these are precious to me..." And she sucks up Megan's tears into the eye dropper, depositing them in the bottle. "Tears of the innocent...," she says, examining Megan's sniffling face. Her eyes meet Megan's. "I wouldn't need you stinking brats if it weren't for—"

"You're hurting me!" Megan interrupts her.

The woman gets off Megan and returns the stopper to the bottle. She rummages around on the top of the table until she finds a partial roll of duct tape. Humming to herself, she peels off a length of the tape and places it over Megan's mouth.

"Okay now, maybe we can get some sort of *peace and quiet around here!*" The last part she yelled angrily directly into Megan's face.

This starts a new batch of tears that get sucked up and deposited into the bottle. The woman stops and cocks her head toward the ceiling where she faintly hears "chick-a-chick-a-chick-a coming from upstairs. She smiles. "That reminds me," she says. Gathering up the bottle and walking back into the kitchen area, she faces the wall that separates the parlor and kitchen area. There is a belly-high counter with cabinets starting eye high and continuing up the wall to house various kitchen items. A large round cast-iron pot with a lid sits on the counter before her. She lifts the lid and leans in to smell its contents. She turns her face to her captive guest. "Well, with dinner upstairs, we won't need this." She smiles at Megan, then turns back and takes the pot and puts the lid back on. Stretching up on her tippy toes, she pushes the pot into the top overhead cabinet with her fingertips. Like several other cabinets, this one has no door. It has been gone for years. The woman turns back to Megan again, smiles a psychopathic smile, and seems lost in thought. The girl looks helpless, scared, and little. The woman snaps out of her thought.

"Oh my, where are my manners?" she says, coming out of the kitchen. While moving into the parlor, she passes in front of Larry, who still hangs from the wall, head down, knees bent but feet on the floor. Blood drips from the wounds from his wrists and forehead to pool on the floor in front of him. The woman pays him no mind as she crosses the room to the dark far corner. She bends to pick up and right another ladder-back chair with another little girl tied to it.

Megan watches her as she spins the chair to face her. The woman's back is to Megan, while the shadows from the candlelight prevent her from seeing in perfect detail. Megan recognizes the little girl.

The woman straightens up and places her hands on her hips, declaring, "This one seems to be dry." Then she one-handed picks up the chair with the child tied in it and, carrying it like a suitcase, marches back across the room and puts it before the table.

Megan sees her friend Jenny, missing a week or more. Jenny is almost comatose with dark circles under her half closed eyes with five perfect x stitches with heavy thread holding her mouth closed. Terrified, Megan Carpenter starts to shiver. The woman has put the chair aside to move a rotten rug that covers a trapdoor to a root cellar below the floor. With an effort, she grabs and hauls on a ring bolted into the floor. The trapdoor lifts with a creak of protesting hinges, exposing a dark maw in the hardwood floor. Megan has to duck her head in order to see the floor just the other side of the table. Picking up the chair with Jenny in it, the woman says, "In ya go," as she tosses the chair and Jenny into the hole as if it was no more than a sack of oats. She stands, looking down into the dark hole, then, getting down on her hands and knees, she reaches in with her free hand.

"Come 'ear, you little shit!" she hisses as her arm moves around in the hold.

Megan whimpers as she watches almost in shock. Slowly, the woman rises with the hair of a child gripped in her meaty hand. Megan sucks in air through her nose in a gasp. It's Tim! He is holding the woman's wrist with both of his hands as his legs kick just out of reach of her. He grunts and groans because his mouth is also sewn shut with heavy thread.

"Little Tim?" the woman asks Megan. "Yes, I see that it is by the look on your face." She tosses Tim back into the dark hole and closes the heavy door with a resounding crash.

Father Spivey's head slowly rises from its slump. He pushes his feet into the floor under him, relieving the strain on his wrists and groans from the pain. Again, Megan struggles in vain with her bonds.

"Shhh!" the woman orders as she cocks her head toward the ceiling again. There's no sound except the wind outside and the creaks of an old house. Father Spivey moans. This sound starts the woman into action again. She turns to the counter she had placed the bottle on. Below this counter is a series of drawers or places where drawers used to be. The counter itself has been eaten away by time and use. There is a fist-sized hole in the countertop above the drawer, and one can see its contents through this hole.

The woman yanks open this top drawer, but it will only open halfway. Something inside the drawer is stopping it. She closes it and yanks it again, to no avail. Megan can hear the utensils inside knocking against the wood of the drawer. Frustrated, the woman slams the drawer closed quickly and then tries to yank it open again, but it's still stuck.

"Goddamn thing!" she says and then leans over to look into the drawer through the hole in the counter, but it's too dark. She pokes her free hand in and tries to moving objects around as she maneuvers the drawer with her other hand. She removes a metal rod with a red handle. It's a butcher's tool for honing the edge of his knife called a steel. The rod itself is eight inches long with a tapered point. She tries the drawer again, but it still only opens halfway. She grunts in frustration as she works the drawer back and forth. She then leans forward over the countertop once again to see if she can see what is obstructing the drawer. Her left hand works the drawer while her right hand, still gripping the butcher's steel, with the handle down and the point up, while bracing her weight against the countertop. Suddenly, soundless against the racket of the drawer, the cast-iron pot she had placed in the cabinet above her came crashing down into the back of her head, driving the metal rod into her right eye, through the socket, and into her brain pan, skewering her brain to the back of her skull. As a reflex, she stands up straight as the pot and lid clatter and thump onto the floor. For a brief moment, she totters there with the red handle sticking out from the socket of her right eye. Megan watches as the woman falls over backward and begins her death throes against the hardwood floor. The girl struggles with her bonds but cannot get free. As the woman's feet stop kicking, all is quiet. Then a dusty, cobwebbed-covered head of a Chihuahua pokes his head out of the cabinet where the heavy pot was and looks down. Rufus gives a tentative whine-type yip and then a defiant bark as he sees the woman lying on the floor.

In the parlor, Father Spivey braces his left elbow against the wall, and grimacing through the pain and a prayer for strength, he levers against the dagger holding his wrist until it pulls free. Gasping for breath, he reaches for the dagger holding his right wrist and pulls it out.

Meanwhile, at the base of the hill, in the middle of the night, in front of the iron gate, under the last street light on Maple Street, half a dozen people have gathered around a deputy sheriff's car parked in the circle of the cul-de-sac.

"I'm telling you, Mr. Carpenter, we've been up there more than once. And there is nobody and nothing but an old house up there."

Megan's frantic father is squared off with the deputy. The small gathering is getting bigger as people from the surrounding houses make their way to the scene. Some parents of missing children called at the news of yet another missing child. This one taken from her own front yard.

"Where else could they be!?" the parent shouts, which bring a chorus of assenting babble from his neighbors and fellow victims.

The deputy holds up his hand for quiet. "Hey, hey!" he shouts over the people gathered around his car. They all quiet for him and listen as he explains, "First of all, that's private property, and I have to get another warrant to—" The rest is drowned out with, "I don't need a goddamn warrant. My boy was taken without a warrant!" a father yells to the deputy. "We can go without you, you spineless..." The rest was lost in the surging mob pressing into the gate. The gate creaks and strains with their weight.

"Goddamn it, people, hold it!" the deputy says, trying to restore order as he pushes his way to the front. He meets resistance but yells and pushes to the front. Then a faint bark from the darkness beyond the gate draws the attention of some of the mob.

"Shhh!" someone said, quieting the rest.

Again, they hear a bark. Closer now. People back away from against the gate as everyone peers into the dark. All is quiet, and then one can hear soft footfalls of several children from up the drive. Then Rufus enters into the edge of the streetlight, trotting before a knot of children's feet. As they draw closer, gasps can be heard as the light climbs up the approaching kids and Father Larry Spivey cradling a small girl in his arms. A sorrier lot has never brought so much joy to so many people. In moments, the gate is separated from its remaining hinge, and the parents are reunited with their children. Umm, and the dog also, definitely the dog.

The End

Jragin

Draconious P. Cinderbreath lived on the side of a semi-active volcano. Sometimes it smoked and vented steam, and sometimes it didn't—mostly, it didn't.

Draconious P. was an adult green dragon who did not like people. Why should he? Practically every encounter with them was a fight for survival.

It was true that, in his younger days, he had enjoyed dropping cows on city folk and roasting a flock of sheep here and there to be eaten like tater tots while watching the people scramble to put out the fires he had started. After all, is this not what dragons do?

His only encounter that did not involve dodging harpoons, spears, or boulders hurled by catapults was a conversation shared with an old wizard. One day, this wizard opened negotiations that resulted in an arrangement lasting the past fifty years.

It happened that Cornelius Van Magewise, the kingdom's resident wizard, came upon the dragon sprawled out beside the main road, picking a boot out of his teeth with the sharp end of a broken lance. It was the wizard's job to rid the kingdom of its dragon problem, and after several failed attempts at hiring dragon slayers, it became obvious to Cornelius that other options must be explored.

That very day, he had hired a reputable dragon slayer to either convince the dragon to "move on or suffer the consequences." But when Cornelius walked up on the dragon lounging against a big rock, picking his teeth, he noticed the dragon slayer's armor strewn about, along with the gear his horse had been wearing the last time the wizard saw them.

A satisfying belch, followed by a perfect smoke ring from Draconious P., left little doubt as to what had happened to the dragon slayer and his horse.

Since then, instead of paying dragon slayers—who were becoming harder and harder to find anyway—Cornelius began paying the dragon directly to not harass the people in the Kingdom of Ore. Such payments consisted of gold coins, baubles, or any item that was shiny or sparkled with crystals.

Why, just the last time, after a botched attempt to kill the dragon by a group of vigilantes, a flock of sheep and a large mirror were accepted as payment. There were no hard feelings over the attempt to ambush Draconious P. after it was explained it wasn't the wizard's idea. The dragon, after all, wasn't entirely unreasonable.

However, this last encounter was the closest anyone had ever come in their attempts to *kill* him, and Draconious P. knew it.

A harpoon had been launched at him from a hiding place as he passed in flight. Had his left elbow not been in the way, he would have taken the harpoon under his left arm—where his dragon scale was weak. The harpoon point entered into the joint of his elbow and broke off, leaving the tip embedded deep inside.

After a few days, it began to bother the dragon and prevented him from extending his left arm. He sat in his lair, looking at himself in his new mirror, until the pain in his left arm became too much to ignore.

Draconious P. had a collection of items which he prized. These he kept upon a mantle high above his cave floor. His most prized possession was a gourd-sized blue diamond that sat in the center of the mantle. Every morning, sunlight would stream in through the cave entrance, hitting the bauble and lighting up the entire cave with a blue brilliance the dragon found pleasing. Not a waking day passed that he did not look over and see it in its place. It gave him comfort. It made his cave a home.

His new mirror, he had placed behind the blue diamond so that it appeared there were two. Draconious P. was a clever dragon.

Even that did not distract him from the pain in his left arm. He could not use it at all. It was swollen and hot to the touch—and in a spot he could not reach. Something had to be done.

On the side of a mountain, away from the dragon problem, a village of simple folk lived who were happy just being mountain folk. They grew grapes and made a very popular wine to trade in the city. It was a common harvest, and everyone in the village benefitted from it. It was a community venture.

Daniel was the village blacksmith. He had his smithy in the village, and his home was just outside it. He married his longtime sweetheart, and they had a daughter. They named her Maddie.

Three years passed, and Daniel lost his wife to a mysterious disease that took her suddenly. Maddie, who favored her mother, was left to care for a grieving father. It is often easier to accept something when you know next to nothing about it. Maddie, being a three-year-old child, knew only that her mommy had gone away.

When Daniel worked, he left Maddie with a widow who had a little girl of the same age. This woman's name was Joan; her daughter's name was Annie.

Annie was a quiet, withdrawn child with brown hair, just like her mother. Maddie was Annie's opposite—blonde-haired, talkative, very curious, and gullible.

Joan didn't mind looking after Maddie for Daniel. She often cooked for both Daniel and Maddie, and they would all eat together before Daniel took Maddie home for the night.

Joan set her cap for Daniel, and he didn't resist. It was a year after the death of his wife that Daniel and Joan were wed. Joan and Annie moved into Daniel's house outside the village.

At first, everything was fine. One day, Daniel came home from the smithy just before sundown. Maddie usually met him at the front door or in the yard, anxious to tell him about her day. Today, she had a problem only he could fix.

"Daddy, I got a splinter," she announced, holding her finger up as she walked up the path.

"Maddie, let your father get in the door," Joan lightly scolded the girl. "He's tired and doesn't want to be bothered when he first comes home."

"Nonsense," Daniel said, lifting Maddie up and holding her on his hip. "What's troubling you today, little porcupine?"

Daniel took her inside and sat with her at the table, listening as she explained how the splinter got into her finger while picking berries.

Daniel was a good father, and he made a point to include Annie in any attention he showed his own daughter. Annie hid behind her mother's skirt most of the time, clutching her favorite doll.

After washing up and greeting his wife, Daniel brought a lamp and some sewing tools over and sat in front of Maddie.

"O-kay, let's see," he said, moving the light closer.

Maddie presented her finger, and after locating the thorn, he said, "Uh-oh."

Maddie looked at him, watching him hold her finger. He looked at her very seriously.

"We're going to have to cut the whole finger off."

Maddie yanked her hand back. "Noooo..." she said, alarmed.

Joan and Annie watched from beside the table, but their thoughts were different. Joan was feeling a flicker of ire and jealousy over the attention he gave Maddie. Annie, who knew and accepted only her mother's love, believed this man truly capable of cutting off Maddie's finger. It confirmed her fears and justified her quiet rejection of Daniel's attempts to be her friend.

"O-kay, let's take another look," Daniel said, winking at Annie across the table. "Maybe we can save the finger."

He deftly removed the splinter, earning a hug and a request to kiss the owie—which everybody knows would hurry along the healing process.

Daniel rarely brought his work home, but sometimes he had things in the way at the shop that he carried back in a wagon. Today, he had an axle from a freight wagon that was too big to unload alone.

Maddie missed her daddy, and while he was home, she followed him most everywhere. Joan would mention this, only to be told that it wasn't a problem.

Annie watched suspiciously from the sidelines.

Daniel asked the girls to help him lift the axle from the bed of the wagon. Annie looked on from the front doorstep while Maddie walked over and climbed into the wagon to help. Daniel and Maddie tried lifting the axle. Daniel, knowing full well the axle was too big but enjoying the time spent with the girls, stood up and stretched his back.

"Well," he said loud enough so Annie could hear, "looks like we're going to have to move the wagon instead."

Maddie looked at her dad with a question on her face.

"Come on," he said, jumping down from the wagon and lifting Maddie down beside him. He grabbed a coil of rope from the wagon and, holding one end, dropped the rest at the back.

Daniel said to Maddie, "Take this over and tie it to that tree."

Maddie, eager to help, took the rope and attempted to tie it. Daniel watched for a minute, smiling to himself, and then walked over to show her how to tie it properly.

Then Maddie helped him tie the other end to the axle. Daniel had her do it several times before she got it right. When that was done, he lifted her into the wagon seat and turned to Annie, asking if she would like to ride too. Annie shook her head no but hesitated.

"Are you sure..." Daniel teased, "It'll be fun..." he said to the little girl.

Joan watched from the kitchen window and couldn't believe her eyes when Annie held her arms out to be picked up. Daniel casually walked over and lifted Annie, acting like it was no big deal.

"Now we can get anything done," he said, setting Annie beside Maddie. "I got both my girls to help."

He climbed into the wagon seat beside the girls and told them to hold on as he nudged the draft horse forward. When the rope pulled tight, they watched as the axle was dragged off the wagon bed. Daniel continued to circle the property, giving the girls a ride before putting the wagon and horse away for the night. Annie and Maddie were instructed in the proper way to do both chores.

Evening closed in, and it was time for dinner and then bed. The two girls shared a bed and each had their favorite rag doll. Annie's was a better depiction of a person—rags sewn into the proper shape with a needlework face carefully stitched onto it. Maddie's was a piece of deer hide with a wad of rag balled up and tied, with a face drawn on it. Several strands of yellow yarn were sewn into the ball, resembling hair. This was Maddie's doll from before her mother died. Maddie would carry the doll head tucked up under the twine-type belt she wore to keep her britches up. Maddie preferred pants over dresses, and that's where Sarah, her doll, could usually be found.

One sunny spring day, Joan woke the girls up early, right after Daniel left for work. "Come on, girls, we're going to pick a lot of berries today. Gotta get an early start—let's go!" Joan hustled them out of bed. She fed them a hearty breakfast and gave them their berry baskets. Annie and Maddie had their dolls tucked or clutched so they wouldn't get lost. Joan had a lunch basket, and the three of them started off for the berry patch.

It wasn't long before Maddie noticed they were taking a different route and asked Joan where they were going.

"We're going to a new place." That was all Joan said. She led the girls farther than they had ever been before, and after half a day's travel, they came to a patch of berries way out on the side of the mountain. They ate their lunch, and once everything was packed away, they began picking berries. Joan placed the girls on either side of her.

"You pick that way, Maddie, and we'll pick this way," she said.

Maddie started picking, and they sang the berry-picking song as they filled their baskets. Maddie sang and picked for the better part of an hour and didn't notice she was all alone.

"Pick a little berry, put it in your pouch, and watch the berry thorns or you will holler ouch," she sang.

Then Maddie stopped and looked into her basket at all the berries. She looked around for Joan and Annie, but they weren't there.

"Joan?" she called to her stepmother but got no answer. She scanned the bushes, trying to make sense of where she was. Maddie called again but only heard the wind rustling through the trees.

Maddie often talked to her doll when she was alone. "I know they're around here somewhere," she said as she started to walk back the way she had come. After a while, the berry bushes stopped—but still no sign of Joan.

"Now don't you worry, Sarah. We'll get home, you watch!" Nervously, she pulled the doll head from her belt, clutched it to her chest, and set off in the direction she believed was home.

It wasn't long before Maddie caught the attention of the local wildlife. A wolf and his mate started stalking the little girl. Maddie saw the wolf and instinctively began to hurry. She took the path of least resistance—downhill—but the faster she went, the steeper the mountain became, until she was running as fast as her little legs could carry her.

The wolves closed in on their prey. Maddie lost her basket of berries but still clutched Sarah tightly. Turning to look behind her as she ran, she saw a wolf closing in. Not paying attention to where she was going, the little girl crashed into a bank of bushes and dropped out of sight.

The wolf, about to snap its jaws on its fleeing victim, nearly tumbled down the side of the mountain where the child had disappeared. The wolf looked at the place where Maddie had disappeared and saw that the bushes grew at the edge of a drop-off. Below, a steep decline broke away, and the tops of trees could be seen far down below. The wolf's mate came over and looked too. They both took note of their surroundings and trotted off to try and salvage the kill at the bottom of the cliff.

When Maddie broke through the edge of the cliff, she fell. She slid for a while and tumbled off the drop-off, free-falling until she hit the upper branches of a tree below. The branches broke her fall. Maddie bounced from branch to branch, each one bending beneath her weight, slowing her descent until, almost gently, the tree seemed to deposit her on the forest floor beside the cliff.

Maddie sat down on the ground, carpeted with pine needles. She broke down and cried as hard as she could. Miraculously, she still clutched the doll head in her trembling fist. Taking deep breaths to fuel her mood, she cried to let the world know that when little girls are scared, angry, lost, and chased off cliffs by wolves, they cry.

When Maddie could cry no more, she hiccupped through her sobs, wiped her nose with the back of her hand, and stood up. She had a scrape on her forehead and plenty of welts from the tree branches. Her face was dirty except where tears had carved twin tracks down her cheeks. Her hair was a chaotic mass of tangled yellow strands mixed with pine needles and twigs that framed a face harboring bright blue eyes. Maddie was in surprisingly good shape for having just fallen off a cliff.

She turned and looked up the side of the cliff from where she had fallen. Still clutching Sarah, she scanned her surroundings and saw trees on a slight slope. It was easier to go down than back up, so she started walking downhill.

Maddie walked for a while and then stopped to listen. She heard water and continued in that direction.

"You need a bath and I need a drink of water," she told Sarah. "We'll go and wait for Daddy to find us by the water." She smoothed out the yarn strands of Sarah's hair as she walked.

Maddie hiccupped one last time and drew a deep, breath-ending cry as she cleared the woods and walked beneath a large green arch of leaves. She picked her way over stones of various sizes, making her way to the river's edge.

"You wait right here! And don't you run off so I can't find you neither!" Maddie told her doll, setting it on a rock before carefully making her way to the water.

All this was being observed by none other than Draconious P. Cinderbreath, who stood in a clearing of rocks beside the river. Maddie had walked right under his leg, passing below him unnoticed. He watched with fascination as this little yellow-headed creature scolded whatever she had left on the rock below him.

Maddie's back was to him as he leaned over to study the doll. He sniffed it, causing it to fall to the ground, then stood up to ponder the situation.

The dragon was every bit as tall as the trees around him. He had never seen a little girl up close before—certainly never one alone.

After drinking her fill, Maddie came back over to the rag doll. "I told you to stay there, Sarah!" she scolded as she picked it up from the ground. "You don't want those mean old wolfs to get you, do you?"

Draconious P. decided to eat the little human. Though small and barely a bite, she was, after all, a human—and humans were nothing but trouble. He leaned over, and just before he opened his mouth, he bumped his bad elbow on his knee, bringing tears to his eyes and causing him to groan and whimper in pain.

Maddie looked up and saw the dragon biting his own lip as tears streamed down his face. He held his injured arm to his chest, cradled in his good arm. Maddie couldn't see the injury but saw the pain on the dragon's face and made the natural assumption.

"Hi, are you lost too?" Maddie asked, looking up at Draconious P.

The dragon got his pain under control and watched the little girl.

"I'm Maddie Smith, and this is Sarah, my doll. Are you a Jragin?" she asked unafraid. "My daddy says Jragins are big like you."

Draconious P. was confused—was this a witch?

Maddie saw the way he held his arm. "What's wrong with your arm, Jragin?" she asked.

The dragon looked down at Maddie, suspecting a trick, but held out his arm for her to see.

"Let me see," she said, almost impatiently.

The dragon shook his huge head and pulled his arm back as if Maddie could somehow reach it.

"Oh, come on, I won't hurt it," she said, standing before him with her fists on her hips. "If you've got an owie, maybe we can make it better."

In a deep rumbling voice that practically vibrated every rock around, the dragon said, "Owie?" Speaking human was a chore and rarely attempted, but he could do it.

"Let me see it, ya big baby. I won't even touch it!" Maddie told him. Tentatively, he looked around but saw no sign of anyone else—only this little human and her doll, Sarah. She must be a witch.

Slowly, he leaned down and brought his wounded elbow to Maddie. She saw the wooden shaft sticking out of the wound.

"You got a splinter, Jragin," she said.

He had leaned over with his right hand bracing his body, his face next to the girl's as she examined his elbow.

"Uh-oh..." she muttered, shaking her head as she looked up at him.

Draconious P. sat back a little, watching Maddie questioningly.

"We're going to have to cut the whole arm off, Jragin."

The dragon stood up, horrified. He clutched his left arm protectively and shook his head vigorously.

Maddie took a deep breath, fists back on her hips. "Maybe we can save it. Let me see it again." She said it as if it would take great effort on her part.

The dragon could only think about saving his arm. He leaned way over, as if doing a one-armed pushup, and brought his elbow right up to Maddie. His face was little more than two feet away from hers.

"Yer pretty big, ya know," she said into his face before reaching for the harpoon shaft.

He instinctively flinched. Maddie stopped and, as sweet as she could, told him, "I won't hurt you, Jragin, but I gotta see how bad it is."

Draconious P. gave a nod, and Maddie put her hand on the shaft and tried to pull it out. It was in too tight, and Maddie was just too small.

She stepped back and looked into the dragon's face.

"We need a long rope and a big bandage," she told him. "And we might be able to save your arm."

He sat back up, blinked three times as he thought, then unfurled his huge wings. Taking a running start, he launched himself into the sky, leaving Maddie alone beside the river.

She watched him until he banked around the mountain and was out of sight. Maddie looked around the clearing. Trees surrounded her in all directions—some across the river and others circling the clearing. She could see the cliff she had fallen from rising above the treetops. It looked like it was getting darker, and night was coming.

The two wolves that chased her off the cliff had made their way down the mountain and were tracking her even now.

Draconious P., eager to help this little person save his arm, came upon a farm a few miles away. He saw what he needed: a middle-aged woman taking her laundry off a clothesline. The dragon dropped from the sky, landing in front of her. She promptly fainted.

Draconious P. grabbed the line with one sheet still attached and took off for the river.

Maddie lay face down on a rock beside the river, showing the fishes to Sarah, unaware that one of the wolves was slinking up to attack her.

Draconious P. saw the wolf and landed behind it, reaching down with his good arm to snatch it up. The wolf did not like being grabbed like that and snarled, biting the hand that held him—only to have the dragon bash its head on the side of a large rock.

Maddie turned at the commotion and, seeing the dragon, said, "There you are!"

She got off the ground, tucked Sarah in her belt, and started toward him. She saw the sheet and rope where he had dropped them—and then noticed his right hand. It looked as if it was bleeding.

Hands back on her hips, Maddie asked accusingly, "What did you do now?!"

Her first thought was that he had hurt himself again.

"Let me see, Jragin."

Draconious P. felt guilty all of a sudden. He looked down at his right fist holding the remains of the wolf. Not knowing what else to do, he popped the wolf into his mouth and ate it.

Then he extended his empty hand to show Maddie. She saw the blood and told him, "Come on."

Walking back to the side of the river, she pulled on the dragon's thumb.

"I swear, Jragin, you need a mommy," she said as she washed the wolf blood from his hand. "Someone has to look out for you."

She examined the hand, saw no injuries, let him go, and made her way over to the sheet and rope—scolding him all the way.

"I don't know how you got to be so big without a Mommy." Maddie stopped and looked at him. "Do you have a Mommy, Jragin?"

He looked back at her, not understanding. "Mommy?" he rumbled.

"Yeah, where's your Mommy?"

Draconious P. shrugged his shoulders. Maddie gave a heavy sigh, picked up the rope, and as she untangled it from the sheet, said, "I had a Mommy once, but she went away."

The dragon looked at the girl, unsure how to respond.

"Well," said Maddie, "we better fix your arm before it gets too dark."

She wrapped one end of the rope around a tree several times, tying it the way her Daddy had shown her the day before.

"Please come over here, Jragin," Maddie said, holding the other end of the rope.

The dragon came to her and offered his elbow. He watched as the girl manipulated the rope with her little hands. Her tongue poked out the side of her mouth as she worked. She glanced up at his huge face and smiled. "My Daddy showed me how to tie."

The dragon noticed her blue eyes and thought of the big blue diamond on his mantle.

Maddie finished and stepped back. "Okay, Jragin, you can sit up now, but don't pull—yet!" she told him sternly.

Draconious P. sat up slowly and watched as the rope played out. When the slack was taken up, Maddie said, "Stop!"

She came forward and rested a hand on his big toe, looking up over his huge, scaly belly. "Okay, you gotta do this fast so it won't hurt," she said.

With his arm poised, he looked down at Maddie and nodded.

"When I say 'now,' you pull your arm away from the tree as fast as you can, okay?"

He nodded again as he stood, ready.

Maddie started backing up. "Get ready... get set... NOW!"

She said it, and the dragon twisted his whole body to the right, yanking his left arm as if throwing a punch. The rope stretched until it drew the harpoon head from the wound, flinging the bloody mess into the treetops.

Draconious P. took a huge lungful of air and roared white fire onto a large boulder in the clearing. Animals for miles around stopped what they were doing and ran. Birds that heard the mighty roar took flight. Most close to the clearing just fainted with fright. Rocks that had balanced against gravity toppled over. The boulder blasted by his fire turned to molten glass.

Maddie covered her ears and took several steps back.

Draconious P. had never felt pain like that before and looked for something to kill. He turned to Maddie with a murderous look on his face.

She stood with her face all scrunched up, hands still over her ears. "Look!" she said, pointing to the bloody harpoon head hanging from an upper branch of a tree.

Still breathing hard, he looked where she was pointing and saw the thing causing his arm to hurt swinging back and forth at the end of the rope.

"See? I told ya!" she said. "Now, let me see it."

As he realized the situation, he looked at his arm and slowly extended it, feeling the difference.

"Come on, Jragin, we gotta clean it and put a bandage on it."

Maddie walked over and picked up the sheet. She had to step back from the rock that was still glowing.

"Wow, you can really yell when you want to. You scared poor Sarah half to death," she said, taking the sheet to the river. "But not me—I knew you were gonna be all better once we got that thing out of you."

She looked back over her shoulder and saw the dragon still standing on the other side of the clearing, watching her and flexing his left arm back and forth.

"Come on, Jragin, you're still bleeding!" She turned to face him. "Don't worry, this will make it feel better, I promise."

The dragon's breathing had slowed, and his anger had turned into the realization that this little human had actually helped him.

He came over and tentatively brought his elbow down to the water beside Maddie.

The girl dipped the sheet in the river and held it over the wound.

As the cool water flowed over the hot wound, the dragon sighed, and smoke drifted out of his nose.

"There now, doesn't that feel better, Jragin?" she asked sweetly.

He nodded as she rinsed the wound again.

Draconious P. was glad he didn't eat this yellow-haired human.

Maddie leaned forward and kissed the dragon's elbow.

"That will make it all better," she said, pushing the wet sheet onto the wound.

"Hold this, Jragin. Sarah wants to kiss it too." Maddie took the doll's head out of her belt and put it to his elbow. She made a kissing sound and told him to be still while she tied the sheet to his arm.

"That's it, Jragin. Leave that bandage on till tomorrow, and it'll be all better."

Maddie smiled sweetly at the dragon, who showed his teeth, trying to imitate a smile. Maddie laughed openly, causing the dragon to laugh too—an unusual sound, this laughter.

"Do you feel better now, Jragin?" she asked.

Sitting beside the river, looking down at the girl, he said, "Feel better!"

"I wish my Daddy was here."

"Daddy?" he asked.

"Yeah, don't Jragins have Daddies too?" The dragon shook his head no. Maddie gave a heavy sigh. "I'm hungry." She looked over at the river. "I wish we had a fishing pole so we could catch one of those darn fishies."

The dragon, eager to please, scrambled to his feet and stepped to the river's edge. He looked at Maddie and tried another smile, causing her to giggle. He unfurled his right wing, took it in his right hand, and stretched it over the river. Then he dipped the entire wing into the water and heaved out about two hundred gallons, flinging it onto the riverbank.

Water cascaded over the rocks, causing steam to bubble up from the rock still hot from the dragon's fire. As the water receded, fish started flopping around on the riverbank. He looked over at Maddie. She was jumping up and down, clapping her hands in delight.

His whole world seemed to swell as he felt like he had just saved the entire world, and he laughed with her.

She stopped suddenly. "Uh oh," she said.

He looked around to see what was wrong.

"We don't got no pan to cook the fishes in," she said.

He looked down at the flopping fish and picked up the biggest one by the head. Holding it out from his face, he cleared his throat dramatically. With one quick glance at Maddie, he blew a stream of fire over the fish.

Maddie squealed with delight and clapped. The dragon held the fish with his talons, turning it until it split open, revealing cooked meat. He leaned down and presented the cooked fish to Maddie.

The little girl sat on the rocks and picked at the fish. "Oooh, hot!" she smiled at the dragon. "Aren't you going to eat too, Jragin?"

The dragon looked at the remaining fish flopping around. He lay down on his right side in front of Maddie, propping his head up with his hand, and started to pick through the fish with his left hand, which felt a lot better.

"When my Daddy gets here, we can use his knife to cut these fishes. He's big and strong too," she said as she ate.

"My Daddy told me all about Jragins, and he was right too." Draconious P. found that he liked listening to the girl talk and felt comfortable with her.

"Where are we going to sleep tonight, Jragin?" Dragons see pretty well in the dark, but not so little girls.

It was getting dark, and Draconious P. could only think of his cave. He sat up and looked toward the volcano miles away. Pointing off in the direction of the darkening horizon, he said, "Sleep."

"Is that where you live, Jragin?"

He nodded vigorously.

"And we can sleep there?" she asked.

Again, he nodded.

"Okay, but you'll have to carry me," she told him as she got to her feet.

The dragon got up too and watched as Maddie tucked Sarah in her belt and reached her arms up to him. He knelt down and offered his hand as she climbed on.

"Don't drop me, Jragin," she told him.

He shook his head at the thought as he gently lifted her up. His big hand closed around her as she grabbed a talon to hold on to.

Draconious P. had never carried anything so fragile before. Maddie had to tell him he was squeezing her too tight once.

She watched between his talons as they took off. At first, she was scared, but it was getting dark, and from where she was, it was hard to see anything. The land below them was all black to her, and above was all dragon. She was, basically, a passenger in the dark.

It wasn't long before Draconious P. landed in the mouth of his cave and sat Maddie down on a pile of coins. Maddie could hardly see at all, and she told him so.

The dragon had a store of treetops he sometimes used as torches. He lit one of these for her.

"Wow!" Maddie exclaimed at seeing the mound of coins she was standing on. "Where are we?" she asked, kicking at the seemingly glowing coins.

"Home," was all he said, holding the burning treetop.

Maddie yawned and told him, "You got a lot of stuff." She laid down where she was and looked up at the dragon holding the torch. It had been a long, busy day, and Maddie was feeling the pull of sleep.

"Good night, Jragin," she said through another yawn, rolling onto her side.

The cave was heated through the floor, so the coins Maddie slept on were warm and soothing to a tired little girl. She was asleep in moments.

Draconious P. tossed the spent treetop out of the cave's mouth and watched as it fell down the sheer side of the volcano. He sat there, one foot dangling outside, dozing the night away.

He was fast asleep when a small tug on the membrane of his wing woke him.

"Jragin, I have to go pee-pee," Maddie whispered, knuckling the sleep from her eyes.

He looked down at her, puzzled. "Pee-pee?" he repeated, unfamiliar with the term.

Maddie nodded and reached up to be picked up.

The dragon gently lifted her and sat her on his big belly.

She pointed toward the cave's mouth. "Out there."

Draconious P. cradled the little girl in his hands and rolled forward, dropping out of the cave into a freefall down the side of the volcano. The drop was sheer and exhilarating; they picked up speed as they fell. Maddie squealed in fright, but when the dragon opened his wings, they caught the air and leveled off just above the treetops.

Maddie clung to the dragon's talon, peeking through his massive fingers as they skimmed the trees. She laughed and giggled as they followed the contour of the river, banking into a wide turn over the water. The dragon chuckled with her as the landscape blurred beneath them.

They passed a small village where the river widened. People stood out on a dock, mouths agape, as the dragon and girl soared past.

"Hi!" Maddie shouted, waving between the dragon's talons.

The villagers screamed and scattered—some dove into the river, others ran for their lives.

"Jragin, we have to stop!" Maddie yelled into the wind.

Draconious P. found a clearing along the river and flapped his massive wings to slow their descent. He landed gently and lowered her to the ground.

Maddie scrambled out of his hand, clutching herself as she ran to a bush.

The dragon peered over the top.

"You're not supposed to watch, Jragin!" she scolded.

He sat back, blinking. When realization dawned, he murmured to himself, "Pee-pee."

Maddie emerged from behind the bush, holding her doll's head under her arm as she tied up her britches. She fastened Sarah into her string belt and made her way to the river to wash her hands.

"You always gotta wash your hands after you go pee," she informed him.

"Why?" the dragon asked, curious.

"Mama says if you don't, you'll get sick. Do you wanna get sick, Jragin?"

He shook his head.

"Then you gotta do it."

He nodded solemnly.

Maddie looked around, then let out a long sigh. Her lower lip trembled, and big tears welled in her eyes. She looked up at her enormous friend.

"Can you help me find my Daddy?"

The dragon lowered himself to her level, his snout just inches from her face.

"Where?" he asked sincerely.

She wiped her cheek and placed her hand between his nostrils.

"Maybe he's up on the cliff," she said, gently touching his scales. "You know, where those poopy old wolves were gonna get me and Sarah."

Draconious P. didn't know about the wolves, but he remembered where they had met—and he knew about the cliff.

Leaning into his snout, she added softly, "I'm sure Joan and Annie told him where we were."

The dragon sat up and thought for a moment, then leaned forward and picked Maddie up. Unafraid, she gripped his talon as he brought her to eye level.

"Maddie want Daddy? Jragin find Daddy. Sarah and Maddie stay here."

She smiled and squeezed his hand. "Can't we go too?"

"Jragin look faster lone."

Maddie's smile faded. "But what if a mean old wolf comes to get me and Sarah?"

The dragon considered this. Then he brought Maddie to a nearby tree, setting her in the top.

"Hold on," he said with a chuckle.

Maddie hugged the upper branch tightly.

Then Draconious P. took a deep breath and began to stomp and roar with such ferocity that wildlife for miles scattered in terror. Some animals burrowed underground, some leapt into the river and sank, birds flew into each other in panic, and a few creatures simply fainted.

When the dragon finished his theatrical display, he returned to Maddie, huffing and puffing, a wide grin on his face.

"No wolves for Maddie and Sarah," he said proudly.

She reached for him, and he gently lifted her from the tree and placed her on the ground.

Pulling Sarah from her belt, Maddie scolded her doll. "Okay, Sarah, you're safe now. Jragin chased all the poopy wolves away. So I don't wanna hear any more about it."

Then, to the dragon, she said, "Thank you, Jragin. We'll wait right here for you to get back with Daddy."

Draconious P. looked around to get his bearings, then launched into the sky. He soared toward the cliff where he and Maddie had first met, scanning high above the mountain for signs of life.

He spotted a group of men felling trees and dropped into a nearby clearing.

The woodsmen screamed and scattered. Draconious P. began snatching men up one by one and sniffing them, hoping to identify "Daddy" by scent.

"Daddy?" he bellowed at the panicked group.

When none seemed to be the one, he took off again and spotted another gathering on the side of the mountain. He landed in another clearing, scattering people once more—except for one man.

This man stood still, holding an empty basket, looking completely lost. He didn't appear any different to the dragon—except that he didn't run.

Draconious P. closed the distance in one heavy step. Leaning down to sniff him, he declared:

"Daddy!"

Then he scooped Daniel up like a toy and launched himself off the mountain.

"That poor man!" said one of the people left behind. "First he lost his little girl, now eaten by a dragon."

"Yeah," said his companion. "Talk about bad luck."

Daniel had been searching for his daughter since the night before. After hearing that a little girl was lost in the woods, a group of villagers had come together to help him. They caught up with Daniel the next morning, along with an expert tracker who had led them to the discarded berry basket. Reading the signs left behind after the chase, the tracker explained that it appeared the wolves had chased Maddie.

Daniel was still absorbing this information when the dragon dropped in.

The dragon's presence couldn't compete with Daniel's grief. As Draconious P. flew, he held Daniel in both hands. He didn't squeeze, but he wasn't about to drop him either. Daniel had lost his hold on the basket and was hanging on mostly out of reflex. He realized he was in trouble and had just begun to grasp the situation when the dragon banked a turn and landed beside a river, dumping Daniel onto the rocks near the water.

"Daddy!" the dragon announced.

Daniel rolled onto his back, staring up at the monstrous beast standing over him—when a familiar squeal caught his attention. He sat up in time to see his daughter running across the rocks toward him.

"Daddy!" she yelled, throwing herself into his arms.

Daniel was stunned. He held back a sob as he pulled her close.

"Maddie," he whispered into the side of her neck, tears filling his eyes. "Oh Maddie, I thought I had lost you, honey."

Maddie pulled back slightly, her arms still around his neck, studying his face.

"I got lost, and the wolves were gonna get me, and Sarah was scared, but I wasn't. I felled off a cliff, but a tree caught me and, and—"

Daniel hugged his little girl to him again, relief washing over him. Then it registered—there was a dragon foot, ten feet away. Still holding Maddie, he got to his feet, wrestling with the impossible reality that a full-grown green dragon had just plucked him off a mountain and brought him to her. He looked up at the towering creature.

"Maddie want Daddy," the dragon said, gazing down at Daniel.

"Daddy, this is Jragin," Maddie said with a grin. "He's my friend. He lives in a cave with lots of money. He had a splinter, Daddy, so I helped him. I want to keep him."

Daniel was still overwhelmed.

Just then, Draconious P. said, "Oh!" and suddenly ran off into the trees, crashing loudly through the forest.

Maddie realized she had left Sarah on a rock and scrambled out of Daniel's arms to retrieve the doll. Still stunned, Daniel watched her walk confidently across the rocks, chattering as if this were any ordinary day.

"We ate fishes, and Daddy, Jragin can cook fishes with his mouth! And he flied with me and Sarah—Sarah was scared, but I wasn't."

She scooped up the doll and started back toward Daniel. The sound of crashing trees returned. The dragon appeared again and stood in front of them.

"Where have you been, Jragin?" Maddie asked.

"Pee pee," was all he said.

Maddie put her fists on her hips and glared at him. "Jragin! Do you wanna get sick?" she scolded.

The dragon blinked, not quite following what she meant, and then began walking to the river to wash his hands. Daniel watched, dumbfounded.

"I swear, Jragin, you need a mommy!" Maddie continued. "It's a good thing me and Sarah found you, or you'd be a mess."

The dragon seemed to enjoy the attention. He shook his hands dry and turned to Daniel.

"Maddie bossy," he rumbled.

Daniel laughed. The dragon laughed. And Maddie laughed too.

It was then decided that the dragon would take them back to where the searchers were waiting. Daniel described the village where they lived and told the dragon he was welcome to visit anytime.

When Draconious P. landed and gently set Daniel and Maddie down on the grass, a few of the searchers stepped out of hiding, unable to believe their eyes.

"I am in your debt, dragon," Daniel said as he backed away, holding Maddie close.

"Maddie save Jragin," the dragon replied. "Daddy and Maddie friends."

"You come see me, Jragin," Maddie told him. "I can't come to your cave. You gotta come see me."

Draconious P. began to feel uncomfortable with all the people staring at him and started to fly off.

"Wait, Jragin!" Maddie cried, scrambling out of Daniel's arms. She ran to the dragon and wrapped herself around his toe. "I love you, Jragin."

Draconious P., who had never experienced love before, bent down and picked Maddie up, bringing her to eye level.

"Maddie is Jragin's friend," he rumbled.

"I'll miss you, Jragin," she said softly.

He nodded.

"You take Sarah, Jragin. 'Cause you don't got no mommy or daddy, and someone's gotta look out for you."

He took the rag doll between the talons of his other hand and studied it. Then he showed his teeth to Maddie in what could only be described as a smile.

She laughed and hugged his thumb.

Then he stooped down and put his friend, Maddie, on the ground. As he launched himself off the side of the mountain, he heard her yelling, "Bye, Jragin!" Then he was gone.

Three months went by; Daniel had separated from Joan, for reasons undisclosed to the gossiping villagers. A new girl watched Maddie when Daniel didn't take the child to the shop with him, which was most of the time. He never tired of her chatter, and always thanked his lucky stars he had not lost her.

One summer day, a procession of the King's Guards rode into the village. It was obvious, by the fact that they escorted a very elaborate coach, that they were here on very important business. It stopped once to ask directions to the blacksmith's shop. By now it had gathered quite a following. This—whatever this was—was big doings in the village.

The coach and its riders pulled up in front of the blacksmith shop. Daniel came out, wiping his hands on a towel; Maddie came out beside him, just as grimy as her father. The footman stepped off the back of the coach and put a step in front of the coach door. He then opened the door for an old man in a blue robe with yellow moons and stars sewn into it. The old man stepped from the coach.

"Who is Maddie Smith?" asked the old man.

Daniel picked up his daughter and held her protectively.

"What is this about?" Daniel asked.

The old man stepped forward, eyeing Daniel and Maddie.

"I am Cornelius Magewise, Wizard to the King; I've come to fulfill an agreement with one Draconious P. Cinderbreath."

Daniel and Maddie looked at him with blank stares. Maddie looked at her daddy, expecting him to explain. He shrugged his shoulders.

"A very large green dragon?" the wizard said.

At this, Maddie gasped. "Jragin!" she squealed.

Cornelius responded, "Quite."

He turned and snapped his fingers to the driver of the coach. The man was set in motion. He turned and retrieved a black lacquered box, which he handed down to the footman, who promptly brought it to the wizard. Cornelius opened the box and presented it to Maddie. Inside was a very large, sparkling blue diamond sitting on a bed of velvet.

"For you, my dear."

In a cave, in the side of a volcano, a dragon took a deep, contented breath and drifted off to sleep. The dragon slept on a bed of gold and silver coins. His most treasured items were sitting on a mantle high above the cave floor. Two gold statues flanked various items, but one was obviously sitting in a place of honor.

Sitting in the very center, before a gilded mirror, was a deer-hide rag doll with a drawn-on, faded face. A few strands of yellow yarn hung from her sorry head. But no item in the dragon's vast treasure pleased him more.

The End

Planets of the Apocalypse

N.A.S.P
(National Aeronautics Space Program)
April 12, 2015

"...I don't care who's in charge over there, someone get me that Carmen kid. I've got three days to... whatever his name is, I need facts and he's the only one who seems to be making any sense."

Gene Oldham slammed the phone down and turned to scowl at the bustling office pool spread out below him. His office literally overlooked a pool of twenty other desks that provided him with various bits of information gathered by several different sections of N.A.S.P. There were no partitions to separate the work areas. A huge plexiglass wall with a map of the Solar System stood on one side of the great room, with Gene Oldham's balcony office on the other.

Gene Oldham was a stout, bullet-shaped man sporting a crew cut and a perpetual scowl that made him seem bigger than he actually was. Grey hair had just started to appear at his temples, adding to the illusion that he was always at odds with life.

Gene watched as his second in command, Miss Kerry Reynolds, led a young man of about twenty-five years old up the stairs to his office. Kerry was the perfect opposite to his gruff manner.

"Sir, this is Corey Whitman. Mr. Whitman wrote the thesis you've been studying."

"Mr. Whitman, this is our senior exec, Mr. Gene Oldham," Kerry said as she stepped aside so the two could shake hands.

"Glad to know you, son. Have a seat," Gene said. Corey sat in a chair facing a cluttered desk.

"Ms. Reynolds said that…" Corey started, but Gene cut him off, waving his hand.

"I'm going to be straight with you, Carney. I've got a situation. In three days, I'm due to testify to the facts presented in your thesis. There's a One World Committee meeting supposed to vote on a multi-trillion dollar space budget—all in response to rumors that a doomsday event is going to happen. So what I need now are facts."

Kerry stepped forward. "Mr. Whitman just graduated from M.I.T., majoring in Astronomy and Space Aeronautics. He was the youngest…"

"That's just great, Ms. Reynolds. So he needs a job. You're hired, son. Now, your first assignment is to convince me that it isn't all bullshit so I can convince this committee to fund a program that will save the human race."

Corey sat up a little straighter. "Oh, it's not… um… B.S., sir. Historical records state, time and time again, the planet Phoenix has entered Earth's orbit around the Sun, only to disrupt the natural balance of Earth's ecosystems—not to mention throwing it off its axis. This, in turn, pushes Earth further away from the Sun, lengthening the years…"

Corey counted these points off on his fingers as he spoke.

When Gene interrupted him again, "Hold it, son; we're talking about what's going to happen, not what has happened."

"That's just it, sir. All of this is prologue to the coming event."

"The catastrophic event has happened before?" Gene asked skeptically.

"Yes, sir. It *has* happened before—many times. The planet literally envelops Earth, choking off the Sun and killing anything that survives the main event."

"And this has happened before? I mean, on *this* level?" Gene asked.

Corey pulled out a small iPad and, referring to it, said, "It's probably what happened to the dinosaurs. There are records of it happening in 2239 B.C. and—"

"If that's so, why weren't we all killed off then?" Gene interrupted, clearly impatient.

"Well," said Corey, "we almost were."

Gene leaned over his desk, planting his hands on the clutter of forgotten paperwork. He glared at Corey. "Well?"

Kerry, still standing off to the side, interjected gently, "He's talking about the Flood, sir. You know, Noah and the Ark?"

Gene looked at her with a skeptical frown.

"What's interesting," Corey continued, referring again to his iPad, "is that it's believed the passing of the planet itself isn't the most catastrophic part—but rather the impact from the debris trailing it."

He scrolled and added, "And then again in 1687 B.C., 1135 B.C., and in 583 B.C.—a man named Thates accurately predicted the very year when Planet Phoenix returned."

Gene came around his desk and reached for Corey's iPad. "Where are you getting this information, Conney?"

"It's *Corey*, sir," Corey replied as he handed over the device.

"What?" Gene asked, staring at the screen.

"My name is Corey, sir. You keep calling me—"

Gene cut him off, "Corey!? Well, of course it is. Who did you think I was talking to?"

Referring to the iPad screen, Gene squinted. "Who is this Jason Brashears? He seems to be an authority on this crap." Then, barking toward Kerry—who was already moving—he said, "See if we can get this person down here ASAP. And get Coleman a desk with a proper-sized computer!"

Turning back to Corey, he handed the iPad back. "This guy Brashears—is he your only source of information? And what does an M.I.T. student think is going to happen when this Planet Phoenix crosses our path? When?"

Corey squirmed slightly in his seat. "Um... 2040, sir. And actually, I'm a graduate of M.I.—"

Just then, the phone rang. Gene snatched it up and began barking into it.

Kerry gently got Corey's attention and led him down the stairs.

"Sometimes Mr. Oldham is gruffer than he intends," she said as they walked. "Don't let it bother you. It took three years before he started calling me Miss Reynolds."

She paused, then asked, "Is this your sole source of information about these planetary events?"

"Uh, no. Not exactly," Corey replied. "Although he does seem to be the best—or at least the most consistent."

They stopped at a desk with a computer terminal.

"This is yours. Management will be up later with a contract. Any details can be worked out then. Any problems—here's my direct line," she said, handing him a card.

"Your first assignment is to track down this Jason Brashears and get me the info. I'll reach out to him too. Your major was Astronomy, right?"

Corey nodded.

"I need a projected, detailed path and an estimated time of arrival—both worst and best-case scenarios as it applies to Earth. And put it in layman's terms. Any questions, call me anytime."

With that, Kerry left him to get settled.

On a West Texas ranch beneath a hot pre-summer sun, a stocky man rose from the fence he was mending. Barbed wire spools and various tools littered the ground beside him. He stretched his back and watched an approaching vehicle bounce over the uneven dirt road, trailing a cloud of West Texas dust. There was no wind.

Recognizing the oncoming truck, he walked over to his own and turned off the music blaring from the open door. Since he was the only person out there, he wondered what could be so important. The dirty white truck bounced up the road and slid to a stop.

The passenger door flew open, and a disheveled woman in a thigh-length skirt with the unmistakable look of the city spilled out.

"Jesus Christ!" she exclaimed, yanking down the hem of her skirt. "You couldn't drive any faster?" she shouted into the cab, where an old man in denim jeans and a cowboy hat handed out her briefcase. The woman slammed the door.

The old man pulled forward and brought the open truck window up to the man mending the fence.

"She said it was urgent, something about the end of the world." The old man leaned out the window and spat on the dusty ground. "Bring her back with you," he told the man.

"I got her, Dave. Thanks," the man replied as the truck pulled away.

"That old man drives like a maniac! He actually aimed for the potholes and knew I had no seatbelt," the woman said, adjusting her clothes. Picking up her briefcase and brushing hair out of her face, she approached. "Jason Brashears, I presume?"

The man nodded. She stuck out her hand. "Kerry Reynolds. I'm with the N.A.S.P."

Jason removed a glove and shook her hand.

"I understand you wrote several books concerning the coming of a planet that has a history of causing problems with ours."

Jason took off his hat and wiped his bald head. "Yeah, I suppose I did," he said, waiting.

"An astronomer has spotted what looks like an asteroid field with a main body heading in the direction of our solar system," Kerry explained.

Jason still waited.

"You don't seem surprised," she said.

"Have you read any of my books on this?" he asked.

Kerry walked awkwardly to the truck in high heels and placed her briefcase on the tailgate. She talked as she opened it, taking out a stack of large photos and a book.

"I read *When the Sun Darkens* on the plane. These photos are infrared images from the Hubble, and these..." she handed him another stack of pages, "are computer projections of the object's path relative to Earth. It seems your projected date of 2040 coincides with—"

Jason, studying the papers, interrupted her. "So what do you want from me? I mean, it seems like you have confirmation, so...?"

Kerry faced him. "Our branch of the government is meeting with other heads of concerned countries in two days. We, the N.A.S.P., are to brief the President on the facts and help create a contingency plan in case..."

"In case?" Jason repeated.

"In case it's a doomsday event. Some scientists say there's a 40% probability..."

Jason held up a hand as he studied the documents, then walked over and leaned against the truck.

"What is the time duration between these photos?" he asked, holding up two glossy 8x10 images of space.

Kerry came over and looked. "I don't know what makes you think they're not from the same time."

He pointed to a circled group of white dots in one picture. "See here?"

She nodded.

He changed to another picture. "And here?"

Another nod.

He flipped again. "And here? And here?"

She looked at the images, then at him. "I don't see any difference."

"You see this mass of stars here?" he asked. "In this photo, see how the light seems to bulge out on this side? And here, how this speck appears separated from the central mass?"

She examined them again. "Well, that's only a speck or something. Maybe a flaw in the photo."

Jason shook his head. "These are ultra-high-resolution infrared photos. They've been translated by computers designed to eliminate flaws. The photos themselves are taken in several spectrums of light—there can be no mistake."

She looked at him, not quite comprehending.

"Everyone's looking at *this*," he said, indicating the circled group of spots. "But *this* is what you're missing. And *this* is the doomsday event."

Kerry still looked confused.

Jason sighed. "That first group you know about is Planet Phoenix, coming toward our solar system. But following it is *another* planet. Either one by itself would disrupt Earth's ecosystems—volcanoes, earthquakes, the works. Together? They'll throw Earth off its axis, bombard the planet with debris and continent-sized asteroids or comets. It could extinct life as we know it."

"All life?" she asked, glancing down at the photos.

"You mentioned this in your book, but..." she trailed off.

"I wrote another book all about this second body of planetary activity—when it passed into our solar system."

She looked up at his weathered face.

"You have to come and brief my boss on this so he can warn the President."

Jason looked back at her. "What good would that do? Don't you get it? This is Armageddon with a twist. No one gets out alive. Or if some do, they'll die under a canopy of dirt and dust that'll eventually wipe out whatever's left."

Kerry put her hand on his arm. "They have a plan to colonize Mars."

Jason gave her a funny look.

"Russia, China, Europe—they'll all be there, working as a federation, looking for solutions. If it's as you say, then the only answer is to get off this planet to preserve the human race."

He took off his hat again and wiped his bald head with a sweaty handkerchief, looking off toward the horizon.

"We have to convince them to pull together and do this for everybody," Kerry said.

Jason replaced his hat and looked at her.

"You *have* to help."

"You people have never come together on anything," he said.

"Well, we'd better on this. Or that's it, right? You said so yourself."

Kerry began gathering her papers and photos, stuffing them back into her briefcase. "I have to get back. Are you coming or not?" she asked, brushing her hair from her face again.

"I'll be in my mid-sixties when this happens," he said, turning to her. "I've given this a lot of thought and doubt it'll do much good, but what the hell—let's give it a go."

He started collecting his tools and gear and loading them into his truck.

"Conley! Conley, where are the latest photos on the Phoenix Group? And where is Miss Reynolds? We gotta plane to catch!" Gene Oldham yelled at the young man scrambling to gather various photos and computer charts.

"I, um… here are the latest pictures and the charts that coincide with—"

Gene cut him off again. "Can you explain these in layman's terms so I can—"

"I'm here, Mr. Oldham," a familiar voice said as the *clack, clack* of heels approached. "This is Jason Brashears, and he'll accompany us to the meeting. He's been hired as a consultant."

Gene turned to face them, hands full of papers, which he shoved into Corey's chest as he rose from his desk.

"Good. Here, kid—explain all this on the way. You two follow me; we gotta plane to catch. Gene Oldham, glad to meet you," he said, taking Jason's hand and shaking it on the way out.

As Gene walked away, Kerry rolled her eyes and mouthed, *"I told you,"* and smiled quickly as she followed her boss.

"Jason Brashears. Here, let me help you," Jason said, introducing himself to Corey.

"Corey Whitman. I read your books. It's what—"

"Come on, you two! We ain't got all day!" Gene yelled from across the room.

Later, aboard Air Force One, the President sat at the head of the table as his advisors, consultants, and "yes" men occupied the remaining seats. Attendants stood at the ready as the meeting continued.

"So, what you're saying is this was prophesied in the Book of Revelations?" the President asked.

Jason answered, "Yes, Sir. But you must understand—that prophecy was written well over 2,000 years ago, in terms that the people of that age could understand… or at least pass on."

Another person spoke up, "That prophecy was inspired by God Himself—as is the entire Bible. And if God wanted us to go to Mars, He would have told us."

"This is Reverend Pat Donahue," the President said by way of introduction. "Reverend Donahue is the head of the Christian Coalition for Christ."

Jason turned to the Reverend and said, "Perhaps He is."

"I don't follow you," the Reverend said.

Jason explained, "We have the prophecy of the Sun darkening and the Moon turning red. We have historical documentation of this very thing happening. We also have data proving that in 25 years, it's going to happen again. We, as intelligent men, know the only way to prevent the extinction of our species is to not be here when it happens. Perhaps our Creator has put all these things before us to aid us in our quest to survive."

Reverend Donahue looked at Jason. "It's blasphemy to presume to know what God Almighty intends for His people. Maybe this is a test—and we should all place our trust in Him."

An advisor spoke up. "Yeah? Explain that to the other religious sects who'll also decide whether to proceed or not. Look—all this information tells us that in the year 2040, we're going to experience a catastrophic event that will, in all likelihood, destroy Earth. What are we going to do about it?"

Gene Oldham said, "I agree. Something must be done. And for now, I have all the facts I need. Thank you, gentlemen, for attending this meeting."

The Federation for Planetary Survival launches its first shuttle to Mars.

A TV talk show host leans across a desk, talking to his guest during a commercial break as the studio audience applauds.

"Hello, and welcome back to *The Baxter Reed Show*," he says into the camera as the applause dies down. "We've been talking to Corey Whitman of the World Save Program. We're glad you could join us." He then turns to Corey, seated to his right.

"Corey, you wrote a thesis that was very instrumental in convincing the heads of government to actually pull together and colonize Mars—is that correct?"

"Yes, it is. But my expertise was more along the lines of astronomy," Corey answered.

"Meaning?" asked the host.

"Meaning, I spotted the Phoenix Group first."

This got some titters from the audience.

"In truth, I was only repeating information already provided by someone else."

"Dr. Jason Brashears, I assume?" Baxter said.

"That's correct," answered Corey.

"We'll get to Dr. Brashears in a moment. I've been informed that the dome shells for the bio-domes have been manufactured in space and are, as we speak, en route to Mars. Can you tell us about that?" he asked Corey.

"Of course," Corey said, leaning forward. "Actually, the Chinese developed a polyurethane substance that is grown. Its elasticity is phenomenal. If it's punctured, it stretches to the point where it gives—then retracts to actually close off the hole. It's truly a remarkable substance."

"So, if say, an asteroid hits it, it won't shatter?"

"That's correct."

Baxter referred to his notes. "They say these domes are literally ten miles wide, two miles high, and can hold over 150,000 people."

"That's true. 160,000 are scheduled for each, with room to grow crops and build treatment plants, etc."

As Corey finished, the audience murmured and then applauded.

After the applause, Baxter asked, "And how many are planned?"

"Approximately 100 are planned, but technology is moving so fast, we could easily see more diverse designs that would enable us to build more."

More applause.

Baxter asked, "As I understand it, water has been found up there. Is that true?"

Corey looked at the audience. "There have been six teams of people on Mars for five years. Some are drilling and finding water; others are experimenting with the soil to see what will grow outside the dome unaided, and what needs to be grown under the dome, as it were."

"And they're having success?" asked Baxter.

"Oh, absolutely—in all fields, as it were."

More applause.

"Mr. Whitman, it's rumored that the shuttles being built will hold more people than the Cowboy Stadium. That seems colossal. Is it true?"

"Yes, it's actually as big as that particular stadium. Not quite as tall—but as big."

Oohs and *ahhs* came from the audience.

"And how do you get something that large off the ground?" asked Baxter, astonished.

"That," Corey stated, "is something I'm not allowed to discuss."

"What do you mean, not allowed to discuss?"

Again, Corey faced the audience and the camera. Looking very uncomfortable, he said, "There's a secrecy clause that binds me to silence on any propulsion or technical matter."

Baxter appeared surprised. "You mean, even though the entire world is in a joint effort to do this, we're still keeping secrets from each other?"

Corey nodded.

"That's incredible." Baxter turned back to the camera. "When we come back—our next guest will talk about the coming Apocalypse and its origin."

Applause.

As the director signaled that the camera was off, Baxter leaned in as the studio audience talked among themselves. He said to Corey:

"I understand you can't talk about this on the air, but off the record—is it true they have developed an anti-gravity device? I mean, I'm sure they'd have to, in order to get something that large off the ground."

Corey shifted in his seat. "Really, I'm not allowed to discuss it. Besides, I'm not the person to ask regarding that subject."

As the *Applause* sign lit up and the show came back on, Baxter asked, "Who's that person?"

Corey shrugged his shoulders as the director cued the host.

"Welcome back. Our next guest seems to have started it all. He's authored several books detailing upcoming events, including the worldwide bestseller *Nostradamus and the Planets of Apocalypse*. Please welcome Dr. Jason Brashears!"

The audience applauds as Jason crosses the stage. He smiles sheepishly, waves to the crowd, and shakes Baxter's hand before taking his seat between Corey and the desk.

As the applause fades, Baxter, holding Jason's book, says, "Welcome to the show, Dr. Brashears. I understand you started all this with your research on the events mentioned in your book. Care to tell us a little about that?"

Jason sits up and leans forward. "First of all, I didn't start any of this—and the doctorate is honorary. I'm flattered, but it's just Jason."

Baxter raises his eyebrows. "Modesty! That's a rare quality on this show."

The audience laughs and applauds as Jason nods politely, clearly a little embarrassed. When the noise dies down, Baxter continues, "So tell us about your research, Jason."

Jason explains the appearance of mysterious planetary bodies throughout history—their recurring effects on Earth, and references found everywhere from the Bible to hieroglyphics on the Pyramids of Giza, even the return of the Annunaki.

"Fascinating, simply fascinating," says Baxter, turning to the camera. "Now we come to the part of the show where you, the audience, get to ask questions. Let's see... you there, third row."

The camera pans to a man standing as an usher holds out a microphone. He shifts uncomfortably. "So, if 100 domes are built and they hold 160,000 people... that means only 16 million people out of Earth's entire population will be saved. Is that right?"

Corey nods. "Yes, that's correct."

The man presses on. "So how do I become one of the lucky ones?"

The audience applauds.

Corey shrugs. "I'm sorry, I don't have anything to do with that decision."

Someone shouts from the audience, "I bet you two have seats though, don't you?"

The crowd begins to stir. Baxter tries to restore order. "Now, now—everyone will get a chance. Please calm down. Next question—yes, the man in the white shirt."

The audience settles. Another usher holds the microphone.

"This question's for Dr. Brashears. You claim the Bible mentions this event—the darkening of the sun—but you skip over the parts where God spares the faithful. Shouldn't we trust God to deliver us from this catastrophe?"

Scattered applause follows.

Jason leans forward. "All I've done is compile documentation of historical events. I'm not trying to influence anyone's faith."

More shouting erupts. Someone grabs the microphone. "But you say we should leave the planet or we'll all die!"

Jason tries to respond. "I'm not saying you should do anything—" but his voice is drowned out by the crowd.

Baxter signals for security, who move in quickly and escort the man out.

Suddenly, a man in a *W.W.J.D.* T-shirt stands and pulls a gun, aiming it at the stage.

The audience erupts in screams. As people scatter, three shots are fired. All hit Jason.

Security tackles the shooter.

Baxter and Corey scramble to recover from their evasive dives and rush to Jason.

Corey kneels beside his friend, stunned. Blood pools beneath Jason's body. Corey takes his hand. "Jason, hang on. Help is on the way."

Jason struggles to breathe. Blood bubbles at his lips. "I... I didn't—" he whispers, his chest soaked in red.

"I'm here, Jason. Just relax. Help's coming," Corey says, though fear floods his eyes.

Jason grips Corey's jacket with his bloodied hand, pulling him close. "I didn't start anything," he gasps—then dies, releasing his grip.

Medical staff rush in and attempt CPR, but it's too late.

Corey is dazed as he's led offstage. In a private restroom, he scrubs Jason's blood from his hands.

In the mirror, he sees a man in a suit he rarely wears—blood staining the lapels. He looks older than his 35 years.

Suddenly, the door bursts open.

Kerry Reynolds rushes in. "Oh my God! We were told you were shot!"

She spins him around, checking for wounds.

"They shot Jason," Corey says, hollowly.

Satisfied that Corey is uninjured, Kerry relaxes. "Why?" she whispers.

He shrugs and leads her out of the restroom.

Later, in the back of a limo, Corey watches a crowd of picketers swarming the studio entrance. Signs read: *Repent! God is Coming. Trust in God, Not Mars. Jesus Is Coming to Get Us All.*

Flashing lights from ambulances and police cars paint the night in chaos.

Kerry sits beside him. "You've got that Lockheed visit tomorrow. Are you up for it?"

Corey nods. His phone rings. He checks the ID and answers. "Hi, Dad… No, I'm okay… Yes, someone was shot. It wasn't me…"

Kerry pats his arm, then returns to her day planner.

"I know, Dad. And she would be right… but Mom's gone… and—" he pauses, listening. "Okay… Thursday. I'll be there for the weekend… I love you too. Bye."

He closes the phone and turns to Kerry.

"I'm heading to Minneapolis on Thursday to spend the weekend with my dad."

Back at the hotel, they had barely stepped through the doors when Corey's assistant, Benny, came running up to him.

"My God, Corey—we thought you were shot!" Benny grabbed Corey by the shoulders, eyes on the blood staining his suit.

"They shot Jason," Corey said, trying to push past him.

Another man approached, hand extended. "Mr. Whitman, I'm Joe Swankston from Lockheed."

Corey shook his hand, still moving toward the elevators. "Mr. Swankston, pleased to meet you. Could you give me a few minutes to clean up? It's been a—"

"Of course, of course. It's just that your visit to the facility got bumped up to today due to… um…"

"They're going to test it today?" Corey interrupted, stopping in his tracks. "We just thought—"

Swankston stammered, clearly trying not to reveal too much. "I'll be right down, Mr. Swankston." Corey turned to his assistant. "Benny, would you take Joe here to the bar while I change clothes?"

Kerry held the elevator door open for Corey. As they rode up, he asked, "Are you coming to the hangar with us?"

"I can't make it," she replied. "There's a lot to do for Gene's big retirement send-off, and I'm supposed to take the reins after that."

Corey smiled. "I forgot about your promotion. Congratulations, Kerry. Please tell Gene I wish him well—he deserves his retirement."

As the elevator stopped, she asked, "You're not coming?"

He stepped out. "No, I'm going home for the weekend. I need some time, and my dad wants me there. I may not have the chance again."

"Okay," she said, "Call me with the details and have Benny take the—"

The doors closed before she could finish, but he knew what she needed. With a heavy sigh, he went to his room.

Later, en route to the hangar, Joe briefed Corey and Benny in the back of the car.

"So the first big ship going up can come back, you see—"

"To get more people," Benny finished.

"And supplies. These first few flights carry just as much material as personnel. Most of the passengers—if not all—are builders in some capacity."

They passed through the third and final checkpoint. Benny rode shotgun while Joe and Corey sat in the back, sorting through papers and photos for Corey's trip to Minneapolis.

"Wow, is that the hangar?" Benny asked, pointing at a colossal structure on the horizon.

Corey looked up. "No," he said, leaning forward to get a better view. "That's the ship."

Joe turned, grinning. "See this strip in the road?" he asked.

Both Corey and Benny noticed a painted line down the center, assuming it was a divider. Joe aligned the car with the strip and engaged autopilot.

"I've heard about those," Benny said, marveling at the driverless vehicle.

"Lockheed developed the AutoPilot system for Earth roads. Now we're taking it to Mars—for transportation between domes."

Corey watched as buildings came into clearer view. "So those cube-like structures are human cargo containers?"

"Correct. Each person will be packed between two water mattresses for the first three days of flight. The takeoff acceleration pulls too many G's for the human body—up to double your body weight pressing down on you. Floating in water reduces that strain."

"I don't get it," Benny said.

Corey explained, "It's like lifting something heavy underwater—it feels lighter."

"Ohhh, right." Benny pointed to the rows of stacked cargo cubes behind the massive ship. "Can we go there?"

"Not this trip," Joe replied. "That's why we're on the strip. 'The powers that be' are directing our tour to the propulsion lab." He used air quotes on the last line.

Benny and Corey exchanged a look. Joe shrugged. "Hey, it ain't my show."

When the car stopped, the doors opened automatically. A man in a lab coat approached, hand outstretched.

"Mr. Whitman, I presume?"

He shook Benny's hand.

"No, sorry—I'm Benny Redman, Mr. Whitman's assistant. This is Corey Whitman."

"Excuse me, Mr. Redman." He turned to Corey. "Mr. Whitman, what an honor. I'm Josh Morton, lead engineer. I understand you had a hand in developing the… um… device." He glanced sideways at Benny and Joe.

"That's true. Benny has clearance."

"Of course! No offense meant."

Benny smiled.

"The first thing I want to show you is the takeoff gear," Josh said, leading them beneath the ship while Joe remained with the car.

"Now, you know these aren't designed to land again—on Earth," Josh said as they approached four massive tires under what looked like a giant shock absorber.

The ship's underside towered fifteen feet high, and the tires consumed at least ten of those feet. Corey looked off into the distance, noting the dozens of similar wheel assemblies.

"They come off," Josh said, grinning.

"What's that?" Corey asked.

"The wheel assembly detaches at takeoff."

Corey and Benny stared at the massive tires.

"So that means…" Corey began.

"Yes—it means once it lifts off, there's no room for error," Josh said. "You have a 15-minute no-error window to launch. Once it's up, it's not coming back—not to Earth, anyway. And without that extra weight, the ship performs better. Skids are built in for landing on Mars. Eventually, the ship itself becomes building material."

Josh pulled out a walkie-talkie. "Start the sequence."

A humming noise began.

"Here—it's not loud, more like a vibration. It'll make your ears itch," Josh said, handing them earplugs.

As they inserted them, the massive structure overhead creaked and groaned.

"Look!" Benny pointed to the shock absorbers.

They watched as the pillar-like shocks slowly expanded.

"Hydraulics?" Benny asked.

Josh smiled and shook his head.

"You mean…?" Corey asked.

Josh nodded.

"What?" Benny asked.

"It's the anti-gravity device," Corey answered. Then to Josh, "How much?"

"Eighty-two percent," Josh replied.

The ceiling continued to rise. Benny watched the shocks double in length.

"It works off the Earth's magnetic field," Corey said.

"Like putting two magnets together with reversed poles," Josh added.

"So they repel each other," Benny said, eyes wide. "So at liftoff, this thing weighs only 18% of its real—"

"And those wheel assemblies just roll off the tarmac as it lifts off?" Benny asked.

"Oh no. The strip that brought your car here also controls the wheel assemblies. They're reused on the next ship," Josh explained. "Now, I'm afraid that concludes our tour."

"Can we go inside the ship?" Benny asked.

Corey remained quiet, lost in thought.

Josh continued as they walked back. "There's not much to see inside. It's a honeycomb of containment units—cargo, people, animals, materials. Only the pilot's area is different."

"What about the cold fusion propulsion system?" Corey asked.

"This ship has four cold fusion engines. Combined with centrifugal launch, it'll hit cruising speeds of 30,000 mph—puts us on Mars in under 100 days."

"That's fantastic!" Benny said.

Josh beamed. "We launched two freighters from China five months ago. This one will arrive around the same time."

As they reached the car, Benny asked, "What's the name of this ship?"

"Why, the *Enterprise*, of course."

"Get out of here!"

"No, really. It wasn't my idea, but once I heard it… I agreed."

Corey smiled, taking one last look at the towering vessel before climbing into the car.

Three days later, Corey sat in his dad's living room, going over new photos from the Space Center.

"What'cha doing, son?" his dad asked, coming into the room.

Corey looked up and saw an older version of himself.

"These new photos of the approaching mass just came from Kerry. I'm going over them."

He sat back and, after removing his glasses, massaged the bridge of his nose.

"I made some soup," his dad said, sitting down.

Corey stared at his father.

"What?" his dad asked.

"I don't know, Dad. I'm just… immersed in this project, and I feel like it's a struggle just to breathe sometimes."

His dad leaned forward. "Whatever happened to that girl you met in college? What was her name—Joyce?"

Corey thought about it. "That was a long time ago, Dad. She moved on," he said.

"Well, maybe you should too," said Whitman Sr.

Corey just sat there.

"Let's face it, son. According to you, this thing is gonna wipe us all out or turn us back into cave men. You told me you have two seats on the last shuttle. Well, I'm not going with you. I won't leave your mother, but you can take some girl and move on."

Corey had thought about that. He knew his dad wouldn't go. But he still hadn't found the right girl.

"The thing is, Dad, I never have the time to go out and find *the one*."

"Make the time. You say this thing comes in fifteen years—make the time, son."

Just then, Corey's cell phone rang. He picked it up and saw it was Kerry.

"Yes?" he said, then listened. "Okay."

He ended the call, went over to the computer, typed in some commands, and sat back. His dad came over and sat next to him.

"What is it?" he asked.

"Kerry said that, according to the math, the second body of mass behind the Phoenix group is gaining on it."

He indicated the spots on the screen.

"Here is Phoenix, and this"—he pointed to another spot—"is the second group."

He typed in new instructions. The images on the screen began to move using time-lapse photography. They watched as the two spots shifted. Corey typed in more commands, and the computer confirmed that the second mass was moving faster than the first. He asked for an ETA.

The estimate showed a 98% probability that the second mass would combine with the Phoenix group right as it reached Earth's orbital path.

"Is that bad?" Corey's dad asked.

Corey smiled, then laughed.

"What?" his dad said.

Corey turned and looked at the old man.

"Nah, not really. I mean, before we were just facing annihilation— now we're facing *super* annihilation."

Several days later, as Corey was packing to return to Houston, his dad handed him a wooden box.

"I want you to take this with you."

"What is it?" Corey asked, opening the box.

"Just some things," his dad said. "Some family things."

He pulled a handkerchief from his pocket and blew his nose.

"Dad..." Corey said, looking into the box. He was moved.

Whitman Sr. said, "You know that park by the machine shop where we used to go when your mother was alive?"

Corey nodded, holding a wedding photo of his parents.

"I proposed to her there, by that duck pond."

Corey looked at his father.

"Dad, I'm not going anywhere for at least fifteen—"

His dad held up a hand.

"I won't be around that long, son. The doctor says my cholesterol is going to kill me, and I'm not changing my diet to save my arteries."

"But Dad..." Corey began.

His dad took the photo, placed it in the box, and closed the lid.

"Just take these things and pass them on to yours, when you finally have some. You *are* gonna have some, aren't you, son?" He stuffed the box into Corey's suitcase.

"I hope so, Dad."

"You *hope*?" his dad said. "You *hope*? Promise me you'll at least carry on the family name, boy."

"I promise," Corey said, closing the suitcase.

January 2038

Kerry Reynolds, now Executive Administrator, walked across the office pool, approaching the big board.

"Benny, come here, please," she said, facing the Plexiglas wall that, with so many notations on it, was nearly unrecognizable as a map.

Benny approached. Corey was at his desk in front of the celestial board, eating his lunch.

"Yes, ma'am," Benny said.

Kerry pointed. "What notation is this?" she asked.

"Those are active volcanoes, ma'am. We have sixteen active ones in the U.S. alone," Benny answered.

Kerry looked at him. "And this notation?" she said, pointing to a mass of marks that seemed to cover the American continent.

"Oh, those are earthquakes, ma'am."

"Are all of these above 6.0 on the Richter scale?" she asked.

"Ah, no. Some are smaller, but they're so remote that—"

She cut him off. "You see that this board is hard to read with all these size-metric events, right?" she asked.

"Yes, ma'am," he said, looking at his feet.

"And I specifically said no earthquakes under 6.0 on the Richter scale, right?"

Benny nodded.

"So, would you please clean this off and record the Chicago earthquake for me? I need to get an idea of what's going on. I have to brief the Vice President today and need an update. Start at yesterday, would you?" Kerry asked, laying a hand on his arm.

The small contact relieved the man's obvious intimidation—she, as the boss, had over him.

"Thank you, Benny," she said.

He smiled. "What about the volcanoes?" he asked as she turned away.

"If they're still active, leave 'em," she said, walking over to Corey's desk.

"Hey, boss lady," Corey said, smiling as she approached.

She pulled up a chair, and with a heavy sigh, sat facing the board, watching as Benny started cleaning it up.

"Still going to Minneapolis tonight?" she asked.

"Yeah," he said, gathering the remnants of his lunch and dropping it into the wastebasket. "It's their anniversary, and I like to be there. There will be a time when I can't, so..." He left it hanging.

Kerry patted his leg in a friendly manner. "I know. I still go visit my twins' grave on our birthday," she said.

"I didn't know you were a twin," he said.

She looked at him and smiled. "There's a lot you don't know about me, Corey." And she winked.

He laughed out loud, and she smiled.

Benny turned and looked back, paranoid he'd messed something up.

They both waved, two old friends sharing a laugh.

"I thought you'd promised your dad that you'd find a significant other," she asked him.

"Why? Are you looking to catch?" he asked.

"No, not me—I have a beau. Besides, I'm too young for you," Corey laughed again. "But thanks for asking."

She smiled. "Yeah, who has the time right now? How is Jeff, by the way?"

Jeff was Kerry's partner and had been for years. He was a Native American from Arizona who made it clear he wouldn't be leaving his home planet for any reason.

Corey liked Jeff. His best description of Jeff Foote was a practical man of common sense, set in his ways.

"Are you coming by tonight on your way to the airport?" she asked.

"Yeah, Benny's driving me. I told him we'd be stopping to see you. I don't know who's more intimidating to old Benny—you or Jeff," he said.

She laughed, remembering a party where Benny and Jeff met. Benny had been drinking, and when Jeff was introduced, Benny raised his hand and said, "How!"

Jeff looked Native American—over six feet tall, dark complexion, black hair, and even blacker eyes.

"Here, let me show you 'How,'" Jeff responded, taking Benny's raised hand and folding all his fingers down except one, then poked Benny in the eye with it.

There was no malice, but Benny stepped lightly from then on around Kerry's beau.

"You two ever gonna tie the knot?" Corey asked.

"We have already," she said.

He looked at her and smiled. "We had a ceremony under the stars and were joined by Native American customs."

Corey sat for a moment, thinking.

"I'm a Squaw," she said.

He looked at his friend. "You're not going, are you?"

She shook her head. "No, I'm giving my two passes to Benny," she said.

Corey looked at Benny's back as he worked on the board. "Does he know that?" he asked.

Benny had two passes of his own, but he also had two children, and no matter how much he begged, the Space Committee only allowed two passes per person on the shuttle to Mars.

"No," she smiled, "not yet. I'll tell him at Christmas."

Corey thought about that.

"You may want to tell him sooner, Kerry. He's wrestling with this problem daily. The last ship leaves next year, and I think he's planning to send his kids alone."

"I know," Kerry said. "Jeff said the same thing. But what if we change our minds?"

Corey chuckled. "Jeff won't change his mind," he said.

"No, I guess you're right. Hey, Benny!" she said.

Benny stopped what he was doing.

"Now?" Corey asked, surprised.

"Why not?" she said, waving Benny over.

Benny came over with a troubled look on his face.

"It's about the Vesuvius volcano, huh? It's venting and has a history..." Kerry waved him to silence.

"No, Benny, you're doing a great job. Jeff and I aren't going to Mars—we want you and Helen to have our seats!" she said.

"You need to be there to raise your kids," she added.

Benny stood stunned. His eyes welled up and spilled over.

"I..." he started to say.

"I know. Actually, it was Jeff's idea. I'll get you the forms today. Fill them in, get them back to me ASAP, and I'll take care of the rest."

Kerry stood up to go, and Benny grabbed her in a big hug.

Corey watched as Benny sobbed into Kerry's neck.

"Benny, you take the rest of the day off. Go and tell Helen," she said soothingly.

He stepped back. "Helen," he said, wiping his eyes.

"Thank you, Miss Reynolds. Thank you..." he said as he backed away.

"Don't forget, you gotta pick me up at 6:00," Corey reminded the retreating Benny.

Benny waved and jogged out the door.

Kerry wiped a tear from her cheek and said, "Well, at least they will go to good use," meaning the passes on the shuttle.

Two days later, on a street in Minneapolis, Corey stood at the corner of an alley, watching the park where his parents had fallen in love. From across the street, he remained in the shade of an old building, observing the many people camped out there.

Due to the frequent earthquakes caused by approaching planets or asteroid fields, people had been displaced or were too afraid to sleep in the surrounding buildings. Things were falling apart.

He remembered this park from his childhood. The machine shop next door had been his dad's business. The hardware store beside it was his uncle's. He had a history here. This was home.

"Come on, Mister, you can't stay here!" said a voice.

Corey felt a very small hand tug his finger. Looking down, he saw a little girl, perhaps four or five years old, dressed in worn but clean clothes. Her blonde hair was tied into two pigtails.

"We gotta go!" she said as her grip slipped. She fell backward and landed on her butt.

Corey stepped forward and picked her up. Before he could say anything, he felt the ground tremble. He staggered forward and leaned against the building at the mouth of the alley.

A mighty crash exploded behind him, jolting the concrete beneath his feet and sending him to his knees. The entire corner of the building had dislodged and collapsed exactly where he'd been standing moments earlier.

"Jesus," he whispered, clutching the girl tightly.

"Duke said we gotta go in there," she said, pointing.

Corey stood up just as the ground began to shake more violently. A boy, no more than eight, dashed out of the alley and grabbed the corner of Corey's jacket, pulling him urgently.

Corey followed, half-jogging, half-stumbling as debris rained down around them. Midway down the alley, they reached a pair of angled metal double doors. The boy grabbed a chunk of concrete and began hammering on them.

Corey stood by, holding the girl's head against his chest as the world seemed to collapse around them. He looked back and saw masonry, glass, and fragments of buildings crashing to the ground.

The noise was deafening.

He felt a tug on his jacket. One of the doors opened, and the boy pulled him inside.

Corey ducked through the door, which slammed shut behind him. It was dark, but the boy kept tugging his sleeve.

A loud crash hit the door just as they moved further into the shelter. A red emergency light flickered on as they entered a room full of children.

Another door slammed shut behind them. Corey dropped to one knee, bracing himself with one hand as the ground continued to tremble. Plaster and pieces of ceiling pelted him. He stayed in a three-point stance, clutching the girl.

And then—Silence.

It stopped as quickly as it had begun.

Corey sat back, still holding the girl, her tiny arms trembling around his neck.

The Earth gave one final shudder, then fell still.

A few seconds passed in silence. Then the murmurs began. Children talking, some crying, others whimpering.

"Okay now, I think it's over, kids," said a female voice.

In the dim red light, Corey could make out children of all ages sitting against the walls of what appeared to be an old fallout shelter.

A woman approached and gently took the girl from Corey's arms.

"Boy, you were a lucky little girl, Annie. This nice man came just in time." She glanced around. "Duke? Where are you?"

The second door creaked open again, but Duke did not return.

The little girl, Annie, pointed at Corey. "He almost got smashed!"

Still shaking, Corey stood. The woman looked at him.

"I'm afraid she's right," he said. "In fact, had it not been for her and the boy..."

Just then, the lights flickered on.

Kids began moving around. Several bolted toward the now-open crash door. Everyone was covered in dust.

"Miss Smiff, I gotta go potty," a small child said, tugging on the hem of the woman's dress.

She handed Annie back to Corey and picked up the child. "Alright kids, let's go back upstairs," she said, walking toward the door. "We probably have a mess to clean up."

About twenty kids followed her out.

Corey waited until most had gone, then followed. As he climbed the second flight of stairs, he heard the woman calmly giving directions to the children.

At the top, he entered what looked like a dormitory. The woman came around the corner, straightening her dress and brushing dirt from her face.

All the children appeared safe. None seemed older than thirteen.

"Miss Smith, all the pots are on the floor in the kitchen, and the dining room's a mess," a girl around thirteen reported.

"Thank you, dear. Will you and Millie take care of that for me? We must get lunch started."

She turned to Corey. "Perhaps you'd like to freshen up a bit."

She had a distinctive Midwestern accent and couldn't have been more than thirty, though the dust made her look older. Holding Annie on her hip, she started brushing off Corey's coat.

"Here now," she said, tugging at the plaster-covered jacket. "Go into the boys' room over there and wash your face. You've got a cut on your forehead that might need stitches."

She gently pushed him toward a door marked **BOYS**.

Annie waved over her shoulder. "Bye!"

Corey smiled and waved back as Miss Smith carried her and his coat down the aisle between two rows of beds.

He entered the bathroom and stood over a waist-high sink. Leaning toward the mirror, he saw himself covered in dust. He brushed back his hair, revealing its natural brown streaked with gray at the temples.

He washed his face, revealing a manageable cut.

"'Scuse me."

It was the small boy from earlier, holding up his hands.

"Oh," Corey said, lifting the child so he could wash them.

Suddenly, the door slammed open and three boys bounded into the room, clearly on some unsupervised mission. They halted when they saw Corey.

"Don't mind me, boys. I'm just passing through," Corey said as he set the small child down.

The little one dried his hands on his shirt and bolted toward the door. One of the older boys held it open for him.

"Are you here to adopt someone?" one of the boys asked.

Corey dabbed at the cut on his forehead with a paper towel.

"I'm afraid not. I was visiting the park when the earthquake started."

The boys looked at him differently now.

"Say," he said, tossing the paper towel in the trash, "how come you all came to be in a shelter when the earthquake started?"

The boys stared at him.

"How did you know it was coming?"

One of the boys pulled out a cigarette and lit it, practically daring Corey to say something. Corey looked at the cigarette, then at the boy. The boy met his gaze unflinchingly.

One of the boys answered, "Duke told us."

The first boy threw an elbow into the one who had spoken and gave him a sharp look. Passing the cigarette to his friend, the first boy said, "What's it worth to ya?"

Corey looked back at the boys. Just then, someone tried to get into the bathroom, but one of the boys had his foot blocking the door.

"Get outta here, we're busy!" one of them yelled.

A younger voice on the other side swore they'd tell Miss Smith.

"Yeah, what's it worth to ya?" repeated the boy guarding the door.

"Five bucks," Corey said, digging into his pocket.

"Man, that won't even get us a pack of squares," the first boy scoffed.

"Five bucks a piece," bartered the smoking boy.

"I've got ten," Corey said, holding out the bills.

The boy, who seemed to be the leader, snatched the money from Corey's hand. "Deal," he said, pocketing it.

"Duke?" Corey asked.

The boy nodded. "Duke's the one who saved your ass out there. Yeah—he is a freak."

Corey frowned. "How did he know the quake was coming?"

Taking the last drag from the cigarette, the boy said, "Duke knew and told Miss Smith. Last time she didn't listen, and one of the kids got hurt pretty badly."

Just then, a sharp banging came at the door.

"You boys unblock this door! Jake, I know you're in there. I've told you boys before…"

Miss Smith was laying down the law.

"Oh crap!" said the boy with the cigarette. He handed it to Corey and pulled his friend away from the door, causing it to swing open.

All three boys ran out, leaving Corey standing there holding the lit cigarette.

"…and you boys had better not—Jake, I smell smoke in there!" Miss Smith said as she entered the bathroom. Seeing Corey, she stopped.

"Oh," she said.

Corey stepped over to the toilet and dropped the cigarette butt in.

"It wasn't mine," he said defensively.

Miss Smith just smiled.

A smaller boy pushed past her and began using the toilet.

Corey moved to leave, and she stepped out of the way, letting the door close behind him.

"No really, I don't smoke," he insisted.

"I guess those boys made you hold that cigarette, huh, Mr. Whitman? You'd think a man of your age and standing would be a better influence on these boys."

"I…" Corey started to respond.

She stood waiting for an answer. He noticed she had cleaned up a bit too.

"Hey, how do you know my name?"

Just then, a girl came down the aisle between the beds and handed him his suit coat.

"Here you are, Mr. Whitman. We got as much dust off as we could," she said sweetly.

He immediately checked his coat pocket—his wallet was there.

Corey looked at Miss Smith, who was starting to turn red.

"You looked at my driver's license, didn't you?"

She stood speechless.

"We thought you were from Social Services," said the girl. Other children began gathering around.

Corey opened his wallet. "What else did you look at? My *standing*? Is that what you said?" He was beginning to enjoy turning the tables.

"I didn't mean to pry. I only thought you were..." she stammered.

She stood about 5'8", probably in her mid-to-late thirties. Nice figure, auburn hair, freckles—and, Corey thought, quite attractive.

"Being nosey is what you were doing," he said with a cagey smile.

The older girls watching giggled behind their hands.

"I don't have to take this," Miss Smith said, briskly walking away up the aisle.

"Come, girls, we have lunch to make. Jake, you get this bed area situated. Joey, I want—" She trailed off into a list of orders as she disappeared through another door at the far end of the dorm.

Corey chuckled to himself. Looking down, he saw the little girl who'd saved his life earlier. She held up her hands, and he picked her up.

"Annie, right?" he asked.

Annie nodded.

"I'm Corey," he said, following the small group of girls up the aisle.

"We only wanted to see who you were," one of them explained.

He put a hand on her shoulder and said, "Don't worry about it. I'm not angry."

The girl smiled, clearly enjoying the attention.

"Is Miss Smith always so bossy?" he asked.

Three older girls walking with him and Annie giggled and nodded.

They entered the kitchen, where Miss Smith was spreading peanut butter on about forty slices of bread.

"Sandy, get me a jar of jelly opened and—" She looked up and saw Corey. "Are you staying for lunch, Mr. Whitman? If so, you can help."

She said it while bustling around the kitchen.

Corey sat Annie down on the counter, draped his coat over her, and started rolling up his sleeves.

"Corey," he said.

Miss Smith turned back to him. "What?"

"Corey," he said again. "My name is Corey. But you knew that already, didn't you?"

She blushed again. The prepubescent girls around them laughed.

"You girls, hush!" she said.

"Do you prefer Miss Smith or...?" he asked, spreading peanut butter on the remaining slices of bread.

"You can call me Molly, if you wish."

And he did—from then on.

Later that night, Corey was still there. After treating the entire orphanage—all 28 kids—to pizza, he and Molly talked well into the evening.

"So it's just you and 28 orphans?" he asked.

She nodded.

"I can't believe the system would just abandon you like this."

Molly eyed him over her wine glass. "Well, you of all people know the world is coming to an end," she said in a mocking sort of way. "I mean, it's been widely known that this oncoming planet is supposed to wipe out mankind. Who cares about a bunch of orphans?"

Corey thought about that. "You'd think it would be the other way around."

"Oh, at first people and different organizations were happy to take the kids. The youngest ones went first, then..." She trailed off. "We used to have over 200 kids here. Now it's only 28 or so. They run off sometimes, never to be seen again."

He looked at her from across the small kitchen table. "What about you?" he asked.

She picked up the wine bottle and emptied it into their glasses. He liked the way the tip of her tongue poked out between her lips as she concentrated on pouring.

"What about Mr. Whitman?" she asked. "I mean, what's your story?"

She got up and took the empty bottle to the trash.

"I've been here at the orphanage since I was twelve years old. And it looks as if I'll be here until the end," she said, returning to the table. "I won't leave my kids."

Corey leaned back in his chair. "Why hasn't anyone adopted Annie? She's what—four? Five?"

Molly sighed heavily, settling back down.

"Annie is four years old. And they have. Duke always finds her and tries to stay with whatever family she's in. She cries a fit if he can't stay, so..."

"Is he her brother?" Corey asked.

"No. But he thinks he is."

"So what's Duke's story?"

Molly got a far-off look on her face.

"Duke was brought here when he was no older than Annie. As far as I know, he's never said a word. Sometimes he'll 'hoot' when he's really excited. Other than that? Annie says he talks to her all the time. Maybe he does. But to the rest of us..." She left it hanging.

"Several people have tried to adopt him, but he won't leave. He doesn't want to, I guess. And when Annie showed up, it was as if he adopted her. She was such a little thing."

Molly looked across the table at him.

"Why? Were you thinking of adopting them?" she smiled.

He was silent for a moment. "Maybe," he said, as if the thought had just occurred to him.

"Because you can't take one without the other," she told him.

They drank their wine in silence—Corey thinking, and Molly not wanting to ruin the chance to put two of her kids in a good home.

"So what would I have to do?" he asked.

"You mean to adopt?" she said.

He nodded.

"Prove to me you're a good, responsible person who can and will provide the kids with a good home," she said.

"That's it?" he asked.

"I told you, Mr. Whitman—we're on our own here."

Corey slept in the old administration office and was up early. He had doughnuts delivered.

Molly woke to the sound of cheering children. She quickly brushed her teeth and hair, threw on a housecoat over her nightgown, and went to see what the fuss was about.

She poked her head around the doorjamb and saw what looked like the entire orphanage sitting or standing around the administration desk. Corey, with Annie on his lap eating a doughnut, was surrounded by all the kids.

Jake was on the phone. "Yes, ma'am... Yes, ma'am. And Ernie can come too?" he asked, then did a silent fist pump in his buddy's direction. "Okay, and thank you," he said, handing the phone to Corey.

"We're going to Nebraska!" he shouted to Ernie. All of the kids cheered.

Jake saw Molly in the doorway and ran over.

"Miss Smith! Me and Ernie are going to Nebraska!" he said, throwing his arms around her in a big hug. Ernie ran over excitedly and high-fived him.

Corey had one hand covering his ear as the kids chattered loudly.

"Where's Nebraska?" Ernie asked.

"It's in California, ya idiot. Who cares—we're going!" Jake said.

Corey, still on the phone, said, "I will, Mrs. Oldham. And thank you." He hung up.

"Now listen, Jake," he said as the noise died down, "both of you—these people are older. They're more like a grandma and grandpa. But a better pair you couldn't ask for. You'll have to look out for them too, you understand?"

"Yes sir, Mr. Whitman. And they got horses?" Jake asked.

They both did a dance when Corey said they did.

"What is all this?" Molly asked.

The entire room erupted with twenty-some explanations at once—even Duke, who stood beside Corey and let out a couple of excited hoots, feeling the moment.

She held up a hand, and the room fell silent.

"Mr. Whitman?" she asked.

"Corey, please," he said. "I'm getting these kids happy homes."

Molly looked on, stunned. The room suddenly burst back into chatter.

"Me and Cyndi are being adopted, Miss Smith!" a girl told Molly.

"Yeah! And Mr. Whitman's cousin lives on the beach in Oregon and is—Miss Smith, I'm going to New York City!"

Corey smiled broadly as tears welled in Molly's eyes and spilled down her cheeks. He stood, confused, as the kids quieted once more while Molly left the doorway. Every eye turned to Corey.

He sat Annie in a chair just as his phone rang.

"Yes?" he answered. "Hi Jeff... yeah, that's right. Could you hold on for a moment? Here, talk to one of the kids—I have a situation."

He handed the phone to a twelve-year-old girl. "Talk to Jeff, Summer."

Then he made his way to the hallway where Molly had been. Duke followed. Reaching the corridor, Corey wasn't sure which way she had gone. Duke tugged his hand and led him to a closed door, then knocked. He looked up at Corey for a moment, and when Molly asked through sniffles, "Who is it?" Duke ran back the way they had come.

"Um, it's me," Corey said, watching the boy retreat down the hall.

The door stayed shut.

"What do you want, Mr. Whitman?" Molly asked, still sniffling.

Corey stood silently, looking down. He wasn't used to this feeling and didn't know what to say.

"Well, first of all, why can't you call me Corey?"

A cheer rose up in the distance as the kids celebrated another adoption. Footsteps echoed down the hallway.

Joey appeared, breathless. "Mr. Whitman that Indian guy said he'd take the rest of us!"

Corey placed his hands on the boy's shoulders to calm him. "All six of you?" he asked.

"Uh-huh! He said we'd be the Brady Bunch. Is it true he lives on a big ranch?"

"One of the biggest in Arizona," Corey said.

Just then, the door opened. Molly stood there, dressed, eyes puffy, trying to look pleased.

"Did you hear, Miss Smith? We're all adopted!" Joey said, barely able to contain his excitement.

"Yes, I heard, Joey. That's wonderful news," she replied, wiping her nose.

"Shouldn't you guys be packing?" she asked him gently.

Joey stopped, glanced at Corey, who nodded, and then bolted back down the hallway.

"It seems you've been busy," she said.

Summer walked toward them, still on the phone. "Yes, Mr. Foote, I will. He's right here." She smiled smugly as she handed the phone to Corey. "He wants the rest of us to come to Arizona and live there," she said.

"I heard." Corey smiled, taking the phone.

Summer stood beside Molly, who pulled the girl close.

"Jeff, what happened?" Corey asked into the phone, glancing at Summer.

"You don't say... and Kerry's okay with this? Uh-huh... I know..." He laughed.

"Yeah, they'll be coming back with me. Okay, I will. Tell your squaw congratulations for me, okay? Bye."

He closed the phone and looked at Summer.

"What did you tell him?"

She gave a smile befitting her name. "I didn't say anything. I just answered his questions."

"And he said he'd take six kids, knowing you're all girls?"

She kept smiling and shrugged.

"What sort of person is this, Mr.—I mean, Corey?" Molly asked.

"Well," Corey said, leaning against the doorframe, "Jeff and Kerry live on a large ranch outside Flagstaff, Arizona. They don't have kids of their own, but they raise just about every kind of animal you can think of. They're good people."

They spent the rest of the day making travel arrangements and helping the kids pack. Corey did everything he could to reassure Molly the children were in good hands. Many of them, having long given up hope of being adopted, were buzzing with excitement about their new families.

Corey fielded so many questions about his friends and what to expect that he hardly had time to think.

Three limos arrived to take twenty kids to the airport. Corey and Molly left Summer in charge while they saw the children off.

By six that evening, they were riding back to the orphanage in the back of a taxi. Molly sniffled, still emotional from the sendoff.

"You're sure they'll be alright?" she asked Corey for the hundredth time, wiping her nose.

Corey took her hand. "Well, I am kinda worried about the Pierce family—they took Tammy and Timmy and—"

She playfully hit him.

"I don't mean the adopters!" she said.

"They'll be fine, Molly," he said, still holding her hand. "You know Duke can be a handful sometimes, but as long as you have Annie, he'll stick around and... and..."

She started to break again.

"Hey, why don't you come too?" he asked.

Molly turned to look at him. "You're going to adopt me too, are you?" she asked, sarcasm laced in her voice.

"What else have you got planned?" he said, squeezing her hand.

"You're serious?" she whispered.

He nodded.

"I'm thirty-eight years old," she said.

"So am I," he replied with a shrug.

She playfully hit him again. "You're forty-eight!"

He released her hand and feigned insult, folding his arms across his chest.

"I knew you looked!" she said.

"Driver, pull over! I can't be seen with this nosy woman!" Corey exclaimed.

The taxi driver glanced back through the mirror.

"Oh, shut up," she said, laughing, and took his hand again.

He turned to face her.

"Why don't you adopt me, then?" he said, pulling her hand to his chest. "I've got a great big house with more room than we'll ever need, thirteen dead plants, and two brand new kids—well, one and a half really, but she's growing fast..."

Molly leaned in and kissed him. Then she pulled back, meeting his eyes.

"You know, your freckles stand out when you blush," she smiled, settling into his embrace.

The taxi driver watched them through the rearview mirror and sighed.

January 2039

The planet Phoenix and the second planet, Niburu, could now be seen in detail with just about any telescope. There was widespread panic in some areas—but not as much as you'd expect, and not from the places you'd expect it. All in all, the human race, for the most part, accepted its fate. The remaining people decided: if we're really going out, then we'd go out with dignity.

There were still many who believed it wasn't as serious as the experts said. It was one week before the final ship would launch, and the planets were expected in May. Corey and Molly were resolved to put Annie and Duke on the shuttle with Benny and his family. The two families had become close.

"So, Uncle Benny is gonna be my new daddy?" Annie asked Corey as they finished their evening story time. Duke watched from across the room. He still had not spoken except to hoot when excited. Molly claimed the boy talked in his sleep, and Annie said he talked to her all the time. But when questioned by Molly or Corey, he would simply stare back—unless he could show an answer by taking them to something.

Psychologists said he would grow out of it when he was ready.

"In a way, Annie," Corey said, pushing her hair back from her face. "But I'd like to think I was your only daddy."

"Just until you and Molly come to live on Mars, right? After your business is over, right?" she asked.

"Right," he said.

Duke stirred from where he was sitting. Corey met his eyes and felt as if the boy knew he was lying. Corey looked away.

"Okay, you two, time for bed," Molly said, coming into the study.

Duke, never taking his eyes off Corey, left the room. Annie gave Corey a big hug.

"Yer the best daddy, Daddy," she said.

Molly picked her up. "Daddy says Uncle Benny is gonna be my new daddy until you and him git to Mars next."

Corey sat back in his chair. Later, Molly came in with two mugs of tea. Sitting on the couch where Annie had been, she reached over and patted his knee.

"They'll be alright," she said as he smiled weakly. "If it's one thing I've learned about kids, it's that they're resilient."

She looked at him lovingly. He looked back, thinking how lucky he was to have found her—and how cruel life's tricks could be sometimes.

"What?" Molly asked, feeling self-conscious.

He moved over to where she was, facing her. "What?" she asked again.

"A finer thing I have never known—the family I've found with you," he said, brushing the hair back from her face.

Molly looked at this man she had grown to love. "You, Duke, and Annie," he said.

"Is that why you gave me this ring?" she asked playfully.

"Yeah, that—and I wanted to get in your pants."

She hit him. Hard. "You!" she said, and pulled him to her.

Duke quietly left the doorway where he'd been listening.

The following week was a whirlwind of events. Corey and Molly were married before friends and family: Kerry and Jeff with their six kids; Benny and Helen with their two; Gene Oldham and his wife; Jake and Ernie; and several others. The park was filled with people. It felt like old home week for the group of orphans. No one spoke about the last ship leaving the next day. This was a day of celebration.

The newlyweds said their vows but agreed to suspend their honeymoon until after the children had gone. Corey and Molly, like every other parent—sending off their kids or not—went to extreme lengths to spoil them.

Molly couldn't believe the changes in the young ones, especially Jake. He took to the Oldhams, and they to him, so much so that it was hard to believe they weren't his real grandparents. They celebrated more than a marriage—they celebrated life, with a vengeance.

That night, Corey went through the box his father had given him and added keepsakes of his own: the marriage license, official adoption papers changing Duke and Annie's last name to Whitman, pictures of the family. He taped the lid closed, wrote "Duke and Annie Whitman" on it, and sat back.

He removed his glasses and rubbed the bridge of his nose. He could hear Duke's running feet bounding down the hallway. Like most ten-year-old boys, Duke ran everywhere. Corey felt a twinge of panic as Duke ran into the study.

At first, Corey thought it was another earthquake. Duke had predicted two before—not big ones, but still. When asked how he knew, the boy had only stared back.

This felt different.

Duke ran into the study and grabbed Corey's arm, pulling him.

"What is it, son?" Corey asked.

Duke spotted Corey's glasses on the desk. He hooted once, snatched them up, and ran out. "Hey!" Corey called, getting up to follow.

He found Duke outside the upstairs bathroom. Duke knocked on the door.

Molly's voice came through. "Not now, I'm busy." It was obvious she was crying.

Duke held the glasses out for Corey.

Corey ruffled Duke's hair and said softly, "Thank you, Duke."

He checked the door. It was locked.

"Molly? Please open the door, honey."

"I'm alright. Don't worry," she answered, and movement could be heard inside. The door opened, and she leaned into his embrace.

She said nothing at first. He stood there, patiently holding her while she gathered herself. Pulling away, she smiled weakly and brushed past.

"Go get ready for bed, Duke. We've got a big day tomorrow."

Duke looked up at her.

"Go on now," she said with a smile.

Corey followed her, thinking she was just sad the kids were leaving on the last shuttle.

"Molly," he said as they entered their bedroom.

She didn't stop. He followed her to the vanity where she started brushing her hair.

"Molly, honey," he said, placing his hands on her shoulders.

She met his eyes in the mirror and started crying again.

"It's alright, baby," he soothed, kneeling down. "They'll be okay. And nothing guarantees that we won't be okay too."

She turned to look at him, momentarily composed. "I'm pregnant, Corey," she said.

He was speechless, sitting back on his heels.

"That's right. I was doing well with all this until..." she leaned forward, crying into her hands.

Corey wrapped his arms around her, soothing.

Suddenly, she shoved him away.

"It's not fair! Why do we have to get through this!?" she shouted.

He came forward again. 'It's just not fair!" she shouted once more, pounding on his chest.

He pulled her in. "I know, honey. I know, baby," he said softly as she cried in his arms.

Corey looked toward the bathroom doorway and saw both kids standing there. Annie's lower lip quivered.

"What's wrong with Mommy?" she asked.

"It's alright, Annie," Molly said, sniffling as she pulled away from Corey and held her arms out to the kids.

Annie came forward, and Duke started to follow.

Corey, with his arm still around his wife, held the other out to Duke. "Come here, lad," he said. They all stood there in a group hug. They spent their last night together in the living room. They fell asleep where they sat. They woke up with so much to do, they had no time to worry about anything else. Molly gave orders and couldn't stand being out of sight of her children.

Corey took Duke into the study and sat the boy down. He faced the ten-year-old. "You realize you have to watch out for Annie, don't you, Duke?" After saying this, he realized how futile that statement was. He smiled at his adopted son. "I'm preaching to the choir, huh?" he said. "My dad used to tell me things I'd already know. He would have loved you, Duke. You would have loved him also."

Corey grew serious. "Duke, you're such a special boy with such a strong character, I..." Corey stopped again and smiled at Duke, looking him in the eyes. "No father could be more proud or love you any more than I do. You remember for me that, like my name, yours will be Whitman too, okay?"

Duke looked at Corey's face, feeling how sad he was. "Spiders," Duke said. Corey looked at the boy, stunned into silence. "It's the spiders," Duke continued. "When the spiders and ants hide, I know an earthquake is coming."

Corey laughed, reaching forward and gripping the boy's upper arms. Duke smiled, and then both were laughing out loud. Corey pulled him into an embrace that Duke returned.

"What are you two doing? We have to leave or we'll be late." Molly came in carrying Annie. Corey, winking at Duke, stood and told her, "Guy stuff."

He picked up the cigar box off the desk and, giving it to Duke, said, "My dad gave me this the last time I saw him. Keep it with you, and when you get to Mars, put it somewhere safe."

"What is it?" Annie said.

"Family stuff, little squirrel," Corey said, taking her from Molly and herding them toward the door.

It was pandemonium around the launch facility. People were saying their goodbyes, trying to get a seat, protesting, and protecting those coming to leave. Corey and his family arrived by helicopter and went directly to the departure terminal where Benny and his family were. Goodbyes were quick; Corey and Molly were away before they broke down in front of the kids. They were directed to a viewing area where they watched as the colossal ship sat with last-minute boarding and loading. It was the last ship leaving Earth.

"Do you think they'll be alright?" Molly asked for the fifth time, and for the fifth time Corey assured her they would be.

Corey stood staring out the window as the ship slowly started to move. "I think they will be fine people," he said, and after a minute, "I think our boy will be a leader of men, while our girl will retain qualities that you yourself instilled in all of your kids. The qualities I've grown to love and even envy."

He pulled away and looked down at her. "Envy?" she asked. He nodded.

"Like what?" she asked, looking at him.

"How to be a parent, for one," he said.

She looked at him for a moment longer and thought about their unborn child.

"I know what you're thinking, Molly," he told her. Without speaking, she turned back to the window and watched as the ship moved away from the building.

"I had a dream last night," she said.

He waited with his arm around her. Before she could say any more, Corey felt someone grab his finger. He looked down, and Annie had raised her arms to be picked up. He gasped. Molly's reaction was similar. Duke stood two feet away holding the wooden cigar box. Corey quickly looked at the departing spaceship, knowing in an instant it was too late. He looked back at Duke, his heart hammering in his chest.

"Oh Annie," Molly finally said, picking up the girl.

"Duke!" Corey said, kneeling before the boy, taking his upper arms and shaking him. "Do you realize what you've done? You've killed your sister and you."

Duke stared at Corey, and as his eyes filled with tears, the cigar box dropped, spilling the contents on the floor. Duke yanked himself free and ran.

"Duke!" Corey yelled, reaching for the things and then forgetting them as he stood to see his son disappear in the crowd of people watching the ship depart.

"Quickly, go get him," Molly said, and Corey went. He shouldered bystanders out of the way, running as fast as he could. Catching glimpses when he could and asking when he lost sight. "Did you see a little boy run past?"

Somehow Corey saw Duke as he rounded a corner and raced to catch up. Rounding the corner, he saw it was a cul-de-sac where boxes of trash, mostly packing debris, were piled waiting for pickup. Duke was hiding there, and Corey knew he had to fix this.

"Regardless of the situation, what's done is done, Duke."

Corey called softly, "Please come out, lad, and talk to me." He moved forward a little. "Duke, you didn't know you had to go, but it's alright now."

There was some rustling, then Duke shot out of the mess of papers and tried to run past Corey. Corey barely got a hand on Duke before they landed in a heap. Duke fought to get free, but Corey held him securely in a tight embrace.

"Shhh, boy, it's okay now. Shhh…" Corey soothed.

Duke struggled with all his might and then started to cry.

"There now, it's okay, Duke," Corey said, smoothing the boy's hair back. For five minutes, Duke cried great, wracking sobs that went unchecked.

"Go on now, let it all out, Duke. I've got you," Corey said softly.

"I… I… my…" Duke tried to speak but cried again.

"It's okay, son. I'm not angry with you," Corey said, pulling back and looking down at the boy holding on to him. Corey smiled.

"Whatever happens, we'll be together, okay?"

"I didn't know, I didn't…" Duke hiccupped between words. "I didn't know she… she was gonna die."

He let loose another wail, burying his head into Corey's chest. Corey held him.

"Don't worry about it, Duke. It's going to be alright."

Duke pulled away and looked up at Corey.

"Are we still a fam… family?"

Corey smiled as he sat on the floor, still holding the boy.

"Of course we are. We always will be, no matter what."

"No matter what?" Duke asked, wiping the tears from his face and watching Corey's face.

"No matter what," Corey said.

"My name is Barry," he told Corey.

Corey held the boy out at arm's length.

"Barry… Barry?"

The boy nodded. Smiling, Corey stood up and held out his hand.

"Hi Barry, my name is Corey."

Barry looked at the offered hand, then up at Corey.

"I thought you were Dad," he said, dragging his wrist across his nose and wiping his eyes.

Corey bent down, scooping up his son.

"I am. I'll always be Dad to you."

"And Annie too?" Barry said.

"And Annie too," Corey said, smiling at his son.

"And Mom's baby inside her too?"

Corey looked at Barry.

"How the hell do you know these things?" he asked incredulously.

2040

They made a pact that the impending event would not keep them from living a happy life. They moved to Arizona to be near Jeff Foote and Kerry Reynolds. The kids were everywhere. Once Barry started talking, you couldn't shut him up. Summer and the other kids from the orphanage were unstoppable. They became one big, happy family living in the desert.

As Jeff put it, "There ain't nothin' to fall on ya when the ground shakes." Indian wisdom.

The volcano visible in the distance posed no threat — it was too far away. A guest house was built, and as March approached, the two families merged.

Elsewhere in the world, people fought. They pitched fits, protested, tried to convert to any religion or belief that promised divine intervention. Scientists claimed there was a chance Earth's magnetic field could repel the oncoming planets. While the event would still be catastrophic, it might not wipe out all life on the planet.

"What do you think of that theory?" Jeff asked Corey one evening while the two stood at a split-rail fence, gazing up at the stars. Cattle could be heard just beyond the fence. Barry was sitting on top of it, just one of the guys.

"It's an interesting theory," Corey replied. "But if that's true, then the mass of two planets — each roughly the size of Earth — could repel us out into space and destroy our atmosphere."

Jeff thought about that. "So…"

"So, the end result would still be the same," Corey finished.

"Ear candy for the masses," Jeff mused.

"Can I ride that cow tomorrow, Uncle Jeff?" Barry asked, pointing to a massive Brahma bull standing just beyond the corral. The moon was bright, and while the landscape was washed of color, it was still easy to see beyond the fence.

Both men looked at the boy.

"I can ride him if I can get on him," Barry said confidently. He had taken to ranch life like a natural cowboy — he could and did ride anything.

"First of all, that ain't no cow, kid. That's a twenty-five-hundred-pound monster from Hell who don't like nobody even lookin' at him, let alone tryin' to ride him. What makes you think a little fella like you can ride him — and why would you want to?" Jeff asked.

"I seen 'em ridin' 'em on TV," Barry answered.

Corey laughed. Jeff spat through the fence.

"You ain't even got no hat, boy. What'd you do with that cowboy hat I gave ya?" Jeff had given everyone a hat when they moved to the ranch.

"It got poop on it when I was ridin' that pig the other day," Barry said, pointing to the pigpen.

Both men burst out laughing, and Barry laughed too.

"Son, there's poop all over the place out here. What do you do when you get poop on your shoes?"

"Wipe it off," Barry said matter-of-factly.

"Well, that hat was especially for you. I done an Indian hat dance over that hat, and you can't ride no bull without the luck in that hat. Where is it?"

Barry sat up, thinking. Then he launched himself off the fence, running toward the hog pen.

"Wait!" both men shouted.

"Wait until morning, son!" Corey called after him.

Just then, Lizzie — one of Jeff's adopted daughters — came running out of the house.

"Mama wants you now, Uncle Corey," she said, out of breath.

Corey, immediately worried about the baby, took off like a shot.

"What is it?" Jeff asked Lizzie.

She paused, catching her breath. "There's someone on the phone for him. They said it's an emergency."

Cell phones didn't get good reception in the desert. Most landlines were automated now. Few services that required people to run them were still operational. Most folks just wanted to spend their remaining time with loved ones — not at work.

Corey rushed into the house. Seeing Molly calmly on the phone, he relaxed. She smiled reassuringly when she saw his worried face, her hand resting on her growing belly.

"He's right here," she said, handing Corey the phone. "It's the observatory. Kerry's on the other line."

Still breathing hard, Corey answered. "Corey here."

"Corey, this is Ted Nash from the Arizona Observatory," Kerry said. "He says Mars has moved."

"What?" Corey asked, trying to process the impossible.

"It's true, Mr. Whitman," Nash added. "Mars appears to be moving toward the Phoenix Group."

The two planets converging on Earth had been dubbed the *Phoenix Group*. They were now so close together they could no longer be viewed as separate bodies.

"I don't understand," Corey said.

"Well, Mr. Whitman," Nash continued, "when I first looked yesterday evening, Mars was two degrees off its normal orbit. Our telescope software tracks planetary positioning in real time — and tonight, Mars is sixteen degrees off. To the south."

Corey was silent.

"Do you understand what that means, Mr. Whitman?"

"Yes," Corey said quietly. "Yes... I think I do. But that's incredible." Mars normally orbited in the opposite direction around the sun.

"Kerry, do we have the T-138 here at the—?"

"It's already being set up," Kerry interrupted.

"Thank you, Mr. Nash," Corey said, and hung up. His mind raced.

He took two steps toward the stairs, then stopped, turned, and rushed back to hug and kiss Molly.

"What?" she asked, surprised by the sudden affection.

"Mars is on the move!" he shouted, bolting up the stairs.

Molly, seeing his excitement, decided to follow.

When Corey reached the rooftop platform — set up just for stargazing — he had to wait his turn at the telescope. Two telescopes were mounted up there, one larger than the other. Either could display Mars and the Phoenix Group, but the T-138 was the better of the two.

Corey, surrounded by girls ranging in age from eight to thirteen, finally got behind the eyepiece — just in time to see Mars move into the same frame as the approaching planets.

"Incredible. Simply incredible," he said aloud.

"What, Uncle Corey?" they all asked in unison.

Kerry had come out and claimed the other telescope.

"Oh my God, Mars is moving *backward*," she said, her voice full of awe. As they watched, it did indeed appear that Mars had picked up speed — and was now heading straight for the Phoenix Group.

"How can this be?" she asked, still glued to the telescope.

"I wanna see! I wanna see!" cried several of the girls.

Corey stepped aside and let a smaller girl take his place.

"As you know, Mars has a diameter of 4,220 miles," he explained. "The Phoenix Planet appears to be about the same size as Earth."

He looked around at the eager, wide-eyed faces. Jeff and Barry had come up to see what the excitement was about.

"Earth has a diameter of 7,926 miles," Corey added.

No one responded. A few of the girls looked confused.

Jeff stepped in. "If the Earth were a plum, Mars would be a grape."

"Oooh," the kids chorused, finally grasping the scale.

Corey smiled gratefully at his friend. "Now, there's another planet following Phoenix — the second one. Together, they've created a gravitational pull that appears to be dragging Mars off its normal trajectory."

He paused, gauging the younger kids' expressions.

Jeff translated again. "If the two bigger planets were the *Enterprise*, they'd have a tractor beam pulling Mars toward them."

"*Oooh!*" they repeated, grinning.

Corey chuckled. "It's an unforeseen variable in the equations we've been working with — one we didn't calculate."

All eyes returned to Jeff.

"No one saw it coming," he said.

Again, they turned to Corey, who had returned to the eyepiece.

"Oh my God!" Kerry gasped.

Corey said nothing as he watched Mars move steadily toward the Phoenix Group.

"They're going to collide," she whispered.

Sure enough, as Corey looked on, Mars appeared to blend into the Phoenix Planet — merging visibly through the telescope. He pulled away from the eyepiece, stunned.

"I wanna see!" Annie said, tugging at his side.

Everyone was up on the roof now. Kerry backed away from her telescope too, her face pale.

"Look up there, honey," Corey said, pointing to the eastern sky.

As their heads turned, the sky lit up — a blazing flash marking the impact of the planets 49 million miles away.

The force of the collision altered the Phoenix Group's course just enough to spare Earth. The largest piece, hurtling through space, missed the planet entirely. The second-largest — slowed by the impact with Mars — was caught in Earth's gravitational pull and began to orbit the planet.

It became Earth's second moon.

It was named *Enterprise*, in memory of the Mars colonies lost during the chaos.

The aftermath was devastating. Debris from the collision darkened the sun for three weeks. Meteors rained down during that time, pummeling the Earth. The worst damage struck the Asian continent, where tsunamis devastated coastal regions.

Religious organizations called it the *Hand of God*.

And who's to say it wasn't? After all, wasn't it the Creator who had placed the Red Planet where it was in the first place?

In a news conference after the event, Jeff Foote was quoted as saying:

"What the hell — maybe the Creator just wanted a way to thin out the man population."

Maybe so.

The End

CAT DANCER

In the White Kingdom, on a winter's night in the keep of a Duke, a woman struggled to give birth. Her screams of pain echoed throughout the west wing of the keep.

There was always a price to be paid for motherhood, and tonight, the cost was high.

The Duke was said to be a cruel man, one who did not tolerate failure. He had been granted a favor from the King of the White Throne and took a White Priestess as his bride. What he did not know was that in doing so, he would never sire a son. A boy had never been born to a White Priestess of the Golden Light. Ever.

The monastery was a matriarchy, and the daughters of this line were destined to serve the White Kingdom in whatever capacity they were needed. The White King's own bloodline came from this monastery and would again, should the need arise. After all, one might question who a child's father was — but a mother could never be in doubt.

On this night, the Duke awaited the birth of his son. It *would* be a son — because the Duke had declared it so. The last time he had found himself in this position, the child had been a girl. Neither the mother nor daughter survived childbirth. Or so it was rumored — evidence of the Duke's wrath.

Measures had been taken to ensure this birth did not end the same way. After all, the woman in labor was no ordinary bride. She was a High Priestess of the White Order.

Another contraction surged through her.

"Bear down with it, luv! That's it — now push!" said the midwife.

The woman half-sat up and strained, drenched in sweat, her voice rising into a scream that seemed to scrape the soul.

"She's bleeding too much," the midwife said.

The physician moved to her side and examined the flow of blood. "She is," he confirmed, turning to the woman in the bed. "You must relax the birthing canal."

The woman's eyes went wide with fury. She grabbed the physician by the front of his robe and yanked him toward her.

"Relax? You vile man! May you rot in hell! I *am* doing everything I can! I don't see you doing anything!"

She bared down again, gritting her teeth, holding on to him like an anchor.

"That's it, luv. I can see her head," the midwife said from between the woman's legs.

"*His* head," hissed the physician, straining against the woman's grip.

"Push, my lady, give it one good—there you go." The midwife stepped back, cradling an infant. The grip on the physician's shirt loosened, and he moved toward the midwife and her charge. First, he checked to confirm the babe was truly a girl, then tied and cut the umbilical cord.

"Quick now," he said, moving to a tapestry on the wall. Behind it was a hidden panel leading to a secret passageway. In the dim corridor stood two wet nurses, each holding an infant born within the hour. He quickly checked the first baby, then glanced at the second. Unwrapping the first bundle, he revealed a squirming baby boy latched onto the wet nurse's nipple. Lifting the infant from her arms, he turned to the midwife to exchange the babies. The moment the boy's mouth left the nipple, he began to wail.

"Hurry now," the physician urged the midwife, whose part had been rehearsed many times. She took the boy to the woman's waiting legs while the man closed the hidden panel. The midwife smeared the crying infant with the blood and fluids from the birth.

The door opened. The Duke entered.

The physician hovered over the woman, who appeared to be asleep. The midwife pretended to tie the cord, then turned, holding the wailing, squirming, bloody bundle up for the Duke to see. He looked between the infant's legs, straightened, and glanced at the unconscious woman. Then he surveyed the room, nodding first to the physician, then to the midwife.

"Well done," he said.

"Excuse me, my Lord," the physician said, placing fingers on the woman's neck. The Duke, still fascinated by the bundle sucking greedily on the midwife's finger, looked at the physician.

"I think your wife has expired," he said, straightening the woman's limbs. The Duke glanced down at her prone form, then back at the babe.

"You're sure?" he asked.

The physician nodded.

"But my son is healthy?" the Duke pressed.

The physician took the baby and examined him.

"He appears to be in excellent health, my Lord."

"Well then, I should say the trade was a good one."

The future Duke, tiring of the fluid-less finger, began to cry again.

The realm is divided into nine Kingdoms, with the central Kingdom, the hub, being the White Kingdom. The easiest way to describe the continent and its Kingdoms is to compare it to a wagon wheel with eight sections, the central hub being the ninth and governing Kingdom. The Northern Kingdom is the Blue Kingdom, and its contribution to the nine Kingdoms is no less important than that of the Southern Kingdom, or the Red Kingdom. In the west are the Brown Kingdom and in the east the Black, while northwest are the Orange Cloaks. Northeast is Grey, southeast is Yellow, and the Druids and Rangers are, of course, Green. Each is important and holds its own station in the Nine Kingdoms.

Peace was not always something that could be achieved through diplomacy. At times, war was the only path to peace. It was not always a harmonious relationship between the nine Kingdoms. This is where our story truly begins.

A battle had taken place, for whatever reason, between the Black Kingdom and the Red. It appeared from the battlefield that there were no winners. There were survivors, but not many. For a solid square mile, the battlefield revealed what was obviously a fight fueled by hate. Nobles lay bleeding or dying beside peasants and simple soldiers. Horses either lay dead on the field of battle or wandered aimlessly on the fringes.

As with war and battles, there were scavengers and mourning widows of the men who fought. Throughout the battlefield, women in dresses whose hems dripped with the blood of the war's casualties walked among the dead and dying. Moaning and sometimes wailing could be heard from the women who had found the remains of their mates. Children were few, but they were there, holding the skirts of their mothers, though they could not understand the horror that life sometimes holds.

A man in expensive armor and decent clothes was on his hands and knees, vomiting into the bloody grass, bleeding from several cuts, none worse than the one on his upper left arm. One could see the beat of his heart by the waves of blood that pulsed from this wound. He was without his sword—it had been forgotten, and he had no need of it anymore. He looked up and saw acres of the dead and dying. His eyes started to lose focus, and he fell face-first into his own filth.

"Look, here's a good one," a man in mismatched clothes said as he approached the fallen warrior. He wore a fine, though bloody, cloak over a rotten and stained shirt. Pants of rotted leather, also bloody from a day's scavenging.

"I think he still breathes," said his partner, carrying an armload of scavenged goods.

"Not for long," said the first man as he raised his cudgel, bringing it down on their newest victim's head. The two stripped the fallen warrior of everything but his small clothes, then moved on.

Later, as the sun set, another person passed the fallen warrior. She was a stout woman with a small child—a Red Priestess looking to absolve any living soldiers of the Red and soothe their dying with reassurance that they would go to a better place. Some she could save; she made an effort to do so.

The child at her side stared on in wonder, never leaving her side except once. While the Red Priestess was consoling a dying man, the child walked over to the man with the cut on his arm. She looked at his face with great interest; she could be no more than seven years old. She had blonde curly hair and striking blue eyes. The man's eyes opened halfway and tried to see the child before him. She wiped the blood from his brow.

"Myrial, come away from there!" the Red Priestess said from across a portion of the battlefield. The child seemed not to hear. She looked at the man's upper arm, still oozing blood. The woman called to the child again as she held the hand of a shivering soldier but could do no more than watch as the child laid her little hand over the man's upper arm, covering the wound. Light seemed to emanate from under her hand. The man gasped and convulsed once before sinking into a deep sleep. When Myrial removed her hand, the wound had closed; her handprint remained.

Since the Red army and the Black army had met in the Yellow Kingdom, it was the Yellow monks who played a neutral role in dispatching the survivors. The man they found alive but unconscious seemed not seriously injured. There was a knot on his head, several cuts and bruises, but nothing too serious. They put him in a wagon with the other survivors who were too injured to care for themselves.

When he woke, he didn't know where he was or how he came to be there. His first contact with a monk was when he was on his hands and knees in his small room, trying to find his way to the privy.

"Here now, my son, let me help you," a voice said as a pair of sandaled feet came into his view on the floor. Two strong arms lifted him to a standing position. He held onto the man in the yellow robe as the room continued to tip and tilt.

"Are we at sea?" the man's voice was rough and raspy from disuse. The monk laughed. "No, my son, you have been in that bed for one full turn of the moon," said the monk.

They made their way out of the room to the privy, where the monk left the man to do his business.

"Where am I, and how did I get to this place?" asked the man as he rejoined the monk.

The monk let the man lean against him as they started back to the room.

"You were part of a battle, do you not remember?" asked the monk.

"No, I remember nothing," the man answered.

"Do you not even remember your own name?" asked the monk as he helped the man back into bed.

The man thought about it as he lay back, looking at the ceiling.

"Ross, I think," he said. "My name is Ross."

"Pleased to meet you, Ross. I am Brother Peel," said the monk.

The monastery was maintained by monks of the Yellow Kingdom, supported by the surrounding nobles as a place for their young to practice hand-to-hand combat techniques taught by veterans. The monks kept a garden and provided shelter for fallen soldiers until they healed and moved on or stayed, providing whatever skill they had to better the monastery.

Some veterans had lost a limb in past battles and were unable to get past it. Some had nowhere to go or had lost their sight and could not make an honest living. Some were just lost in their own hell and could not be reached. These men had a place here and either taught or worked if they could; none were ever pressured to leave.

For these reasons, the nobles supported the monastery—that, and the training of their young.

Ross slowly gained his strength and became a caretaker of a part of the monastery. He swept the flagstones in the courtyard, as well as the practice hall when not in use. He carried buckets of water from the well and hauled in vegetables from the garden. Anything the monks asked of him, he did without complaint.

Ross rarely spoke. It seemed he could not remember where he came from or how he came to be in a battle. Here's your passage cleaned up for grammar, punctuation, clarity, and flow, while keeping your voice intact:

"Perhaps you are a noble from one side or the other, and people are looking for you?" Brother Peel said one day, trying to help Ross remember. "Maybe you have a family."

Ross thought about that very thing when he allowed himself to dwell on it. "I think not. I have no woman's face haunting me at night, but..." He stopped, lost in thought.

"What?" asked Brother Peel.

"There is a girl with blonde curly hair..." He let that trail off, adding, "I do get the feeling that I have been in other battles, though."

"Could this child be your daughter, do you think?" asked the monk.

"I know not. I just know she comes to me in my sleep sometimes," he said.

Brother Peel asked Ross, "You cannot rush things like that, my son. Would you care to teach the lads? I know you have skills in that area—I have seen you exercise, and you move like no man I have ever seen."

Ross looked at the monk. Brother Peel turned red and looked at the floor. "I too used to be a soldier, and have trained." He looked up at Ross. "But I have never seen anyone train like you," he said.

"It didn't seem to help me in the last battle. I may not be a good soldier," Ross said.

Brother Peel gave a heavy sigh and got up from where he was sitting. "You are welcome here regardless," he said, and left Ross.

—m—

Days turned into weeks, and weeks turned into months—until two years had passed. The one thing that perplexed Ross the most was the small white handprint on his upper left arm. Sometimes at night, in a dream, he would wake and remember a curly-headed child looking into his very soul, and the mark on his arm would tingle. He would sit there in the night, absentmindedly rubbing the spot on his arm, trying to make sense of the dream.

After two and a half years, Ross's memory had not improved. He had his health and had become a regular fixture around the monastery. He minded his chores in the morning and did exercises to strengthen his body and open his mind. He found that a good two hours of calisthenics daily improved his state of mind as well as his body. Ross had gotten hold of a quarterstaff that had seen better days and used it to aid him in his workout.

He always worked out at the end of the day and always alone. Sometimes he would get the feeling that someone was watching him, but he did not feel threatened by it—so he put it out of his mind and never mentioned it to anyone.

Rarely did Ross have any contact with the students and did not go out of his way to make friends or carry on long conversations with the older veterans who lived in the monastery with him. He was never rude and was always helpful when needed, but he would always end a conversation before it got too personal. Ross was a loner, and it was understood.

One day, while carrying two buckets of water for the kitchen, Ross had to walk through the courtyard while training sessions were taking place. There were perhaps twenty of the more advanced students with practice swords sparring with each other. A one-armed veteran named Cal was drilling the finer points of swordplay into them. Their ages ranged from sixteen to twenty—all sons of nobles. Ross had on a brown robe tied at the waist and carried two buckets full to the brim with water.

"Hey, Cal," one of the older students called out to the one-armed instructor, "how come that brother is always wearing brown? Isn't he good enough to wear the Yellow?" This particular student was the Earl's son and was feeling like showing off.

The one-armed instructor told him, "That's enough, Warren, back to your sparring."

Ross ignored this exchange and passed out of earshot for the rest of what was said. The chore generally took three trips, and Ross was normally seen as no more than background—so it never occurred to him to take a different route to deliver the water.

"Hey, brown monk!" the student said, moving in to intercept Ross. "Do you not know when your betters are speaking to you?"

Ross stopped and set the buckets down. "What is it you require of me, my lord?" Ross asked. He was aware of two things: first, Warren was just showing off for the other boys who had gathered around. The second was that he himself was a guest here and did not want to jeopardize his position.

"They say you're pretty handy with a slop bucket," said the Earl's son. He looked around at his friends as they chuckled at his jest. Ross did not respond but stood there looking at this youth, waiting for him to finish.

Warren unsheathed his practice sword, which was dulled and little more than a metal stick.

Absolutely, Bea! Here's your cleaned-up passage with polished formatting for easier reading—paragraph breaks placed where natural pauses and scene shifts occur, and consistent indentations for dialogue:

"Warren, you are not here to harass the monks. Get back to your sparring, or your father will hear about this!" Cal said, shouldering his way through the boys standing around.

Warren turned to Cal. "My father pays for you to live here, old man. Your place is not to order me around but to teach. I will do as I please," said the pompous youth, turning back to Ross and sizing him up and down.

Ross was of average height, mid-thirties, with a scraggly beard and sandaled feet—nothing special. Nothing to concern the Earl's son. Warren was taller, younger, cocky, pampered, and too sure of his position as the ranking noble's son.

"Give me your practice sword, Jem," Warren said, reaching behind him without taking his eyes off Ross. The boy handed the dulled sword to Warren, and the others knowingly spread out to give them room.

"This is the last time I—" Cal started to say.

"Silence!" said the Earl's son. A couple of Warren's friends pulled Cal back.

Warren placed the practice sword's hilt in Ross' left hand.

"Let's see how well you handle a sword," Warren said, stepping back and taking a defensive stance.

Ross looked down at the sword in his hand, turning it and feeling the old familiar weight. It felt good.

"Defend yourself!" Warren said, swinging his sword.

The blow struck Ross in the upper part of his left arm, sending a shock down his arm and loosening his grip on the practice sword. The sword dropped to the ground, and as the clang died away, nervous laughter could be heard from the other boys. Cal shook his head in shame for the boy.

"I knew you were a phony," said Warren in disgust. "You have the rest of these country folk fooled, but I can spot a fraud when I see one."

Ross looked up. "Will there be anything else, my lord?" he said to the youth.

"Yeah, there will be. Pick up that sword," Warren said, waving his sword around. He moved as if to strike Ross again. One second Warren was standing there; the next he was airborne, flying backward, and Ross was leaned all the way over with one foot lifted chest high, rock steady.

Warren landed with a thud and a grunt as his sword and his butt clattered across the floor. Warren rolled over, trying to catch his breath. Several boys ran to help, but Warren angrily pushed them away.

"Get away from me!" he rasped.

Ross lowered his foot, looked around, nodded to Cal, picked up his buckets, and continued on to the well.

Ross pumped water for the buckets, and Brother Peel caught up to him at the well.

"There you are," the monk said, approaching Ross. "I'm afraid young Warren has gone off to tell his father about today's events."

Ross stopped what he was doing and looked at his friend. "The Abbot has been informed and is concerned that this may become a reason for the Earl to pay us a visit."

"I have had no dealings with the Earl and am unaware of the implications," Ross said.

Brother Peel stood wringing his hands nervously. Ross noticed this and gave a heavy sigh.

"While the Earl is our main benefactor, he is also known to be... unreasonable at times," said the monk.

Ross looked at the monastery and thought about the time he had spent there. He looked back to Brother Peel and smiled a knowing smile. "I understand," he said.

He saw the Abbot as he came out of the main building.

The Abbot of the Yellow Monastery was a well-loved and well-respected man. He was known to be a fair man. Abbot Gaston was also a practical man. He walked up and laid a hand on Brother Peel's shoulder, calming him. Ross liked the Abbot.

"I have spoken to Cal and know what happened. I am sure young Warren will tell a different version to his father, though," said the Abbot.

Abbot from having to say the words.

The Abbot smiled gratefully.

"There are other elements to think about, my son," said Abbot Gaston.

"I understand completely," Ross said.

"I appreciate all that you and this monastery have done for me while I have been here," he said sincerely.

The Abbot reached for Ross' hand and, gripping it, passed a small leather pouch. "There is strength in you; what's more, there is honor. Know, too, that we were blessed by your being here."

The Abbot released Ross's hand and, turning to Brother Peel, said, "Take him to the closet before he leaves," then left them.

Ross looked down at the leather pouch. He could feel the coins inside.

"I cannot take this," he said, offering the pouch to Brother Peel.

"It would shame him for you to return it," the monk said, pushing the offered pouch back to Ross.

"Come, we have much to do," he said, leading Ross back to the buildings.

Ross didn't have much in the way of personal belongings: a cloak, a pair of boots, a change of clothes, his robe, and the staff—all donated but in good repair. A sack of food was brought, and in moments Ross was ready to leave.

He looked around his room, where he had lived for the better part of three years, and sighed.

Brother Peel put a hand on Ross' shoulder, trying to comfort his friend. Ross shouldered his pack, and the monk led him down a hallway.

"I have something to show you," Brother Peel said as they walked. "These things were either donated or picked up from spent battlefields." He came to a door Ross had never entered before. Brother Peel pulled out a key on a string and unlocked the door.

"Some of the instructors gave up more than limbs when entering the monastery." As he swung the door open, he stepped to one side.

On one side of the small room was a cable with daggers, knives, and various small weaponry. Above that, hanging on the wall, was armor and helms, some ornamental and very expensive, some plain but serviceable. Some metal, some leather or wood. On the whole, it was a small armory of the first order.

The other side of the room had another table with bucklers, greaves, and maces. Above this table, hanging on the wall, were swords of various makes: big two-handed broadswords, bastard swords, longswords, and shortswords. Shields and staffs were also there. Everything in this room looked well attended.

Ross stepped forward and looked without touching until his eyes fell on a particular sword. This sword was in a plain leather scabbard, but one could tell this sword was anything but plain. He set his pack down and leaned his staff against the table. With reverence, he lifted this sword from the wall. Its hilt had room for two hands; the guard had an image of a cat engraved into it. There was a crosspiece at the end of the sword that had an orb which resembled a cat's eye. He half exposed the blade, revealing a double edge and mirror-like finish. He slid the blade back home and handed the sword to Brother Peel.

"Do you recognize this blade?" asked the monk holding the sword.

"It was another life," Ross said, picking up the staff and shouldering the pack. As Brother Peel replaced the sword, Ross picked up a simple dagger from the table and looked at the monk questioningly.

"Of course, anything you need," Brother Peel said.

"And this staff," he said. The monk nodded and they left the room, locking the door as they left.

Several brothers and some of the old veterans came out and offered their hands in farewell before they came out the front of the monastery. Nearly the entire staff and most of the monks gathered to watch him go. He had barely got to the end of the property when five horses came galloping up and stopped before him. Several brothers and the Abbot started walking out to Ross as the dust settled at the end of the walk.

Of the five horses, four had riders: The Earl, Warren, and two men who looked to be about the Earl's business, whatever that business could be. This time it looked to be business of the rough kind.

"There he is, Father!" Warren said to the imposing figure beside him. The Earl nodded to the two burly men-at-arms who promptly dismounted and approached Ross, intent on subduing him. One had a length of rope; the other looked as if he was accustomed to bending other men's wills his way, forcefully if need be. Both were armed.

Ross lowered his pack to the ground, holding his staff loosely. He stood waiting. The two men came in as if any opposition was out of the question. They were not used to opposition.

As soon as the two came in range of the staff, it seemed such a simple thing for Ross to sweep their feet from under them and set them on the ground. Ross picked up his pack and moved it out of the way. Seemingly unconcerned, he took off his cloak and covered his pack; his back was to the two men seated in the road. Ross turned casually, twirling the staff as he watched the two men-at-arms gain their feet.

Both looked fit to be tied at being bested in front of the Earl by a simple monk. They unsheathed their swords.

"Here now, I forbid this...!" the Abbot started to say as the Earl raised his hand for silence. The two men-at-arms looked back to the Earl questioningly.

"By whatever means necessary," he said to the two swordsmen.

They turned back to Ross and moved in, one from the left, the other from the right. You could hear the whirl of the staff and the 'thwack' of contact on the fingers of the hands holding the swords. Ross seemed to dance around these men effortlessly and when he came to stand still, both men were again sitting in the dirt, gripping their throbbing fingers, their swords lying in the dirt, forgotten.

The crowd responded with a collective gasp.

"See, Father, I told you..." Warren started to say, but the Earl, eyes never leaving Ross, again lifted his hand to silence his son. His two men rolled out of range of the staff, dragging their swords with them, their eyes also never leaving Ross.

"My son tells me you struck him," the Earl said to Ross from his horse.

"Your son, thinking I was weak, struck me first and after I did nothing he moved to do so again," Ross told him.

"He was mad because I was besting him with the practice sword, Father; he kicked me when I wasn't looking," Warren said.

Slowly the Earl turned and looked at his son. For a full minute the Earl did not speak. When he did, he said, "Warren, go back to the keep."

Warren, frustrated, said, "But Father, I—"

"Mind me, boy, or you'll feel the back of my hand!" the Earl said, glaring at the boy.

Warren yanked the reins of the horse cruelly, turning the horse while kicking it into a gallop back the way they had come. The Earl dismounted.

"The boy lies, sir," said the Abbot. "He provoked this man, who was only—"

"Thank you, Abbot. But when I need you to help with matters, I'll ask you." The Earl turned to Ross studying him as he removed his gloves. "Striking the son of the Earl is a treasonous offense," he said to Ross. "Resisting the Earl's offer to accompany him is almost as bad." He said, eyeing Ross.

The Earl turned and looked at his men. He sucked his teeth noisily as he thought. "You just bested two of my best men with a..." he indicated the staff, "stick, you don't appear to even be breathing hard. It is obvious the boy is not telling the truth of the matter."

The Earl looked at the Abbot when saying this. "However, you did in fact strike the son of an Earl, is this not true?" he asked, looking at Ross.

"It is," Ross answered.

"I see," said the Earl, stroking his chin as he studied Ross. "What would you say if I offered you a position teaching my son what you know of fighting?" he asked Ross.

"With all due respect, my lord, I would decline," Ross said. "Your son would use this skill to torment people of lesser standing, and I could not be a part of that."

The Earl looked at Ross for a moment, thinking. "Pity," he said and turned back to his horse. Putting his foot in the stirrup, he paused, looking at his men, who at this point stood holding their swords. "Kill him," he said and mounted his horse.

The two men-at-arms gripped their swords and again closed in from two different angles, though more wearily. The Abbot gasped and ran forward, stepping between Ross and the two men.

"My Lord, you can't be serious!" he said.

The man nearest the Abbot ran his sword to the hilt into the Abbot, lifting his boot to kick the man free of his sword. The Abbot fell, clutching his wound.

"No!" came the cry from Brother Peel as he came forward.

Ross came at the man with the moves of a well-choreographed dance, ducking a swing from the outside swordsman and smashing the end of the staff into the teeth of the man who had just stabbed the Abbot. Ross's momentum carried him by this man, and his next blow swooshed back and crushed the fingers holding the bloody sword. This time the blade did not complete the trip to the ground.

Avoiding another swing by the other sword, Ross jammed his staff into the crotch of the man clutching his hand, causing him to bend at the waist. Ross, having caught the man's sword before it hit the ground, shoved the sword between his neck and collarbone until the hilt rested against his face. This man died before the Abbot.

Ross turned to face the remaining man, using his foot to flick the fallen staff up, catching it deftly. The entire thing was finished in the span of five breaths. The other swordsman swallowed and started to advance.

"Enough!" said the Earl.

The remaining man-at-arms took a few backward steps, not taking his eyes off Ross.

"You have until sunset to be out of the Yellow Kingdom. Make no mistake," said the Earl. "The next time you will die."

The Earl nodded in the direction of the fallen man, and the man-at-arms, seeing that Ross wasn't advancing, sheathed his sword and collected his dead partner, carrying him to his horse and tying him to the saddle, face down. Taking the reins, he mounted his own horse, and they rode away.

Brother Peel was cradling the Abbot's head as Ross came over. The Abbot would not last long.

"I am so sorry to have brought this upon you, Father," Ross said, squatting down. "It was... not... your fault... my son."

The Abbot struggled to say through the pain and the blood in his mouth.

"Shhh, don't try to speak," Brother Peel said, holding the Abbot's head in his lap.

The Abbot gripped Ross's collar and pulled him close.

"It matters… to do what is right… regardless… of…" he paused to breathe, "consequences." He released Ross's shirt, leaving a bloody mark as he breathed his last.

No one spoke for a few moments. Ross looked at Brother Peel.

"I have brought this upon you and I am sorry," he said with genuine sadness.

Brother Peel looked down at his Abbot. "He did not blame you, and neither do I."

"My spots seem a mystery to me," Ross said almost to himself.

"I was not speaking of your spots, my friend. Sometimes things happen according to the maker's will," Brother Peel said to Ross. "We are merely instruments of that will."

With a heavy sigh, Brother Peel looked around at the people standing there. "Let us honor him," he said, gaining his feet.

Several people stepped forward to bear the Abbot back to the main building of the monastery. Ross gently put his hand on Brother Peel's arm to get his attention.

"Do you remember the sword I held in the armory?"

"I do," said the monk, studying Ross's face.

"It seems I may have need of it after all," Ross said.

"Perhaps you will indeed," the monk said. "I'll get it for you."

Ross gathered his things and waited by the road for Brother Peel. Cal came to keep him company.

"That arrogant pup will get a lot of good men killed in battle if he is allowed to lead," Cal said as they stood there.

Ross agreed. "Where will you go?" he asked as they watched Brother Peel emerge from the building carrying the sword.

"I'm not sure," Ross said, watching the monk.

"I hear the White Witches are able to tell a man's past," he told Ross as the monk arrived, placing the sword in Ross's hands.

Cal's hand snaked out and gripped Ross's wrist. "Do you know this blade?" he asked in a serious manner.

"It seems familiar to me."

Cal turned the sword in Ross's hand, revealing the cat engraved on the crosspiece.

"This is a Cat Dancer's blade," Cal said, releasing his hold on the sword.

Ross appeared to be concentrating on a fleeting thought that would not come.

"You must not delay, my friend, the Earl meant what he said," Brother Peel said, concerned for Ross.

"Of course," Ross said, snapping out of his reverie. He unwound the straps on the scabbard and deftly hung the sword across his back with the hilt rising above his left shoulder, tying the leather straps across his chest. It felt right. He picked up his pack, made his goodbyes, and, using the staff as a walking stick, walked away. His friends watched him go.

"What is a Cat Dancer?" Brother Peel asked Cal.

Without taking his eyes off the departing Ross, Cal said, "Legend, mostly." He turned to face the monk. "In the Eastern Continent of Ore, there is a guild that trains orphaned boys that nobody else will have." He looked back down the road. "They train these boys to fight and turn them into men of honor." Brother Peel followed Cal's look down the road, waiting on the old warrior.

"Their training begins as early as possible and some never leave this place. Some are assigned to Lords as personal bodyguards; some are called by a different order, who knows? But as fighting men, they are without equal," Cal said, turning back to the monk.

"That doesn't sound like much of a legend to me," the monk said as they started back to the monastery.

"The legend comes in with the fall—if they fall. That sword, if it is a Cat Dancer's blade, is enchanted with a spell, so they say. When a Dancer falls honorably, he is welcomed into the halls of his brothers and is at peace. But if it is a dishonorable death—like poison, or ambush, or backstab—any such way that is not honorable, it is said their sword will morph a true Cat Dancer into a cat of some sort that reflects the type of man he was or the integrity of his master. I think it's a purity of heart thing," Cal said.

"Now that sounds more like a legend," Brother Peel said.

—⚏—

It was weeks later when Ross walked up on a campfire in the early evening.

"Hail the camp!" he said, as was the custom if you were friendly. He did not get a response, so he walked in, wearily.

What he saw immediately put him on guard. There were four people in this camp, paired up. A fire separated the two pairs. On the left were a man seated and a woman standing. On the right was a young girl with a man who held her close. He was trying to appear casual, but the scene was anything but.

The woman looked to be about thirty years old, with brown hair streaked with white. She was solidly built and would be considered attractive if she didn't look so… angry. The man had his arm around her waist; he looked rough, dirty, and mean. The woman's dress was red.

"Good evening, mind if I share your fire?" Ross asked as he stood holding his staff, his right hand close to the dagger he wore on his hip.

The woman answered quickly, "Please do, we are—" she was pulled sharply into the man holding her.

"We got plenty of company, mister, we don't need no more," said the man holding the woman.

"I know you!" said the girl still being held by the other man. This man smiled through broken, stained teeth.

"We ain't got enough to feed ya," he said, hugging the girl to him. His free hand was hidden from Ross's view behind the girl. He sat with his back to a big rock.

Ross looked at the girl. She appeared to be about ten, with blonde curly hair, dressed like a boy, and big blue eyes that looked scared. She somehow looked familiar.

"Maybe you should find another camp, mister," said the man holding the girl.

Every instinct Ross had told him something wasn't right. Keeping both men in sight, he approached the fire.

Just then, a moan came from behind the rock. The man on the left looked sharply toward the rock. The woman threw an elbow into the side of the man's face, making her move to get away.

Ross looked to the man holding the girl. The girl began to struggle, biting the hand that held her. He grunted, raising the knife that he held behind her.

Ross's right hand moved in a blur as a dagger appeared in the man's throat. He let go of the girl, grabbing for the dagger lodged in his throat.

The man on the left lunged for the woman and had just grabbed her skirt when the tip of a very sharp sword pressed against his throat. He froze.

"Hey now, friend," Ross said, "there's no need for that." He looked up the length of the sword against the man's neck.

"They are bandits, sir," said the woman, yanking her skirt out of the man's grasp.

"They were going to... use us and then kill us," she said, moving to a pack propped against a nearby tree.

The girl disappeared behind the rock.

Ross nudged the man with his sword and the man sat back up.

"Is that true, friend?" Ross asked.

The man looked over to his companion, who by now had stopped struggling to remain among the living, and then looked back at Ross.

"Look, I..." Clang! The woman had gotten a heavy skillet and brought it down upon the man's head. She raised it and did it again.

Ross stepped to stop her from doing it again. She was crying.

"It's over, my lady," Ross said, pulling her to him. She struggled to get away, but Ross held her tighter.

"Easy, woman, I am not your enemy," he said, loosening his hold but not letting her go. She relaxed a bit, and Ross let her cry it out.

He still had the sword in his right hand; his left arm was around the woman when the girl came out from behind the rock, leading a boy of about fifteen summers.

The boy looked to have been beaten and leaned on the girl to stand.

She sat him down, and the woman pulled away from Ross, wiping her eyes.

"We are most surely in your debt, sir," said the woman.

"I was not fully aware of the situation until you made your move," he said as he sheathed his sword.

The woman looked down at the unconscious man again.

Clang!

Ross winced as she whacked the outlaw. She sniffed once more, wiped her nose, straightened her dress, and went to tend to the youngsters.

Ross watched her as she went over to aid the boy. He took his gear and set it against the same tree where the other packs were stacked. He removed a leather strap to bind the outlaw's hands, but found it wasn't necessary. He looked over at the woman—her back to him—and shook his head in admiration. Then he stood and went to retrieve his dagger from the other outlaw.

Ross removed anything of value from the two men, piling it up to be disposed of as needed, and then went over to the trio.

"How is the lad?" he asked.

The boy was thin but tall and lanky. *He will be a big man,* Ross thought. He had light brown hair and brown eyes. The woman seemed to have things under control—she hovered over the boy like a mother hen. The girl, though young, had an air of authority. She straightened up and turned to Ross.

"He'll be okay."

She tilted her head in thought as she studied him. "You're... Ross?" she asked skeptically.

The woman's head came up and she, too, looked at Ross. He was surprised by the question.

She knew my name—how?

"I am," he said slowly.

The girl stepped toward him, swung her little fist as if throwing a rock, and hit him in the chest.

"Where have you been?" she demanded.

Ross was speechless.

"Myrial! Have you lost your senses?" the woman said, coming over to stand by the girl.

"You're supposed to be my protector—I chose you!" the girl said, clearly upset.

"You?" the woman asked, almost accusingly. "This is the one?" she asked the girl, who stood angrily, arms crossed, glaring at Ross.

"My lady has me mistaken for someone else," he said, looking from the girl to the woman.

The woman stepped forward and kicked him in the shin.

"Ow!" he said, hopping away from the pair.

"We could have been killed!" said the irate woman.

"Are you two addled or something?" Ross snapped, intercepting the girl as she came toward him. She reached for his left arm. He grabbed her wrist reflexively. She looked at him, and he released her.

She slowly reached up and pulled his sleeve to reveal the handprint on his arm.

Realization dawned.

He recognized her—from the dreams.

"My lady..." he whispered in awe, looking at the girl before him in a new light.

"This is the part where you take a knee," said the woman.

Ross looked at her questioningly.

"Myrial is heir to the White Throne," she said, indicating the girl.

"Isn't there a king on that throne? Last I heard, he was alive and well. Besides, if this be his daughter—"

The woman interrupted him.

"The King, Willard Whiteborn, died without leaving an heir. Myrial is keeper of the flame and next in line for replenishing the King's line."

Ross stood, looking from one to the other, at a loss for words.

"The King's line comes from the White Priestesses of the Golden Light Monastery," the woman continued, taking the girl's hand in her own. "The hierarch is the keeper of the flame—or, as you might say, of the King's line. Only the hierarch of the order can sit the throne if something should happen to the king and his heir. Myrial is the last of the true-born. Only she can pass the test and take the throne."

"What is the test?" Ross asked.

"Her blood must ignite the White Rose on the Throne of Kings," she said.

"This must take place during the Summer Solstice Festival in the White Kingdom."

"And if she is not there at that time, what then?" he asked.

"Already, armies are being gathered to vie for the Crown of the Nine Kingdoms. In short, sir—civil war, until a new bloodline is established."

Ross looked around, giving a heavy sigh.

"So how did you come to be here without protection?" he asked.

The boy stood up unsteadily.

"I am their protection," he said, clearly still affected by the beating.

The woman went over to steady him.

"We must get to the White Castle in time for the festival," she said. "We were on our way when these two attacked Fletcher and threatened to—"

She stopped, glancing at the girl.

Ross nodded, sparing her from saying it aloud in front of Myrial.

"I am not a child, you know!" Myrial said. "I know what they were going to do."

She turned to Ross.

"Did you not feel the pull?"

"I do not know what you mean," he said.

"Once the mark is placed," she explained, "choosing you as my personal protector, you're supposed to seek me out if we ever get separated. Did you not feel the pull? I thought you were dead!" she said, hitting him in the chest again. Then she stepped back and crossed her arms, stern-faced.

"Well, he's here now," said the woman, starting to gather their belongings, "and we've got to move this camp or prepare for more uninvited guests."

Ross stepped over to the boy to check on his injuries. He spoke softly so their conversation couldn't be heard.

"Not to overstep my station, sir," Ross said to the boy, "but if you'll permit me to travel with you—two swords are better than one."

He saw that the boy's injuries would not prohibit him from traveling.

"My name is Ross," he said, offering his hand.

The boy straightened a little taller and shook it.

"I'm Fletcher Greenborn," he said, trying to match Ross's strength in the handshake.

"Well met, Fletcher Greenborn," Ross answered, trying to put him at ease.

All at once, Fletcher slumped slightly.

"What is it?" Ross asked.

"I... uh... don't have a sword," Fletcher said miserably.

Ross smiled, placing a hand on Fletcher's shoulder and pretending not to notice the crack in the boy's voice.

"No matter," he said, leading him over to the outlaws' belongings and handing him a sword.

The boy took it with reverence. The blade was tattered and well-used, but Fletcher didn't notice. Holding the sword, he looked at Ross with a question in his eyes.

"I'll help you learn to use it," he said, putting a reassuring hand on Fletcher's shoulder.

"Are you two going to help or play with your swords?" the woman asked, shouldering a pack.

Ross looked at the boy. Whispering, he asked, "Is she always this bossy?"

Fletcher rolled his eyes and nodded.

"I saw that, Fletcher Greenborn!" she said. Myrail laughed behind her hand, and Ross started grabbing things to carry. In moments, they were on their way.

"What is my lady's name?" Ross asked the woman as they walked.

"I am Emalee Redborn, governess of Myrail Whiteborn," she said. "She's been with me since she was smuggled out of the White Kingdom."

"Why was it necessary to smuggle her out of the White Kingdom?" Ross asked.

"That's a long story, and now is not the time," she said. It was a half-moon, and easy to follow the footpath. Ross was content to let Emalee and the boy lead while he dropped back. Besides, Fletcher seemed to know some woodlore as he led them through the forest.

They made camp and, after placing a watch, were able to rest. The next morning, after breaking their fast, they packed up and set out again.

"We must move cautiously," Emalee said after discussing their route and possible dangers. They walked until midday.

"Why was Myrail hidden from the White Kingdom in the first place?" Ross asked Emalee as they broke for the midday meal. The two youngsters were off gathering things for the camp.

Emalee took a deep breath.

"It wasn't necessary for Myrail to be anything but a normal little girl—until the king died without leaving an heir," she explained. "We lived in a small village in the Red Kingdom, and one day we were visited by a messenger of the White Monastery. But it wasn't just any monastery. It was the Golden Light Monastery of the White Kingdom—*The* Monastery."

Ross just looked back, not understanding. Emalee sighed heavily and continued, as if explaining the obvious.

"The Golden Light Monastery is the direct bloodline of the White King. Only the granddaughter of the High Priestess inherits the ability to choose her protector or pass the test to take the throne. It skips a generation. No one knows why. Myrail was supposed to be High Priestess after her grandmother but... she'll now sit the White Throne— provided we can make it to the White Kingdom in time."

"Why not simply seat her grandmother?" Ross asked.

"She cannot pass the test," Emalee said with another sigh.

"I thought you said—" he began.

"The test has to be performed before the priestess's first letting," Emalee interrupted, averting her gaze. Ross didn't follow.

"Her first letting...?" he asked, confused.

"Yeah, you know—'the red moon,'" she said.

He still looked blank. Emalee turned scarlet.

"Her first *flow!*" she blurted, looking embarrassed.

It finally dawned on him. "Oh... her... first... She has to take the test before her..." Now *he* turned red. "But she's only—what—ten?" he asked, abashed.

"Are all men as daft as you, Ross?" she asked. "First, some girls are quicker than others at... becoming a woman. Second, the Black King is determined to become the next bloodline to the Central Kingdom. And finally, two other kings are about to toss their swords into the mix to vie for the Central Kingdom. So if we don't get Myrail to the White Kingdom in time—"

He finished for her, "Then we have civil war, and there may not be another chance to seat Myrail, because..."

"That's right," she said. "And it's up to us to get her there."

"She's so little to have all that on her shoulders," he said, almost to himself.

"She is stronger than she looks," Emalee said, looking at the girl with Ross.

On the road, it was explained that the Central Realm was bordered on the southeast by impassable cliffs. They had to travel halfway through the Yellow Kingdom to reach a switchback road that would allow them to ascend to the plateau marking the White Kingdom's boundaries—the hub of the Nine Kingdoms.

They traveled for three days without incident. Ross showed Fletcher how to hold a sword properly, and exercises that would strengthen his arms and improve his defense.

At the end of the third day, as Ross was practicing with the boy, Myrail watched while Emalee prepared the evening meal.

"Your sword is a barrier between you and your opponent. Once set, instead of moving it, *you* move," Ross told the boy. "But when you *do* set your sword in motion, keeping its momentum until you achieve the blow that ends the confrontation strengthens the strike with the least amount of energy on your part."

He demonstrated how to move with the sword in continuous motion. After a while of emulating Ross's moves, Fletcher said in frustration, "I'll never get it!"

"Actually, you're doing quite well. Nothing comes without work," Ross told him.

"Your natural abilities will always rise when studying something new."

"I don't have any natural abilities," Fletcher said, putting his sword away.

"Sure you do," Ross replied, slapping him on the back. "We just haven't discovered them yet."

Emalee called over that she needed more wood for the fire. Fletcher volunteered and went to get his hand axe. Ross sheathed his sword, wiped the sweat from his face, and found a seat beside Myrail on a log. She had been watching them practice.

"Where did you learn to sword fight?" the girl asked as he sat beside her, watching Fletcher chop wood.

"I don't remember a lot about my past. I woke up in that monastery and knew I'd been in a battle—but not what battle, or what it was about." He turned and looked at her. "For a long time I thought you were dreams. Do you remember marking me on the battlefield?"

She thought about it for a moment.

"I remember seeing you, and I knew you would die if I didn't do something—and I didn't know what to do," she said, shrugging her shoulders. "I just knew I didn't want you to die, so I put my hand on your arm—it was bleeding..."

She squirmed on the log, trying to explain. Ross, smiling warmly, lifted her chin so she looked into his eyes.

"Thank you, my lady," he said sincerely.

She smiled back at him. Emalee, who had overheard, smiled too.

Fletcher, finishing with an armload of wood, spun the hand axe and struck it in a log ten feet away.

Ross saw what he had done and called out to the boy.

"Hey, Fletcher." The boy looked up from gathering the wood.

"Can you do that again?" Fletcher looked confused.

"Can you stick that hand axe in the wood like that every time?" Ross asked him, indicating the axe.

Fletcher looked over at the axe sticking out of the log. Shrugging his shoulders, he said, "I guess so." He carried the wood to Emalee.

"Show me," Ross said, getting up to retrieve the axe.

They spent the remaining daylight hours sticking the hand axe into everything from trees to tree stumps. Fletcher never missed.

"My father was a ranger, and wood lore was our life," said the boy.

"This is one of those natural abilities I spoke of," Ross told him.

"Yeah, but you don't ever see anyone throwing a hand axe in a sword fight," said the youngster, eyeing the older man.

"Sometimes, my friend, it is better not to fight at all. The risk may be too high or the matter too small to shed a man's blood over. And sometimes, it is necessary to kill without a fight," Ross told him.

"Knowing how to throw anything that can tip the odds in your favor when your life is on the line..."

The boy nodded and thought about Ross's words. Just then, Emalee called them to eat.

Several times during the night, riders passed. They always made their camp well off the road. With Fletcher leading them, taking animal trails or paths only he could find, they made their way toward the base of the plateau and the switchback road that led to the top.

Once, a party of armed soldiers with a black banner passed, going in the direction from which Ross's group had come. Fletcher, alerting them, gave everyone plenty of time to hide off the road as they passed.

"Do you think they're looking for us?" Ross asked the Red Priestess after the soldiers had passed.

All three of his companions looked at him as if he were a mental case.

"I don't doubt your word that there are reasons to be cautious, but..." he said. "How could they know about Myrial and her claim to the White Throne?"

"I don't know, but the messenger was clear: 'Stay away from the soldiers of the Black Kingdom,'" Emalee explained as they made their way back to the road.

"This is not their first attempt to stop us from reaching the White Kingdom," she told him. "It is best not to take any chances."

Thinking about it as they walked, Ross asked, "How far to the switchback road?"

"We should start up the plateau tomorrow," Emalee said.

By now, the four were used to each other. They had developed a routine when they camped. They tried to camp near a stream, if one could be found. They paired off to do what needed to be done.

Emalee and Myrial would unpack and prepare the evening meal, while Fletcher and Ross would start a small fire to cook with and gather the wood to keep it going. The boys would then find water and refill all the water bags. If water was near enough, the girls would bathe and the boys would spar—choosing to wash later, if at all. They were, after all, boys.

"When you hold your sword pointed up, you are guarding the spot over your head where there is nothing to guard," Ross told the boy, repositioning Fletcher's grip on the sword to show him what he meant.

"Hold the hilt of the sword up with your wrist bent—like this—pointing the sword toward the ground. Now, without moving your arm, lift the sword."

Fletcher did as instructed, and Ross set him to repeating the exercise over and over while he went over to sit on a log to rest. Ross removed his boots, rubbing his tired feet.

Myrial came over and sat next to him.

"What's he doing?" she asked, seeing the unusual exercise Fletcher was doing. She seemed a little cranky. They were all road-weary and needed rest.

Ross looked at her. "He is strengthening his wrist," he said, rubbing his foot.

"Why? Does he think I'll make him a knight when I'm Queen?"

Ross stopped rubbing his foot and looked at her.

"He's only a stupid boy!" she said.

Fletcher, hearing this, lowered his arm, crestfallen. He let the sword drop from his hand and walked off into the surrounding trees.

Emalee, hearing what Myrial said, watched him go, stunned.

Without warning, Ross lifted the girl up and laid her over his knee. He spanked her bottom with three sharp, open-handed whacks, then stood her up. It happened so fast, she stood there stunned.

"You can't do that to me!" she yelled, mad as hell. "I can say whatever I—"

She never finished, because again, she found herself over his knee. This time, he yanked her pants down, exposing her bare bottom. Three sounding whacks echoed through the camp as his open hand struck her reddening backside. Again, he stood her up. Her lower lip was out as far as it could go, tears streaming down her face. Then she cried openly and ran into the brush, tugging her britches up as she went.

"Why you...! That is treason!" Emalee said, coming at him with a carving knife. Her face was flushed with anger.

Ross stood up to meet her, deftly removing the knife as he sat back down, pulling her over his knee. He held her firm as she kicked and flailed. He lifted her dress and spanked her bare backside four good whacks, then kicked her off his lap into the dust.

She looked up at him from the ground, shocked.

"You... oh you!..." She didn't know what to say.

He moved as if he was going to get her again, and she rolled out of his reach.

"You heard what she said," he stated.

Emalee got to her feet and stood defiantly, literally not knowing what to do.

Finally, she said, "She is heir to the White Throne! You do not strike the future Queen of the realm for having a bad day!"

He stood up. She stepped back, absently rubbing her backside through her dress.

"How dare you...!" she said, stepping in to kick at his shins.

He sidestepped the kick, catching her around the waist and pulling her to him. He easily secured her arms, and before she could protest any further, he covered her mouth with his own, kissing her—then releasing her suddenly.

She gasped, eyes big as saucers.

"Why, I... You!" she said, breathless.

He stepped in and kissed her again. This time, before he released her, she started kissing him back. The kiss was longer, and when he pulled back to look at her face, he saw that her eyes were closed. He watched as she slowly opened them, seeing him differently.

"It is not enough that she be Queen," he said to her, brushing the hair from her face. "It is our job to help her be a good Queen."

He smiled at her.

"If I have overstepped my boundaries, I yield to your authority and accept whatever punishment you deem necessary."

She continued looking into his face as if seeing it for the first time. *He has a kind face*, she thought.

"Good," she finally said. "Now shut up and kiss me again."

And he did.

When they stepped back from each other, she smoothed her dress, brushed off the dust, and said, "I should go and get her."

"No, my lady, I should go and get her. You go and get the boy," he said, and walked off in the direction she had run.

Emalee watched him go, then gave a heavy sigh and went after Fletcher.

When Ross came into the clearing where Myrial was, he saw her beside a stream, standing withher arms crossed over her chest, facing away from him. He sat on a rock and picked up a stick.

"Myrial," he called softly. "Come and talk to me."

She jerked her shoulders away from him as an answer.

"That 'stupid boy,' as you called him, would—and has—put himself between harm and you. He is young, but he would gladly lay down his life for you. And he'd do it because he loves you," Ross told her as he traced circles in the dirt with the stick.

"When you are Queen, they will know the kind of Queen you are by the company you keep—and how or why the people love you. After all that Fletcher has done," he went on, "and would do... you would cast him out as a stupid boy not worthy of his Queen's love or appreciation?"

She turned to face him, her lower lip not out so far. The tracks of her tears could be traced on her face.

"Would you, Myrial?" he gently asked her.

She sniffed and dragged her wrist across her nose.

Slowly, she shook her head as fresh tears coursed down her cheeks.

"Come here, girl," he said, setting the stick down and holding his arms out to her.

She took a couple of hesitant steps in his direction.

"Come on," he urged, waving her to come.

She took another step, and all at once, she ran over, falling into his arms, crying freely, uncontrollably. She was trying to speak but couldn't through her wracking sobs.

"There, there now," he said soothingly, smoothing her hair.

"I know," he said, holding her as she got it all out.

She pulled her head from his chest and looked at him.

"I... I... I didn't mean to... to be so... mean. I thought Fle... Fletcher was going to be..." she hiccupped and wiped her eyes, "...killed when those men..."

Ross wiped her cheeks with his thumb.

"I know," he said. "It's alright," he told her, pulling her to him.

She cried into his shirt some more, and then pulling back, she told him,

"He told us to ru... run when they grabbed him, and then, and then they hit him so hard..."

This brought on more crying. He held her through it all. She straightened up all at once.

"And I called him a..."

When they came back to camp, Fletcher was sitting by himself, sharpening his sword with astone. He did not look up.

Myrial looked at Ross, who nodded to her. She walked over and sat beside him.

Emalee and Ross watched from across the camp as Myrial draped her arm across Fletcher's shoulders. What was said could not be heard.

"You fixed it," she said, linking her arm through Ross's.

"It's what I do," he said, smiling down at her smugly.

She playfully punched him.

They decided, because of the increasing traffic and how tired and road-weary everyone was, to move off the road even further and rest for a day.

Fletcher found a good clearing with a stream to wash clothes, surrounded by trees and completely cut off from the rest of the world.

Emalee took a little more time with her appearance. Ross noticed and told her so. Fletcher practiced his exercises and showed Myrial how to throw an axe.

After the midday meal, the sun was high and hot. Ross had just put his sword away after checking its edge. Fletcher and Myrial sat together, and Emalee sat by Ross.

"Why aren't girls warriors?" Myrial asked—a valid question from a curious young girl.

"Because," Ross said teasingly, "girls can't aim properly."

This drew looks from everyone.

"It's true. Their eyes are too close together," he said as if it were a well-known fact.

Of course, he was met with resistance.

"Let me show you."

Having already removed his boots, he set them at a distance and gathered a handful of small stones. Then he elbowed his way between the two youngsters.

"Ever play pebble-in-the-boot?" he asked.

Myrial shook her head while Fletcher said that he had.

Emalee sipped tea, content to watch from across the ashes of the campfire.

Ross divided up the stones, giving the youngsters their share. He then tossed a stone toward the nearest boot; it bounced off the rim and landed on the ground.

"All ya gotta do is land it in the boot," he said, readjusting himself on the log.

Fletcher tossed and missed entirely. Myrial took careful aim and bounced her pebble off the toe of the nearest boot.

Ross tossed again—this time, the stone hit the rim of the same boot but bounced into the other.

"I meant to do that," he said and got an elbow from Myrial.

"You lie!" she said.

Emalee chuckled.

Fletcher tossed again and hit the boot, while Myrial's stone dropped into the first boot.

She squealed with delight.

"Atta girl, Myrial," Emalee said. "So much for girls not being able to aim."

"That was luck," Ross said, tossing again and missing terribly.

Fletcher dropped one into the boot, and so did Myrial.

"She's got you two—two to your one. You guys had better get moving," Emalee said.

Ross tossed and missed again. Myrial laughed and tossed another into the boot.

"Ha!" she said.

Fletcher missed his next toss.

"Darn!" he said, looking at Ross.

Ross took careful aim and launched his stone, only to watch it sail wide of the mark.

Myrial laughed at him.

"Boy, Ross, you stink at this. Maybe your eyes are too close together," Emalee told him.

Myrial laughed merrily. Everyone laughed.

"Yeah?" he said in his defense. "I've been trying for the second boot. It's further away. Let's see you do it."

He sat back, crossing his arms over his chest.

Myrial took careful aim and dropped one into the second boot.

She jumped up and squealed with delight.

"Why you!" Ross said and lunged for her.

She jumped out of his reach, colliding with Fletcher and spilling them both over the log they had been sitting on.

Ross dove over the log, grabbing the girl.

"Hold her, Fletcher!" he told the boy as the three rolled around in the dirt.

Fletcher held the screaming, giggling girl while Ross blew raspberries on her tummy.

Emalee laughed as she got a pan of cold water and dumped it on the three of them—then the chase was on.

All three of them chased Emalee down until she was cornered, where the whole pile ended up tickling the woman until she laughed so hard, tears were streaming down her face.

"Yield!" she said through her laughter.

"I yield!"

Ross and the youngsters were wet, muddy, and winded. Emalee wasn't in much better shape.

They all spent the remainder of the day cleaning up. Ross shaved the hair off his face using the reflection of a pool of water for a mirror.

Emalee noticed and told him so.

Beneath the stars of a clear summer night, after the youngsters had gone to sleep, Ross and Emalee shared a bed.

"So how is it that you, being a Redborn, came to be governess to the heir to the White Throne?" he asked as she lay in his arms.

"Myrial was born to a Duke of the White Realm. His wife, a White Priestess of that same realm, was an arranged marriage of convenience. The White King owed the Duke a favor for some such deed, and the Duke asked for the hand of a White Priestess.

"Reluctantly, this was granted. It seemed that the Duke was smitten with a certain Priestess. Anyway, the Priestess protested, but she was sworn to do the King's bidding—whatever that bidding was, so..."

Emalee rose up on her elbow beside him, looking at his face as she explained.

"The Duke had been married before, but his wife had died giving birth to the Duke's daughter. It was rumored that the Duke drowned the babe, wanting a son for his first child. This was never proven, though," she said as she traced a scar on his chest with her finger.

"So," he said, figuring it out on his own, "the Duke wanted a son, and the Duke's new wife gave birth to Myrial."

"Yes, and the babes were switched with no one the wiser," Emalee finished for him.

"What of Myrial's mother?" he asked.

"She bled to death after the birth," she told him.

"I was Priestess of the Red Order when Myrial was brought to the Red Kingdom. The Abbot of our monastery put her in my charge, telling me what he could."

Ross rolled over and slid down until he was facing her. He kissed her nose.

"So, it was you who taught her how to toss pebbles?"

She smiled, enclosing him in her embrace.

"Maybe," she said. "I can teach you a thing or two if you like."

For the second time that night, they made love.

The next morning, they packed up, getting ready to leave.

None wanted to break the spell of the previous day.

They ate from their dwindling supplies and started out. By midday, they had made it back to their original camp.

They stopped for a rest before moving on to the road. Myrial was picking berries, and Fletcher was chopping sticks for a fire.

Emalee was removing things from a pack while Ross was off by himself near the road.

He looked over at his three companions, feeling as if something was missing. Instinct drew his hand to his sword.

Everyone was too spread out, he thought, trying to get a handle on what was amiss.

Ross heard something beside him—at the same time, he saw Fletcher's head come up suddenly.

Ross pulled his sword just in time to block a strike from a hidden foe that had been waiting for them.

Ross had been caught off guard but managed to kick his opponent off his feet and backed up to see what was happening behind him.

At the sound of Ross's sword making contact, Fletcher, Emalee, and Myrial turned to see what the noise was.

Two other men stepped out of hiding—one behind Myrial and the other by Emalee.

Everyone in Ross's party was separated by at least thirty feet.

Fletcher stood up, dropping the wood he was carrying. He was also fixed on Myrial.

As if in slow motion—before anyone could act—the man near Myrial grabbed her and pulled a dagger. His left hand caught her under the chin and yanked her head back, exposing her throat. His intentions were clear.

"No!" Ross screamed, surging forward. But his body moved as if underwater, and he knew he'd be too late.

The man near Emalee had already drawn his sword and moved to intercept Ross. All the men were dressed in black.

"For the King of the Black!" the man holding Myrial declared.

Emalee screamed in horror as his hand began to fall—then a spinning hand axe buried itself in the side of his head. He dropped lifelessly to the ground, the deed unfinished.

Myrial ran to Emalee. Fletcher pulled his sword, and the man blocking Ross was cut down so quickly he fell to the ground in pieces.

Ross, seeing Myrial and Emalee were not in immediate danger, turned back to the man he'd kicked earlier. That man, now aware the ambush had failed and his companions were dead, backed toward the road.

Ross turned to make sure the threat was truly over. Fletcher stood guard by the girls, sword drawn. No more enemies.

The man at the road whistled sharply, his gaze fixed on Ross. Ross didn't pursue him—he wouldn't leave his friends just to kill a retreating man.

"Why attack us?" Ross called.

"You'll never make the White Kingdom!" the man shouted back. Another rider approached behind him, leading several horses.

"You're mistaken!" Ross yelled. "We mean nothing to anyone!"

"Oh, there's no mistake," the man said, climbing into the saddle. "The Black Witch said: 'A warrior, a Red Priestess, a boy, and a girl dressed like a boy.' That's you, friend."

"Let's get them now!" said the rider with the horses.

"You go ahead," the man replied. "I want to live long enough to spend the reward."

He kicked his horse into a gallop while his companion hesitated, eyeing the scene, then raced off after him.

Ross went to Myrial, checking her throat. A small nick—barely bleeding.

He rested a hand on her trembling head, then caught Fletcher's eye.

"Well done, lad," he said.

Emalee embraced Fletcher and Ross, with Myrial in the middle.

"What are we going to do?" she asked Ross.

"We must move quickly," he replied, retrieving Fletcher's axe. He noticed the fallen warrior's sword was in better shape than Fletcher's, so he claimed it and handed both weapons to the boy.

"How far until we reach a safe haven in the White Kingdom?" Ross asked.

"We should reach the base of the plateau by day's end," Fletcher said.

"I heard there's a garrison at the top of this road," Emalee added as they gathered their belongings.

Ross looked ahead and could see the looming plateau.

"It looks closer than it is," Fletcher explained. "That's because it's so big."

They traveled the rest of the day and reached the base of the plateau by nightfall.

They camped well off the road while Fletcher scouted ahead. When he returned, he said, "There are soldiers blocking the road. Some in metal armor—I think they're Knights of the Black Kingdom."

Ross studied the boy. "How can you tell?"

"They were the ones giving the orders."

Ross nodded. "Think you could find a way up this hill without using the road?"

"There has to be animal trails we can follow without getting too close," Fletcher said, studying the slope. "But I'm worried about the thinning cover as we climb."

Ross looked and saw what he meant. "Can we do it in the dark?"

"We could," Fletcher said, "but it's risky. We wouldn't see danger coming. They may have posted men up there."

"Good point, lad. But we need to put distance between us and those men. We'll move slow and cautious until we find a place to rest for the night. If we get separated, get the girls to the garrison."

Fletcher nodded.

"What do you mean, separated?" Emalee asked.

Ross rested a hand on her shoulder. "Just in case, my lady," he said gently.

She gave him a suspicious look. "We're not getting separated, though."

"Of course not, my lady," Ross said with a smile.

He nodded to Fletcher, who began leading them uphill. By full dark, they found a usable deer trail. Too tired to continue, they made a fireless camp, set watches, and passed the night uneventfully.

They resumed at first light. By midday, Fletcher called a halt. Everyone welcomed the break, drinking from their water bags and eating some hard bread and jerky.

From their perch, they could see the country spread out below. The trail had brought them closer to the road, but so far, they hadn't been seen—until now.

Fletcher pulled Ross aside. "I think we're being followed."

"Why do you say that?" Ross asked quietly.

Fletcher pointed. "See those men beside their horses?"

Though far off, Ross could make them out. "Aye, I can."

"Well," said the boy, "if we can see them, they can see us."

Ross scanned the slope. Fletcher gripped his arm suddenly, directing his gaze to the side—three men were moving toward them, parallel to their position.

"Ross!" Emalee called, pointing the other direction. Ross caught the glint of a sword blade in the sun—three more men, flanking them.

Ross looked uphill. Still too far to reach the top. At least a full day's travel.

He turned to Fletcher. "You must get them to the garrison, lad."

Fletcher nodded solemnly.

"No!" Emalee said, understanding Ross's intent. "We can all go!" She reached for him.

The advancing men didn't seem to know they'd been spotted. Myrial put a hand on Ross's arm; he covered it with his own, smiling.

Then he leaned in to whisper something to Emalee.

"No!" she gasped as her eyes filled with tears.

He kissed her cheek. "You must."

"We must hurry!" Fletcher said urgently.

Emalee touched Ross's face, tears slipping down her cheeks. "Go," Ross said. "I'll be right behind you, I promise."

"You promise?!" Myrial asked, still clutching his arm.

"I promise. Now go."

She hugged him fiercely, then turned away. Ross waited until they had a lead, then followed—only far enough to rise above the men coming after them.

Then he stopped, clearly visible. The ruse was up.

Below, he saw a group of riders racing up the switchbacks—but they were still far off. One last look at his companions. All clear.

He took a deep breath, exhaled, and drew his sword.

Ross advanced on the three men opposite the road. They were Black Army soldiers—swords drawn, dressed like the ones from the day before.

They spread out on the uneven slope, but Ross had the high ground. He feigned a swing to draw a sword, then kicked the man into his comrade behind him, sending them both tumbling.

The last man closed with Ross and died on the end of his blade.

Wasting no time, Ross climbed after the other group—now behind Fletcher. The boy had stepped between the girls and the approaching men.

The attackers came in single file. Ross picked up an apple-sized rock and hurled it at the rear man. It struck his back, making him turn to face Ross.

The man, winded but on higher ground, swung down. Ross sidestepped and stabbed him in the crotch. The man folded.

Ross grabbed him by the collar, yanked him downhill, and pressed forward.

The other two were closing on Fletcher.

Fletcher stopped and drew his sword.

The boy's sword shook—he was scared. Ross knew he couldn't catch the last man before he reached the boy. The man waiting on Ross was winded; Ross almost had to chase him out of the way before the man stopped and planted his feet, swinging a desperate strike. Ross blocked the swing and began to counter, only to see the man turn and run down the hill. Gaining speed, he literally sat and slid to a stop two hundred feet down the grade.

Ross, breathing hard, turned to catch the third and final man. This one also showed signs of fatigue, but he looked to be in better fighting shape. He closed in on Fletcher. All Ross could do was watch as the man climbed.

The attacker stabbed at Fletcher, who kept his blade steady and moved to the side—just the way Ross had shown him. While the man's sword was on the far side of Fletcher's, the boy lifted his own sword with both hands and slammed the point into the underside of the man's chin. Fletcher pushed the blade into the man's throat, then shoved him off the sword with his foot, sending the body tumbling down the slope.

Ross stepped aside as the dying man passed, then smiled and saluted the boy. Fletcher grinned, wide-eyed and dumbfounded.

"Go!" Ross shouted.

Fletcher smiled down at his friend, quick and boyish, then turned and began climbing the slope after the girls. Ross looked down the grade at the ones who had fled or were injured. They weren't advancing. He glanced toward the road and knew he couldn't let them pass.

He picked up a fallen sword and made his way over to the road. It was steep, with switchbacks. He stood at one, facing the decline between turns. He stuck the extra sword into the ground.

He would make his stand here.

Looking below, he spotted riders approaching. Removing his cloak, he stretched his arms and shoulders. He looked up and saw his friends still climbing. Pride filled him—he wished he could see them all grown up.

The horses' hooves echoed on the road. Ross turned and watched as the riders rounded the bend below. The first two were warhorses, ridden by the Black King's best—Knights, most likely. The road was just wide enough for three horses to run side by side. Four other riders followed, likely regular army. The horses looked tired, but the riders were determined to run him down.

Ross set his sheathed sword on his cloak beside the road. He stepped to the sword planted in the ground and pulled it free, feeling the tremble of the approaching horses under his feet. He raised the sword above his head, letting the blade hang down his back.

The riders were twenty-five feet away when Ross stepped forward and hurled the sword end over end at the inside warhorse. The rider tried to veer, pushing into the outside horses—who were themselves trying to avoid the steep slope. The two warhorses tangled and went down in a heap, with the remaining riders piling up behind them. The mess slid to a stop just ten feet from Ross.

He picked up his sword and stepped into the middle of the road.

The two lead Knights disentangled themselves and stepped away from the mass of tangled horses and men.

"Nice trick," one of the advancing Knights said.

They wore matching steel plate armor. Chainmail covered their arms, and their legs were protected by steel plates on their shins, knees, and thighs. Even their gloves were made of ringed mail. The two stepped apart and drew their swords.

"This is the one I told you about," said one of the soldiers from the pile, approaching. Ross recognized him from the fight in the clearing.

"He is but one man," said the Knight on the left.

Ross feinted a move that caused both Knights to raise their swords in defense. Then he smiled, showing them his sword was still sheathed. They looked irritated.

He repeated the move, this time flinging his scabbard into the mouth of the Knight on the left and immediately stepping to block a swing from the one on the right. The Knight with the bloody mouth came at him in rage. Ross ducked his swing, stepped past him, and struck the back of his knees with his blade. The cut was deep. The Knight went down.

Two more steps, and Ross was among the lesser men-at-arms. His blade whirled. The two soldiers dropped.

Ross stepped away from the dying men and squared off three paces from the standing Knight, careful to stay out of reach of the one on the ground, who could no longer stand.

"Rem said you were good," the standing Knight said. "He didn't do you justice." He waved the two other soldiers in.

Ross launched an attack before the others could close in. The Knight fought defensively and did not underestimate him. Armor protected the Knight well—Ross slipped in a cut here and there, but nothing like the one that had felled his partner.

Ross steered the fight away from the approaching soldiers. He parried a blow from one, ducked a swipe, and, while dancing away, jabbed his sword tip under the Knight's chin, drawing blood but not a fatal blow.

The Knight grabbed Ross's blade with his mailed glove, trying to hold it. Ross, now at the edge of the slope, couldn't back up. He yanked the sword free, but too late to block a cut to his shoulder. He kicked the Knight and turned to face the man who'd struck him.

A stab landed in his back.

The man who had earlier fled had climbed back up the slope and stabbed Ross. Though wounded, Ross stepped past the men and squared off again with the Knight. He was breathing hard, clearly affected by the wound, but still on his feet—his sword held steady, ready.

"Back!" the Knight said, waving his two companions back. Another soldier climbed up from the slope. Everybody seemed winded.

"We can afford to wait. He is finished. Let's wait," said the Knight.

"The longer we wait, the further my friends get," Ross told the man.

"Your friends won't get past the overlook. There are three good men posted up there in case they get past us," the Knight told him, still holding his sword at the ready even though Ross was badly wounded. "I can assure you they are fully capable of dealing with a boy ranger and two girls," he added.

Ross knew he was getting weaker the longer he stood there. He stepped forward in a frenzy of sword swings and attacked the Knight.

The Knight was a first-rate fighter and knew Ross would attack, but he did not think any man in Ross's condition could fight with such passion. The Knight tried to position the fight so that Ross would come close to the watching soldiers. When he saw his chance, he let his sword go and grabbed Ross's sword with both hands, pulling the blade and Ross to him, chest to chest.

"Get him!" yelled the Knight.

The move was designed so that Ross would let go of his sword, but he did not. Ross pushed forward into the Knight until the sword was flat against the Knight's armor plate. As Ross felt the first sword being shoved into his body, he gripped the crossguard on the sword and lifted with all he had, sending the tip of the blade up behind the Knight's chin, through his mouth, and into his brain.

Another sword was thrust into Ross's back. He held on as the dead Knight fell away, leaving him standing with his sword. The two men who backstabbed him backed away and watched as Ross fell to his knees.

"He's finished. Go! If that girl reaches the top, you'll end up worse than that," said the Knight with his legs cut.

Ross fell over with his sword beneath him, as the three remaining men started up the road on foot. The horses had run off long ago. The crippled Knight watched as the sun dipped below the horizon. He noticed when Ross took his last breath, and then, too, lay back to rest, not realizing the severity of his wounds; he continued to bleed out, waiting for help.

Emalee, Myrial, and Fletcher climbed for their lives. They skirted the road and made good time up the animal trail. By now, night had fallen and stealth was their biggest ally. They heard horses pass several times, knowing the road was not far.

Fletcher's sword was sheathed but in his hands as they moved up the plateau. A twig snapped, and Fletcher turned back to shush the girls. That's when he saw two armed men coming up behind them. He immediately rushed back to stand between the men and the girls. A third man came from the darkness of the brush. The moon came from behind a cloud, and Fletcher could see that these were from the Black Army that had attacked them earlier. Fletcher drew his sword.

"Well, boy, are you going to kill us all with that big ole sword?" one of the men said, taunting Fletcher.

The boy stood firm, sword extended the way he'd been taught; it did not shake. Emalee Redborn stepped up beside Fletcher with a skillet in one hand and a carving knife in the other. Myrial came up to stand on the other side.

"I stand corrected, boys; we have an even match, three on three," the man said. The three men laughed.

"Go away!" Myrial yelled, fists balled up at her side. She was crying. She stood there beside Fletcher, tired, frustrated, and very afraid. Then she watched as the mocking smiles seemed to die on the men's faces before her.

Course fur slid under her hand as she stood there. A massive white panther with a low growl moved forward to stand beside her. The three men took a step back. The panther sprang.

—◊◊◊—

Three weeks later, at the Summer Solstice Festival, thousands gathered to witness a new era. A platform had been raised so that the people could view the crowning of their new Queen.

Eight Kings representing the surrounding kingdoms sat before a table. A single white rose in full bloom was all that was on it. Emalee Redborn stood to the side on the platform dressed as befitted her station, in red. A ten-year-old girl dressed in white with gold trim and a gossamer train strolled confidently across the platform. The crowd cheered.

Myrial stopped halfway to the table, turned, and looked back. Impatient like, she patted her thighs with both hands. "Come on!" she said.

A huge stark white panther galloped a couple of steps, then slowed to a trot as he made his way to the girl. The crowd cheered harder as the two made their way out to the table. The panther sat beside her, making the girl look smaller than she was. A low growl rumbled through his throat as he eyed the King dressed in black.

An older lady dressed similarly to the girl gracefully stepped up to the table. She raised her hands to the crown for quiet, and they obliged her. She ran her hand through the fur of the cat and then cupped the chin of her granddaughter. She smiled down affectionately at Myrial.

The lady took a silver dagger and the right hand of the girl. She pricked the finger of the girl and a drop of blood appeared. Eight men in different-colored dress, all wearing crowns, watched as this drop of blood dripped onto the white rose. At first it smoldered, and then flames engulfed the flower.

The crowd could not be contained; they cheered their new Queen. The eight Kings sat back with a collective sigh.

The lady in white lifted a crown and placed it on the head of Myrial Whiteborn, Queen of the White Kingdom. The White Priestess walked over and stood next to Emalee, leaving Myrial to the cheering crowd. A ceremonial sword was brought and placed in her little hands.

Queen Myrial held up the jeweled scabbard to show the crowd; they cheered harder. The panther dragged his rough tongue up the back of her arm, and she hugged him.

Emalee cried freely from the side of the platform as she watched. Myrial's grandmother kindly laid a hand on Emalee's arm, smiling at the woman. The White Priestess leaned in to be heard.

"You did a wonderful job; this kingdom is indebted to you." Emalee smiled and did a slight curtsy. Once more, she leaned in to be heard.

"Does the man you honor know he is to be a father?" she asked.

Emalee's hand went to her stomach as she looked at the older woman, tears pooling in her eyes. They both turned and looked on as Myrial and the panther stood before the screaming crowd.

"He will," Emalee said to herself.

Myrial held her hands up for the crowd to be still. It took a minute, but after seeing their new Queen had something to say, they quieted. She looked out at the sea of faces before her.

"It is my privilege to serve you," she said. It took another minute to shut the crowd up again so she could continue.

"As Queen of the White Realm, I will name my First Knight." She turned to face the side of the platform. "Step forward, Fletcher Greenwalker," she said.

Emalee led the young man out. He stepped in front of Queen Myrial. Her smile to him was breathtaking. She said to the crowd behind him, "Were it not for the courage of this man, I would not be here." The crowd cheered for him. Myrial nodded to him.

Emalee leaned in and said over the noise of the crowd, "This is the part where you take a knee." She smiled at him.

The big panther's head almost knocked her over as he rubbed against her hip affectionately. Fletcher knelt before Queen Myrial. At once the crowd quieted.

"I, Myrial Whiteborn, Queen of the Nine Kingdoms, name this man Fletcher Greenwalker, First Knight of the White Realm, right hand of the Queen."

She placed the ceremonial sword upon his left shoulder, and then the other.

"Rise, Sir Fletcher."

He did. A big burly Knight approached and draped a white cloak with a gold-stitched hand on the back across Sir Fletcher's shoulders. He bowed to his Queen.

The End.

Angels Inc.

FADE IN

Opening bars to "Beyond the Shore" by Bobby Darin play.

INT. Hospital room – Night

Camera shot: Takes in the entire hospital room. Only one patient, a very old man hooked up to all sorts of equipment designed to prolong the inevitable. A middle-aged woman sits beside the bed, weeping quietly while facing the old man in the bed. Across from the woman stand two impeccably dressed men (ages upper thirties to forties). One in a light-blue suit and the other dressed in a white suit. Their suits fit perfectly. They seem out of place in the room.

Music fades for dialogue. We can now hear the beeping of the monitors.

FIRST MAN (blue suit)

Better suit up. He's lived a good life.

Both men reach into their inside jacket pockets, pull out a matching pair of sunglasses and put them on. As the monitors beeping begins to slow, the B.9 music stops altogether as the scene holds, and then alarms start to sound. The woman starts to wail, and the drum solo to the Bobby Darin song takes off, while the music hits us full force. At that time, it appears as if a man made of white light sits up out of his corpse on the hospital bed. The light is so bright we cannot make out the features of the man. The crying woman seems oblivious to this. The two men in suits step back as the man of light swings his legs over the side of the bed. Bobby Darin croons on. The blinding light fades to reveal a younger version of the man. He's now in his thirties. Bobby Darin croons on. The blinding light dims, and we can begin to make out features.

MAN OF LIGHT

WoooHooo!

He hops off the bed. He is dressed casually and seems happy.

MAN IN BLUE SUIT (smiling warmly)

Hello, Mr. Devereau.

MAN IN WHITE SUIT (also smiling warmly)

Well done, sir!

The two men in suits remove their sunglasses and begin to guide Mr. Devereau toward the door of the room. B. G. – activity is bustling in the room with hospital staff. Everyone, including the young lady, who is still weeping, is oblivious to the men in suits and Mr. Devereau. The three step out into the hallway and approach an escalator going up into clouds. Mr. Devereau stops at the foot of the escalator. He puts a hand on Mr. Blue suit's arm, stopping him as well.

MR. DEVEREAU

Where is she?

The man in blue suit looks at Mr. Devereau, not following his question. Mr. Devereau looks to man in white suit, who shrugs his shoulders in ignorance.

MR. DEVEREAU (on the verge of panic)

She's gotta be here! Where is she?

MAN IN BLUE

Who, Mr. Devereau?

MR. DEVEREAU

My wife! She's been dead for ten years.
She's supposed to be here!

Mr. Devereau looks from one man to the other.

MAN IN BLUE (uncomfortably)

Eh hem…

Mr. Devereau focuses on man in blue

MAN IN BLUE (loosening his collar)

Aaaaah…she might not have made it, sir.

The men in suits move Mr. Devereau onto the escalator. As they rise, the hospital and all its busyness recedes into the floor as the B.G. turns into fluffy clouds.

MR. DEVEREAU (exasperated)

What!? What do you mean she didn't make it!
Where *is* she? Where am *I*?

Mr. Devereau keeps turning from one man to the other for answers. They seem uncomfortable, looking everywhere but at Mr. Devereau. Man in white reaches for Mr. Devereau.

MAN IN WHITE

Relax, sir, everything is okay, we can…

Mr. Devereau yanks his arm away.

MR. DEVEREAU (excited)

Let me tell you something, Mister! That woman
was a saint! She took in more strays than the
SPCA. Not just cats and dogs either. If there
was someone, anyone, that needed help, she was
the first in line to help. They were on first-name
basis with her at the shelters and soup kitchens, blood
banks! Why she had her own parking spot! She gave
enough blood to drown Dracula…

MR. DEVEREAU (cont.)

And then you tell me that she wasn't good enough to…

WOMAN (at top of escalator)

Ben!

Mr. Devereau and the two men look up the last ten feet of the escalator.
A woman, standing with her fists on her hips. She is in a summer dress
and about the same age as Mr. Devereau.

MRS. DEVEREAU

Ben, why are you yelling at these nice men?

MR. DEVEREAU (in awe)

Eleanor!

The two suited men step aside as the escalator comes to the top, depositing them before the waiting woman. The Devereaus embrace, and the two suited man high five each other as Bobby Darin and his orchestra fade back in full swing.

SUPERIMPOSE
ANGELS INC.

The two men watch as the Devereaus move away, their arms round each other, into the busy area beyond the escalator.

There does not appear to be any kind of ceiling and the landscape is all white. It is calf deep in a sort of mist/fog and any walls or doors that are seen are white. People dressed in all fashions seem to be going about their business singly, in pairs, or small groups. Like a half-full train station. The two men meld into this semibusy area as the camera view lifts.

We catch up to the two as they walk.

MAN IN BLUE

Another perfect job.

MAN IN WHITE

What's next?

A woman in a long white robe approaches

WOMAN IN WHITE ROBE

Well, if it isn't Ru ben and Toby, the dynamic duo.

The two men stop and wait for her.

RUBEN (man in white suit)

Tabitha, how…quaint.

Tabitha looks them up and down, tsking.

TABITHA

It's good you're wearing your Sunday best because the boss wants to see you two.

The two men exchange looks.

TABITHA (enjoying herself)

It seems you two have blown it again.

TOBY (man in blue suit)

What's he want with us?

TABITHA (starting to move away)

I don't know, but I wouldn't keep him waiting.

The two men watch her go as she melts into the busyness of the area.

TOBY

Might be anything.

RUBEN (with a heavy sigh)

Well, we won't know until we go see.

The camera angle rises as the two men move into the bustle of the scene. Mist swirling about their feet as they walk.

Cut to another misty area that *could* be outside. Cloud like B.G. with multiple escalators either rising into the clouds or lowering into the clouds below. These escalators are all going somewhere, none coming in. A lone desk sits off from the array of escalators. A lone man sits at the desk, long-sleeve dress shirt, black suspenders, and black armbands. A black thin tie and a visor surrounding a futile attempt at a comb-over job on a bald head. The man is skinny, early fifties with half-moon reading glasses perched upon a thin, narrow nose. The desk top is very organized. Ruben and Toby approach.

TOBY

Here to see "The Rock."

Ruben looks at Toby like a parent would an unruly child.

The man at the desk slowly looks up at the two men standing in front of him. His eyes staying with Toby.

RUBEN (to man at desk)

Hello, Percy.

PERCY (to Toby)

"The Rock?"

Toby shrugs his shoulders

RUBEN

Forgive him, Percy, he has the Spartacus syndrome. It can't be helped.

Percy turns his gaze from Toby to Ruben, raising an eyebrow in question.

RUBEN

My colleague believes us to be in trouble, so he feels the need to compound the issue...Spartacus syndrome.

PERCY (beginning to smile)

Ooooh...well (looking at Toby), I don't know that you *are* in trouble, but he wants to see you two as soon as you come in.

Percy motions them toward an area beside an escalator where the mist swirls heavily. Ruben and Toby approach, and the mist clears to reveal a plain door with frosted glass that has "Peter" painted on it. Ruben reaches to knock, but before he can...

BEHIND THE DOOR

Come in!

The two men exchange looks before entering.

INT. OFFICE

The office is small and much cluttered, almost cramped. A big man in a light-colored robe, bearded with long hair (late forties) sits behind the desk, studying papers before him. File cabinets with open drawers are within reach. A ficus tree and an old-fashioned water bottle complete the look. There are two chairs before the desk.

PETER (without looking up)

Don't sit down, you're not staying.

TOBY

It was Mrs. Devereau's idea, Boss. She told us
Mr. Devereau was a prankster all his life...

Peter looked up and lifted his hand to stop the explanation.

PETER (to Ruben)

What's he talking about?

Ruben shrugs his shoulders, pretending ignorance.

TOBY

Well, what's this about then?

Peter shuffles through some papers and, after finding the one he wants,
reads...

PETER

Harvey Baker.

Ruben and Toby groan audibly.

TOBY

Again, Boss?

RUBEN

We've been down there five times already.

PETER

I know, I know. But this time you're to bring
him in.

The two men look stunned.

RUBEN

But I thought...

Peter holds up his hand again.

PETER

Yeah, we all thought he'd get over it, but
free will is free will. Here is your destination
papers (handing them some papers) and send
Percy in as you're leaving.

The door opens, and Percy is there holding folders and waiting for Toby
and Ruben to leave. They walk out, and we hear...

PETER (to Percy)

I need the folders...

Percy steps past the two men and into the office.

PERCY

The Jenkins, Johnson, and Jones file, I took
the liberty to...

The door closes on the rest, and the scene changes.

EXT. DAY – DOWN TOWN STREET – SEMI BUSY

Camera view is from across the street. A man stands on a sidewalk
just back from the curb. He has messy brown hair (wind-blown),
midthirties, casually dressed. He is intently watching the traffic. Cut
to oncoming bus and then back to see the same man watching the bus.

The camera pulls back to show Toby and Ruben standing across the street from this man watching him. The bus comes into view as the man steps off the sidewalk into its path. Just before the bus strikes him, he makes eye contact with Toby and Ruben. Our view stays with the man in the street. The bus bats the man's physical body off screen as we hear tires squealing and breaks screaming along with crashing sounds. The man appears to have passed through the bus and is standing in the middle of the street. Any further traffic seems oblivious to him and the approaching two angels.

RUBEN (to a bewildered Harvey)

Harvey, it's time to come with us.

Toby and Ruben walk up as several cars pass through them unnoticed. We hear traffic noise in the B.G.

TOBY (reaching for Harvey)

Come along now, Harvey, you're holding up
traffic.

This gets Toby to look from his partner. Harvey looks stunned from the unfolding events.

HARVEY (tentatively)

Who are you?

Taking his arms, Toby and Ruben start walking Harvey across the street.

RUBEN

Why, Harvey, we are your guardian angels.
I'm Ruben, and this is Tobias. We have come
to take you home.

They walk on either side of Harvey, directing him to an escalator that appears to disappear into white mist going up.

> HARVEY (stopping at the foot of escalator)

Wait...I'm dead?

> RUBEN

Hmmm...*dead* is such a final word, don't you think, Tobias?

> TOBY (nudging Harvey onto escalator)

Indeed. We like to think of it as "passing on." Come along now.

> HARVEY (getting excited)

Wait...if you are my guardian angels, why didn't you stop me?

> RUBEN

Oh, Harvey, we *have* stopped you, but I'm afraid this time you left us no choice.

Toby rolls his eyes and nods in agreement.

> TOBY (counting on fingers)

Let's see...the first time you tried to poison yourself, remember? You spent six hours puking your guts out. And another two days on the toilet. Then there was the time you were going to jump off the Metro building.

RUBEN (cont.)

But tripped over a guide wire and broke your leg. Remember?
That was us.

Harvey follows the dialogue like a tennis match.

TOBY

Then my personal favorite was when you locked
yourself in the garage with the car motor running.

RUBEN

But you couldn't keep the motor running
long enough to fill the garage.

TOBY (starting to laugh)

Remember banging your bad leg on the car door?

HARVEY

That was you?

RUBEN (nodding and laughing)

Yeah, when you went to fix the motor, the hood
came down on your head.

Unable to continue through fits of laughter.

TOBY (laughing harder)

Knocking your face into the air cleaner and…and
breaking your nose!

Harvey's lower lip comes out, and he is about to cry. The two angels continue though fits of laughter, oblivious to Harvey's emotional state.

RUBEN (through tears of laughter)

Remember the two black eyes? And…and the neighborhood kids calling you raccoon monster?

TOBY

They threw rocks at you and even…even (laughing too hard) your own dog didn't know you.

Both angels were bent over in fits of uncontrollable laughter. Harvey stood between them as the escalator continued to rise. Tears finally spill over his cheeks, and a wail starts to come from him. Ruben and Toby straighten up, wiping tears from their eyes and got control of themselves as the escalator tops out.

RUBEN (sniffling as laughter fades)

Oh, Harvey, we don't mean anything. We're sorry.

TOBY (trying to console)

Yeah, you'll be okay, Harvey. Trust us.

This brought on another fit of laughter from the two angels as they exit the escalator to the same area as before. Harvey is crying freely now and could not be consoled. As they walked Harvey over to a door marked "Debriefing," they get themselves under control. The door opens before they could knock. Tabitha is standing there with eyes only for Harvey.

TABITHA (smiling sweetly)

Hello, Harvey, we've been expecting you.

Harvey looks to her with big hopeful eyes. She moves aside to let him pass. Someone immediately hands him a purring little kitten. His face lights up.

HARVEY (through fading sobs)

Mi…Mi…Mittens?

Harvey looks hopeful at the person handing him the purring ball of fur. They all smile while leading him away. Tabitha comes out of the doorway, pulling the door closed behind her.

TABITHA

What did you two clowns do to him?

TOBY (defensively)

We didn't do nothin'.

TABITHA (eyeing them suspiciously)

Come on, we have a briefing to go to.

They all start walking through the misty area.

RUBEN (to Tabitha)

You were expecting him?

TABITHA

Of course not. We never know exactly when suicides are going to show up.

TOBY (pretending to be shocked)

So you *lied* to him!

TABITHA (defensively)

No, I tried to calm him down after you two...did whatever it was you did to upset him.

TOBY (sarcastically)

Yeah, we pushed him in front of a bus.

RUBEN

Why do you always assume we do wrong?

TABITHA

Because your track record does you little credit.

Ruben and Toby exchange looks as the three of them pass into a room half filled with other people.

INT. CLASSROOM-LIKE ROOM – EVERYTHING STILL WHITE. PEOPLE MINGLING AUDIBLY

As the three newcomers take their seats, an instructor or watch-commander-type person takes the podium at the front of the room. He bangs a gavel for attention. People range in various fashions, ages, and gender. The atmosphere is casual. Maybe twenty people seated where thirty could sit.

INSTRUCTOR

All right, you guys, settle down we've got assignments to get to.

The class came to order.

INSTRUCTOR (cont.)

Barney, Ted, nice work on the school-bus thing.

People turn toward two men, making mock bows and offering congratulations.

INSTRUCTOR

That natural disaster is going down today, and Peter wants to bring that group into debriefing through the back. We'll need six more angels to assist.

Various hands go up as chatter among the rooms occupants grow. The instructor points out to six angels and bangs the gavel.

INSTRUCTOR

Now I need someone special to visit a nursing home.

Groans throughout the room. No one volunteers.

INSTRUCTOR

We have a young woman who has had a hard time, and her time is up. Someone needs to go and get her *and* do a once over on the nursing home.

TABITHA

What happened to her?

INSTRUCTOR

It seems she was assaulted at an early age and mentally never recovered.

INTERESTED PERSON

How young is she?

INSTRUCTOR

She just turned eighteen.

RUBEN

How long has it been since…?

INSTRUCTOR

Seven years.

ANOTHER ANGEL

She's been in the nursing home for seven years?

INSTRUCTOR

She has no family. Well, she has a dad, but he's in prison for….umm, killing her attacker. (Pause while the classroom responds to tragic situation) We need a gentle touch with this one.

No one speaks up. The room quiets down.

INSTRUCTOR

Tabitha, this might be perfect…

TABITHA

I would, but I have that homeless thing.

Instructor eyeing people, who find anywhere else to look but at the instructor. Quiet chatter can be heard.

Then a small voice from the back.

SMALL VOICE

I'll go.

The room's noise dies down.

INSTRUCTOR

Who said that?

A boy, previously unnoticed, stands up from the back of the room. He is maybe ten years old. He's wearing a slightly baggy black T-shirt; new jeans, rolled at his ankles; with black old- school Keds on his feet. His hair is almost shaggy, down to his collar.

BOY

I'll go.

INSTRUCTOR

Gabe! Okay then. Gabe has the nursing home.
None of *you* need worry yourself.

Everybody thanks the boy, who shrugs it off.

INSTRUCTOR

All right, there are things that need taking
care of in your boroughs. Shane, you can't
be late on the jumper.

Shane acknowledges the instructor as people get up and the class disperses.

INT. INTERSECTION OF TWO HALLWAYS – ONE DARK, ONE LIT – NIGHT

Our view is from the lighted hallway into the dark hallway. We hear B.G. noise of nursing-home TV droning on in the B.G. with occasional loud voices, dishes clanking. At the end of the dark hallway, a door opens. Streetlights silhouette a small person coming into dark hallway, the door closes, and the hallway is completely dark again. Gabe emerges from the dark into the lighted hallway. His attention is immediately drawn to an old man leaning against a wall facing away from him, counting on his fingers and mumbling to himself. Gabe looks on for a moment and then moves away. The boy looks into several open doors as he walks down the hallway. As he reaches one, a boney hand reaches out and grabs his arm. An old woman in a wheelchair.

OLD WOMAN (elated)

David! It's so nice to see you!

GABE (smiling compassionately)

Hello, Mrs. Davis. It's so nice to see *you*.

MRS. DAVIS (pulling her hand back)

You're not *David*!

GABE (soothingly)

No, but I *am* a friend.

MRS. DAVIS (on the verge of tears)

Where's David?

GABE (he placed her hands over her heart)

He is here.

A serene look comes over her face as Gabe leaves her and continues down the hall. He looks back once; and we see Mrs. Davis sitting in the doorway to her room, hands still over her heart with a dreamy, faraway look on her face. Gabe comes to another room, steps inside, and stops just inside the doorway. The room is a standard nursing-home room. A nurse is fussing around as a stream of dialogue comes from her as she goes about her duties.

NURSE (Ms. Day)

Oh, Rachel, your daddy sent you another picture.
Girl, that man *loves you*.

The girl in the bed has a vacant look on her face. She is in her late teens and does not respond to anything.

MS. DAY

Let me get this messy ole thing off you now. How
about that yellow nightdress? I'll show you the
new picture and tell you what your daddy said in
his letter just as soon as I get you cleaned and ready…

She stops and steps back with her hands on her hips, still talking to the unresponsive girl in the bed. Gabe watches from the doorway. The nurse does not see him.

MS. DAY

Girl, you got to snap out of this thing that's
got hold of you. You too young to…

The nurse gives a heavy sigh and goes back to changing the girl's clothing, bedding, etc. Gabe moves back out into the hallway. As he comes to the hallway intersection, the TV sound and voices get louder. He rounds a corner and comes into a rec room. TV, Ping-Pong table, chairs, card tables etc. There are approximately eight seniors in the room scattered about. The first one Gabe comes to is an old man with longish white hair. He is perched atop a chair crowing like a rooster. Two other old residents are standing. One steps back, watching him flop his arms and crow to the ceiling. One is scowling. The other is smiling.

FIRST RESIDENT (scowling)

What's that old fool trying to prove?

SECOND RESIDENT

Why, he's celebrating life.

This draws Gabe's attention, and he smiles at the second resident.

FIRST RESIDENT

What the hell does he have to celebrate?
He's stuck in here with *us*.

Second resident turns to first resident, and over the crowing...

SECOND RESIDENT

We should *all* celebrate the life we've been
given. It is, after all, our finest gift.

FIRST RESIDENT

AHHH! What the hell do *you* know.

The first resident walks away. Caught unaware, a hand comes down on the boy's shoulder. An old woman, who must have been very pretty in her youth, has come up from behind Gabe. Gabe turns to see her.

OLD WOMAN (confused)

Where are all the paintings?

Gabe reaches up and places his finger tips on the old woman's forehead.

GABE

The paintings are *here*, Mrs. Cain.

The scene hangs for a moment as the woman's face transforms into a smile.

GABE

Can you see them?

MRS. CAIN (breathless)

Ooooh…

Gabe pulls his had away from her forehead, and there is a perfect yellow rose in his hand. He hands it to her. Her face lights up as her eyes fix on it.

MRS. CAIN (in awe)

It is so beautiful…

She takes the rose and is lost in its beauty as she turns away, smelling its fragrance.

SECOND RESIDENT (oblivious to Gabe)

Come on, Billy, let's go see what's on TV.

The man on the chair starts to climb down with his friend helping him. As resident no. 2 pushes the chair back to the wall, Gabe locks eyes with the crowing man.

GABE

Thank you, Mr. Williams.

Mr. Williams does a mock salute, and his friend takes him by the arm and leads him away to the TV area. Gabe surveys the room once and then goes back down the hallway, the way he came. He rounds the corner, and we see Ms. Day come out of Rachel's room. She has the medication tray in her hand. Ms. Day looks down and sees a coin on the carpet.

MS. DAY

Why look at that. It must be my lucky day.

She bends and picks it up. She then notices the old man leaning against the wall with his back to her. She does not see Gabe.

MS. DAY

Hello, Mr. Jones.

We can see Mr. Jones cringe when she addresses him. She approaches him.

MS. DAY (jovial)

I've been looking all over for you, Mr. Jones,
and here you are.

MR. JONES (almost whimpering)

(trying to press himself into the wall)

Please don't hurt me.

MS. DAY (soothingly)

No one is going to hurt you Mr. Jones. I promise.

Gabe watches as she gently rubs the old man's back. He cringes at first but is soon soothes enough to look at her. She smiles at him reassuringly.

MS. DAY

It's time for your medication. You know, your *youth* pills. These will help you grow your hair back.

Unconsciously, his hand goes to his bald head. He smiles, showing very few teeth. Ms. Day laughs, and he laughs with her. Gabe is moved by the scene. He watches as she leads a happier Mr. Jones away.

Start Sarah McGloughlins song, "In the Arms of the Angels."

Gabe enters Rachel's room once more. He approaches the bed and picks up the picture on the nightstand. It is a simple frame and is of a young girl and a grown man. They are happy in the picture. He sets it back on the nightstand. He reaches over and slips his hand into the girl's limp hand lying on the bed. His other hands fingers trace over her forehead, brushing strands of hair from her face in a loving manner.

GABE (softly)

Rachel…

The girl's body shudders. Her chest rises and falls with a heavy sigh.

GABE (softly)

Wake up now. We have much to do.

Her eyes blink, and her head turns to look at Gabe. He smiles and continues to stroke her forehead. She returns his smile.

GABE

It's time to come home.

He helps her to sit up. She looks around. He helps her swing her legs over the side of the bed. She looks past him and sees the picture beside the bed and slowly reaches for it.

GABE (still smiling)

Don't worry, you'll see him again.

Gabe takes Rachel's hand again as she slides off the bed to stand beside him. She smiles down at him. They leave the room. The camera angle follows them to the door and hold on the empty doorway. It is but a moment before Ms. Day enters the room and approaches the bed. Rachel's body is still in the bed, but there is a peaceful look on her face. Ms. Day notices. She slowly approaches the bed, sensing something is different. She feels for a pulse, and her face falls.

MS. DAY (whispering)

Oh, Rachel.

Ms. Day wipes a tear from her cheek as she looks around Rachel's room. She notices the empty picture frame and picks it up. The scene hold as the music plays, then fades to black.

INT. OFFICE POOL – MANY CUBICLES – MIDDAY

Sound of office busywork. Various phone conversations, typing on computers, and a radio drones on.

Jimmy Daniels, age twenty-six, office worker. One of twenty such in office pool. Clean-cut, good-looking, professional working his way up the corporate ladder. Pictures displayed in cubicle indicate he is a family man. Wedding ring on finger verifies.

A man pops his head above cubicle partition, intruding on Jimmy doing his work.

INTRUDER

Jimmy Dan! Wha da ya say, pal?

JIMMY

What do you want, Sal?

Pushing back from the computer, leaning back as if stretching his back, looking up at Sal.

SAL

Oh, come on, Jimmy ole pal, you know you're
moving up today. Hell, I'm surprised you haven't
got the call yet.

JIMMY (smiling smugly)

That's right, slug, no more looking up your
big fat nose every morning.

SAL

You're gonna miss ole Sal when you're upstairs
kissing corporate butt just to get the key to the
executive bathroom…gotta go.

Sal, noticing someone coming, drops behind partition.

Female, sharply dressed in conservative business attire, enters Jimmy's
cubicle.

FEMALE

Jimmy, you're wanted in the boss's office.

Jimmy bounds forward, literally hopping up, smiling broadly at female,
as if greatly anticipated moment had arrived. Affected by Jimmy's mood,
female smiles back, shyly.

FEMALE

Do you think this is the promotion you've
been waiting for?

He reaches out and lightly grips her upper arms.

JIMMY

I don't know, Kim, but I got a feeling.

He spins her around, trading places with her, so he's now in the cubicle
entranceway. He reaches over, snatching his suit jacket off the hook and
rolls out of cubicle, leaving Kim alone with the radio still on.

INT. PERSONEL OFFICE – OUTSIDE HALLWAY

Looking through the glass in the door. "J. J. Boyle, Supervisor" painted on pane. MAN in shirt sleeves and tie sits behind desk talking on the phone looks up into camera and waves to come in. Door opens. Jim comes into view, entering office. Inside office, man on phone continues talking while waving Jim into seat in front of desk.

                    J. J. BOYLE (on phone)

     No, no, he's right here…yes, sir, I'll be sure
     to mention it…yes, sir, I will…you, too, sir, okay,
     goodbye.

Jimmy sits forward in his chair, anticipating. J. J. hangs up the phone, looking at Jimmy solemnly.

                    J. J. BOYLE

     Jimmy, that was Joe Cunningham. As you know he
     owns this whole outfit.

Jimmy says nothing. He is at attention, expecting.

                    J. J. BOYLE (cont.)

     I've got some bad news for you Jimmy. (Heavy sigh)
     You're not getting that promotion at this time, son.

Jimmy looks across the desk incredulously, slack jawed.

                    J. J. BOYLE

     Look, I know you've been counting on this promotion,
     and you deserve it, but Winston from the mailroom…

We watch as Jimmy's face falls and then becomes resolved to the fact. Boss continues to drone on in B.G.

Dejected, Jimmy walks back to his cubicle, where he takes off his jacket, hangs it on the hook beside the entrance. It falls to the floor, forgotten. He drops into chair, exhaling loudly. The radio drones on in background.

RADIO

And finally in the local news, a millionaire loses a heirloom ring. A reward of $15,000. is offered to…

SAL (from over partition)

Hey, big shot, how did it go?

JIMMY (not looking up)

I didn't get it, Sal!

SAL

Wha da ya mean, you didn't get it? I thought it was a shoo-in!

JIMMY

Winston from the mailroom got it, Sal.

SAL

What?

JIMMY

Winston's the owner's sister's kid, Sal. He gets
the promotion. I get the next one.

SAL

That bites, dude.

Kim appears in cubicle entrance. Sal makes cutting motion across throat
to her where Jimmy can't see. Kim looks disgusted at Sal.

KIM

Jimmy?

JIMMY

I didn't get it, Kim. I'll get the next one, I guess.

SAL

Winston from the mailroom got it. Seems he...

She gives Sal a look. Sal disappears.

KIM (squeezing his shoulder)

I'm sorry, Jimmy. Don't let this get you down. It's
a minor setback, that's all.

Kim leaves, and after a moment, Jimmy leans forward, picking up
picture of a smiling woman holding a little girl. Staring at the picture
for a few moments, he gives a heavy sigh, puts the picture down, and
picks up the phone.

JIMMY (into phone)

Hi, honey, it's me....no, I didn't get it....no, it's
got nothing to do with me....

Scene fades and picks up in deserted parking garage. Jimmy carrying
jacket and briefcase, walking to what appears to be the last car in the
garage. Another car comes into view from ramp leading to upper floors.
It slows as it passes

CAR (passenger window)

Say, Jimmy, sorry to hear about the promotion.
That's a tough break man. See ya Monday.

Jimmy never breaks stride. Lifts briefcase, acknowledging person's well-
wishes. Car passes. Jimmy continues to his car.

Jimmy comes to nondescript car, opens door, and tosses in briefcase and
coat. He drops into seat and sits there with one leg outside the car for
a couple of moments. He leans over, opening his briefcase, takes out a
cell phone, and tosses it into the glove box. He pulls in his legs, closes
the door, and camera view goes to close-up of Jimmy in car. He puts
key in the ignition and tries to start car. It doesn't start. We can hear
the starter turning over, but the car doesn't start. He let's go of the key,
and the radio plays.

RADIO

Millionaire who lost his ring has upped the
reward to $20,000 dollars, and when asked...

Jimmy tries the key again, killing the radio. Again, the starter turns
and turns but never starts the car. He lets go of the key, and again, the
radio plays.

RADIO

Cannot reveal the inscription or he couldn't
be sure of its authenticity...

Once more, Jimmy turns the key until we hear the engine go click, click, click. He turns the key off and slams his hands against the steering wheel in frustration. He gets out of car, slams the door, standing beside it, arms akimbo, glaring at it.

At that moment another car approaches. Jimmy looks up.

Music from approaching car gets louder. A four-door town car comes around the corner down the ramp and pulls to a stop. A tinted window on passenger side lowers, and the music is louder. Volume lowers. Jimmy walks over and leans over to look inside.

INSIDE CAR (man's voice over B.G. music)

Jimmy Dan! Hey, man, is everything okay?

There is a buxom blonde in the passenger seat. Jimmy sees driver is none other than Winston, the guy who got his promotion.

JIMMY (straightening up, look of dismay on face)

Hello, Winston. Yeah, I'm all right. My car won't start.

WINSTON (leaning down to see across passenger)

Sorry to hear it, Jimmy. We're on our way to Tillies
to celebrate, come with us.

Jim leans back down, talking over cleavage of the blonde.

JIMMY

No, thanks, Winston, I gotta get home. I'll call someone.

WINSTON

Hey, man, I'm sorry about that promotion thing. That wasn't my idea. Let me make it up to you. Let me buy you a drink, and I'll give you a ride home afterward.

JIMMY

I appreciate it, Winston, but I don't think so.

At that time, a redheaded woman leans over the front seat from the back of the car.

WOMAN IN BACK SEAT (speaking provocatively)

Oh, come on, Jimmy, you can be *my* date.

Through the window, we can see Winston motioning woman to open back door.

WINSTON

Open the door for him, Helen. Come on, Jimmy,
I insist. Hell, it's the least I can do.

Jimmy's resolve is melting. He straightens up and looks around the deserted parking garage.

HELEN (teasing)

Come on, Jimmy, I won't bite...hard.

This brings laughter from both women. Jimmy, breathing a heavy sigh, goes over, opens his car door, retrieving his jacket. He locks his car and gets in the waiting car. The camera watches the car drive out of sight down the parking ramp.

INSIDE CAR: View from back seat, we can see Winston driving. Helen slides over, pressing up against Jimmy, reaching for his tie, seductively.

HELEN

Hi, Jimmy. I like your tie.

WINSTON

Say, Jim, come on over and at least have one drink with us. And then I'll take you home.

JIMMY (taking tie from Helen)

Naw, Winston, I really just want to get home. Thanks anyway.

HELEN

Don't be like that, Jimmy. You could sure make a girl happy if you come with us for a while.

JIMMY (showing wedding ring)

I'm married, Helen.

HELEN (giggling)

I won't tell if you won't.

Winston makes eye contact with Jimmy through the rearview mirror. Smiling, he raises his eyebrows questioningly. Helen presses up against Jimmy, speaking into his ear.

HELEN

Look what I've got, Jimmy.

She opens her hand in front of his face revealing two pills.

JIMMY

What's that?

HELEN

It's "ex," silly.

JIMMY

Drugs?

HELEN (looking exasperated, backing up)

Don't be so naïve.

JIMMY (suddenly)

Stop the car, Winston.

Winston makes eye contact through mirror.

WINSTON

Lighten up, Jim, we're all friends here.

JIMMY (raising voice)

I said stop the damn car!

We see from the outside as the car pulls to the curb. The back door is open before the car stops. Jimmy gets out next to a vacant lot.

WINSTON (over front seat)

Say, Jimmy, no hard feelings, right? I mean this doesn't have to be an issue at work, right?

Winston nods in the direction of the back seat. Jimmy glances quickly at Helen as he's putting on his jacket.

JIMMY

Don't worry about it, Winston. I'm just not in the mood to party tonight. I won't say anything.

Jimmy closes the back door, and the car pulls away. He watches as it leaves. We see Helen blow a kiss through the back window as it leaves.

On the street, Jimmy appears to be alone. The street is empty except for a lone phone booth about fifty feet away. From our view, we can see the empty lot on his left and the dilapidated phone booth in the B.G. A chain-link fence separates the right side of the street from a huge pillar holding up an elevated freeway, where car noise can be heard. Jimmy starts walking back the way they had come.

A VOICE (o. c.)

Hey you!

Jimmy stops and looks around.

VOICE (o. c.)

Say, man, can you spare some change?

Two men in early twenties dressed like street thugs jog up to Jimmy. One shorter than the other. They jockey for position.

SHORT THUG

Got any money, ass wipe?

TALLER THUG (pushing Jimmy)

What, you can't talk?

Jimmy looks out of his element. He takes a step back.

JIMMY

Look, guys....

At that time, tall thug punches Jimmy in the mouth. Before he can recover, short thug punches Jimmy in the stomach, bending him over at the waist. The two thugs commence to hitting, and when Jimmy falls to the sidewalk, they get his wallet and complain that there is only eighteen dollars in it. As this goes down, our POV reveals a city police car turning down the street in the B.G. Instinctively, one thug looks up from kicking Jimmy; backhands his partner in the chest, saying, "Cops"; throws down the empty wallet. The two run off.

Camera view has both Jimmy and approaching cop car in view. Jimmy uncovers his head and slowly sits up. Lip bleeding, one eye is red and starting to swell. Suit is a mess; his knee appears to be bloodied through a tear in pants.

Cop car rolls to the curb. The overhead strobe lights come on. Passenger side window comes down. We see two officers in car.

PASSENGER-SIDE COP (through window)

You all right, sir?

Cop remains in car.

JIMMY (touches lip)

Yeah, I guess so.

COP

Did they get anything?

Jimmy straightens out his leg, examining his knee. He grimaces, sees his wallet beside him, picks it up, and checks what's missing.

JIMMY

Looks like about eighteen dollars.

Cop notices Jimmy's wedding ring and watch still on his hand and wrist.

COP

Well, it looks like we showed up just in time.
You want to file a report?

Jimmy scowls at the cop as he probes his swelling eye, doesn't answer.

COP

We can take you down to the station, maybe
get you medical attention. You can try picking
those guys out of our mug books, maybe catch
the guys that did this to you.

The futility of this statement is not lost on Jimmy. He climbs to his feet, testing his injured knee, wincing from the sudden pain but able to support his weight.

JIMMY

No, Officer, I appreciate it. But I'm just going
to go back to my car and call someone to come
and get me. I'll be all right. Thanks anyway.

COP (relieved)

You're sure? 'Cause we can...

JIMMY

No, really. I'll be okay.

COP

Okay then. We'll be in the area if you need us.

Cop car rolls away, lights going out. Our POV stays with Jim next to
the vacant lot. Beat-up phone booth in the B.G.

JIMMY (to the sky)

For the love of Christ! Can I get a break? Huh?

Behind him, out of his view, the light in the broken-down old phone
booth flickers once and then comes on. Jimmy gives a heavy sigh, starts
to limp down the street toward the phone booth.

Halfway down the cracked sidewalk sits the dilapidated phone booth.
Several of the glass panes are missing, graffiti is its only decoration,
pushed back off the sidewalk it is truly a relic of the past. Jimmy limps up,
leans up against the phone booth that actually moves from his weight.
Bracing his hand on the corner, Jimmy leans forward and spits out blood,
mops his mouth with his handkerchief, grimacing from the cut on his lip.

The phone rings.

Jimmy looks up, squinting from the overhead light inside. He looks up and down the deserted street. He looks at the ringing phone again, thinking.

The phone rings incessantly.

Tentatively, Jimmy steps into the booth and reaches for the phone handset. He notices through the broken glass beside the actual phone, exposed wires sticking out of the back. He lifts the handset.

MAN'S VOICE ON PHONE (faintly)

Jimmy? Jimmy!

Jimmy puts the phone to his ear.

MAN'S VOICE (on phone)

Jimmy, for a minute I thought you weren't
going to answer.

JIMMY (in a daze)

Who...who is this?

VOICE ON PHONE

That's not really important. You could say I'm
your guardian angel, but (laughing) with the
day you're having, I wouldn't be much of a guardian
angel, now would I?

Jimmy looks around as the man on the phone speaks, as if he's being watched.

JIMMY (facing back to phone)

What do you want?

He notices his reflection in metal face of phone, leans in to examine his bloody lip and then swelling eye.

VOICE ON PHONE

Son, it's not what I want. It's what you asked for a few minutes ago.

JIMMY

Refresh my memory.

VOICE ON PHONE

"A break," Jim. You asked for a break, didn't you?

JIMMY (looking confused)

How could you know that?

VOICE ON PHONE (laughing)

That's not important, Jim. You get your break, but you only get one. So don't waste it, do you hear me?

Jim looks around again, outside the phone booth.

JIMMY

Where are you?

VOICE ON PHONE

Never mind that, just remember what I told you, don't waste it.

JIMMY

Yeah, I remember, but I don't understand...
Hello?

Realizing he is talking to a dead phone, he pulls the handset away from
the side of his head, looking at the handset as if that could provide him
with a clue as to what is going on. He sees a wad of gum stuck in the
listening cup, trailing strands of gum to his ear. In disgust, he pushes the
handset away, backing out of the phone booth. He brushes the mess away
and wipes his hand on his pants, leaving gum everywhere he touches.

JIMMY

What the...?!

He is becoming very angry as he wrestles with the mess stuck to his
fingers

JIMMY (yelling at sky)

That's just great! Good one, God! What now!?

Jim kicks the phone booth and, still digging gum out of his ear, starts
down the street in a determined limp.

Back in the parking garage, Jim limps to his car. He unlocks car door,
opens it. Takes off his jacket, throws it into backseat angrily. He starts to
reach in glove box for phone but, on a hunch, digs out keys from pocket.
Inserts key, car starts right up. Stunned, he seems uncertain what to do,
then quickly pulls legs in, shuts door.

We see the car backing out and turning to stop and come forward
starting down the parking ramp. That's when the front tire blows. From
the side, we see Jimmy pounding the steering wheel, throwing a fit.

FADE OUT.

FADE IN.

EXT. FOURPLEX APARTMENT UNIT – NIGHT

There is a small boy sitting at the top of some stairs leading up to the top two units of the fourplex. His knees are drawn up, and he is looking past the camera view intently. Suddenly, his head comes up, and he yells into doorway of open apartment. The boy is five or six years old.

SMALL BOY

He's here! Uncle Jimmy's home!

The boy bounds down the stairs and runs across grounds to parking area.

Camera view changes to Jim's car pulling into park. The front tire can be seen as one of those temporary doughnut tires. As car rolls to stop, the boy is there, excited. The car door opens, and an arm hands out the briefcase. The boy takes it, then his face changes to shock as he sees his uncle's face.

BOY

Uncle Jimmy! What happened to your eye?

JIMMY (climbing out of car)

Oh, I got in a little scrape, but I'm okay
now, Carson.

Camera pulls back as Jimmy and Carson walk together to the apartment stairs. Carson chattering away.

INSIDE APARTMENT, two women are sitting at kitchen table talking. We can hear the radio in the background as Carson's voice gets louder until he and Jimmy round the corner from outside porch.

The two upstairs apartments share a porch that separates them. They both have windows that look out on the porch. Windows facing the same direction, doors facing each other. These windows are in the dining area of the apartments.

FIRST WOMEN (getting to feet)

Oh my God! Honey, what happened?

CARSON (still lugging briefcase with two hands)

Uncle Jimmy got mugged.

The same woman goes to Jimmy and starts to poke at his injuries. Jimmy, wincing, pulls back.

JIMMY

Sarah, don't, honey. It looks worse than it is.

OTHER WOMAN AT TABLE (pulling at boy)

Good, because it looks pretty bad. Carson, it's time
for bed, son. You got to see Uncle Jimmy, now
hop to.

CARSON

Aw, Mom, it's Friday, can't I...

JIMMY

He's okay, Janice. I told him I'd tell him all about
woopin' all them bikers, but after I take a shower.

Jimmy smiles down at his nephew, messing his hair and taking his briefcase.

JANICE

Well, you can tell him tomorrow, tough guy. It's almost ten o'clock, and that's past his bedtime.

Janice gets up to leave.

CARSON

Awww, Mom...

They leave.

SARAH (leading Jimmy away)

Come on, hon. Let's get you into the tub.

Scene fades with the radio playing in the B.G.

IN BATHROOM: Sarah, on her knees beside the bath tub, leaning over the edge to dab a cloth at Jimmy's injured lip. Jimmy sits in water surrounded by bubbles holding an ice pack to his eye.

JIMMY

And then the tire blew, and I kinda lost it.

SARAH (sympathetically)

I'll bet. I'm sorry you had such a rotten day.

The scene hangs as the two quietly share each other's company. The drip of the water faucet can be heard along with the radio in the other room, faintly.

SARAH

Oh, Janice, wants you to look at her water

heater again. She said she smelled gas.

JIMMY

I will tomorrow. It's probably the pilot light again.
I wish she'd meet someone.

SARAH

She will. She's so protective of Carson. Besides
she's got her big brother to look after her.

SCENE FADES.

FADE IN to kitchen table with view of hallway. In B.G. radio is playing
softly on some news channel. We hear Jimmy talking before we see him.
He emerges from the hallway holding little blonde girl cradled in his
arms. He is in pj's and terry-cloth robe, she in pj's and giggling.

JIMMY

And then I did a flying double back,
flip chop socky kick, and down he went.

LITTLE GIRL

Really, Daddy?

JIMMY

Yup, and when the cops came, we put them in
jail so they wouldn't get out.

He carried her into the kitchen area, and as he's one handed making a
bowl of cereal, they chat. Sarah enters the kitchen. Group hug. He sits
the girl up at the table with the cereal.

SARAH

Did you get the paper, hon?

JIMMY

Getting it now!

Sarah, busy in the kitchen, still in her nightgown, makes coffee. Jimmy comes in from getting the paper, sits at the table with little girl, who is slurping her cereal to get Daddy's attention.

SARAH

Matty, honey, don't slurp. You sound
like a pig.

JIMMY

But you look like a squirrel.

Matty smiles at her daddy, cheeks bulging with cereal. Mom comes in carrying coffee mugs and sits. Jimmy is unfurling paper.

MATTY

Daddy, beat up twenty-one bikers last night,
Huh, Daddy?

JIMMY

Twenty-two.

SARAH

Matty, don't talk with your mouth full, and
you shouldn't lie to your daughter like that.

JIMMY

You're right, hon. Okay, Matty, it was only twenty-one.

Sarah playfully punches Jimmy as he, seeing something in the paper, sits up all of a sudden pointing at the paper.

JIMMY

Look at this! I don't believe it!

SARAH (leaning in to look)

What is it?

JIMMY

You know that millionaire who's been all
over the news about losing his ring?

SARAH (absently)

Last night he said he'd pay twenty thousand
dollars reward. Did someone find it?

JIMMY (pointing to paper)

Yeah, see these two? They're the two who
mugged me last night.

We see the picture of the two street thugs holding up a check and smiling for the camera. Sarah reads over text.

SARAH

It says they found it in the coin return of
an old phone booth.

JIMMY

What? Where does it say that?

SARAH (pointing)

Right here, hon. Do you think it's the same
phone booth that...?

The camera view is of the family at the table with the before-mentioned
window that looks out onto the porch in the B.G. The curtain is closed.

An explosion occurs outside the window, pushing curtains inward and
blowing glass and debris onto table. Sarah instinctively reaches for child.
Jimmy ducks and comes up checking wife and daughter.

SARAH (clutching Matty)

What was that!?

The front door is just around the corner. Jimmy runs to it flinging it open
and looking across the porch. Our view is over his shoulder as we see
the apartment next door. Door hanging off its hinges, smoke billowing
out. The window to next door apartment is also billowing smoke. Janice
is hanging out the window, motionless, bloodied. Jimmy runs to her,
lifting her gently from the shattered window pane.

JIMMY (panic in voice)

Janice? Janice!

Sarah comes out of apartment still holding Matty to her chest. She puts
her hand over the child's eyes when she sees her sister-in-law. Blooded,
eyes fixed, dead.

SARAH

Oh my God, Jimmy!

We can see past Jimmy into burning apartment. Lots of smoke, some fire can be seen through the smoke.

JIMMY (shielding Janice from Matty's view)

Get her downstairs, Sarah.

SARAH

What about Carson?

Jimmy's head comes up at that thought, and at that time, we hear Carson scream from inside the burning apartment. Jimmy moves to the doorway, pushing hanging door out of way and shielding his face from heat and smoke trying to see inside

JIMMY (over shoulder)

Go, Sarah. I'll get Carson!

Sarah takes a crying Matty downstairs. We hear Carson yell again. Jimmy makes a decision. He bolts from doorway back across porch into his own apartment. He runs to the sink in his kitchen, tearing off robe as he gets there. He throws robe into sink, turning on both taps. He is impatient.

JIMMY (frantic)

Come on, come on, for Christ sake!

He turns around and yanks open refrigerator door grabbing anything liquid, a jug of something red, a pitcher of tea and pours it all into the robe in sink. He flings the two empty containers to the floor, snatching up the sopping wet robe, putting it on as he runs.

We pick him back up at the door to burning apartment covering his head with wet robe. The camera angle is over his back as we see him enter the apartment. Flames and smoke dominate above his head as he moves towards hallway. He reaches for a door on his right as we hear Carson scream again. Jimmy pulls his hand back and continues down the hallway to the end where there is only one door on his left. We can see flames on the ceiling above his head. The sound of fire is loud.

SMASH CUT to inside bathroom.

Camera view is a wide shot to include the bathtub, bathroom door, and a very small window over bathtub. Carson is crouched in tub. Smoke is not as thick in bathroom but hangs in upper part. The bathroom door opens and then quickly slams behind a frantic Jimmy.

CARSON (gasping)

Uncle Jimmy!

Tears have cut a path down Carson's cheeks. He starts toward his uncle, but Jimmy is there before he can get out of the tub. As he takes the boy into his arms, we see him look up at the too- small window about the bathtub. Jimmy climbs into tub, holding Carson to him. He turns on the water to activate the shower, the water soaks them both.

CARSON (with water streaming down his face)

Are we gonna burn up, Uncle Jimmy?

JIMMY (smiling to reassure)

Of course not, Carson. We're going to get all wet, and then we're gonna run out of here before the fire can get us.

CARSON

Is my mom in the fire?

JIMMY (looking sad)

No, Carson, your mom is not in the fire.
Now we gotta go. Are you ready?

Carson, looking intently at Jimmy, nods his head. Jimmy steps out of the tub and goes to the door carrying Carson.

JIMMY

Hold on tight now.

Carson clutches him around the neck; and Jimmy, with one arm holding the boy, wraps the dripping robe around the two of them and opens the door.

Our view is changed to the hallway. We are behind Jimmy, following him down the burning hallway. He is crouched over as far as he can. Flames completely cover ceiling above him. We can see the apartment open up as he nears the end of the hallway. Just then a gas main blows to Jimmy's left, filling the left side of his path with billowing blue flame. Jimmy veers to the right, through the path of least resistance into the living room and out the shattered living-room window, his only option.

SMASH CUT to outside apartment. On the ground looking up at burning apartment. Our view is as if we were one of the bystanders.

The people standing around number about twenty. All of them are looking up expectantly at the apartment. They gasp collectively as burning curtains come billowing out with sparks and smoke trailing Jimmy as he comes flying out the window. We see him make his decent, but the camera angle is blocked for his impact with the grassy ground. Again, the crowd reacts audibly.

Camera cuts to Jimmy lying on his back in the grass and debris, still clutching Carson. Jimmy's eyes are open looking at the sky. He seems to be having trouble catching his breath. Someone pulls Carson away. Carson has blood on him. He is coughing and crying. We see blood on Jimmy's neck, pulsing out. He is still struggling to breathe.

Camera angle changes to Jimmy's point of view. Sarah comes into view with the sky behind her. She is not holding Matty. She is crying as she reaches for the pulsing wound on Jimmy's neck.

SARAH (frightful)

Jimmy, honey, are you all right?

We see other people come into view. Camera view cuts back to Jimmy's face. He is trying to say something to Sarah, but there is blood in his mouth. B.G. noise is of the crowd saying things like "Doctor," "Ambulance," "911," and "Oh my God," etc.

SARAH (still crying)

Jimmy, baby. Hang in there, honey, help is on
the way. (To the crowd) Somebody do something!

Jimmy reaches up to touch his wife's face. She leans into it and tries to smile reassuringly as tears spill over her cheeks.

Jimmy's POV again. We see Sarah with the sky and smoke. There are a few clouds, and this picture starts to darken.

SARAH (starting to panic)

Jimmy! Oh, Jimmy, don't go, honey. (She looks
around desperately, then back down at Jimmy.)
Jimmy...?Jimmy!

Sarah's image fades into darkness as her voice and all the other B.G. noise fade and echo from far away. The camera stays dark as Sarah's voice echoes into silence. A few moments pass, and her voice is coming back. Distant at first and a bit distorted as if over a small speaker.

SARAH

Jimmy, honey, is that you?

POV is still from Jimmy. An image develops out of the blackness as Sarah's voice gets stronger.

SARAH

Jimmy, say something, honey. You're scaring me.

Instinctively, he answers.

JIMMY

Sarah?

As the image becomes sharper, we see Jimmy's battered reflection in the metal surface of the phone inside the phone booth.

SARAH

Jimmy, where are you?

Camera angle changes to show him in the dilapidated phone booth beside the vacant lot. He is looking into the metal face of the phone with the handset pressed against his head.

JIMMY (reaching for bloodied lip)

I'm...Sarah? Is everything okay?

Jimmy, in disbelief pulls the phone away from his ear, looking at it as if it could provide a clue. He sees the gum. A smile spreads over his face as he reaches up to feel the mess on his ear and starts to laugh.

SARAH (pleading)

Jimmy, what's going on?

Uncaring about the mess, he puts the handset back to his ear.

SARAH

Honey, have you been drinking?

JIMMY (laughing)

No, baby, I'm not drunk. I'm okay and on
my way home. I just got a little hung up
here, is all. I love you.

SARAH

Are you sure? Because you sound different.

JIMMY

No, I'm fine, baby. I'll see you as soon as
I change a tire. I gotta go.

Camera view pans back to show phone booth from above. Jimmy hangs up the phone and practically dances out of phone booth. He woo-hoos to the sky, wiping goo from his head onto his pants. He starts to bound down the sidewalk, limping, only to stop suddenly. Slowly, he turns, looks back at the phone booth. We see the phone booth over his shoulder. The light flickers almost as if winking. Slowly, he limps back, stopping in the doorway. He reaches in and pokes his finger in the coin return, pulling out a gold wedding ring. He brings it to his face to read. Camera shows inscription, "For second chances, Love Pheobe."

FINAL CAMERA SHOT.

Panning back, we see Jimmy limping/skipping down the sidewalk. The phone booth is in view. Ruben and Toby are standing beside it, watching him go.

RUBEN

I liked the gum idea.

TOBY

Thank you. Another perfect job.

RUBEN

Indeed.

Ruben raises his hand and Toby high fives him.

Start song, Billy Vaughn's "Swinging Safari"

As the two angels turn into the vacant lot where an escalator can be seen, they are walking away from us with the phone booth still in view. Toby's arm shoots out, and he snaps his fingers. The light in the phone booth goes out. They rise up on the escalator. Music plays on.

FADE OUT.

The End

www.ingramcontent.com/pod-product-compliance
Lightning Source LLC
Chambersburg PA
CBHW032039240626
47154CB00003B/998